Pampered, fun-loving Laurie Sinclair hates everything about the rough, ugly mining town of Lucky Creek, California. She only left Philadelphia because her wealthy father opened the Monarch Gold Mine—and because Brandon, the man she'd hoped to marry, sent her away. But when Brandon changes his mind, she's ready to pack her bags—until her father is suddenly killed in a mine explosion, and her brother is badly injured . . .

As troubles mount for the Sinclairs, including a ruinous unexpected debt, they save themselves by selling half their mine ownership to Darcy McKenna, a friend of Laurie's late father. Brusque and brooding, Darcy is the opposite of exuberant Laurie. Yet as Laurie stays on to help him in the office, Darcy soon finds himself smiling and happier, while Laurie finds her interests are changing. She might even be falling for Darcy. But her heart won't truly be tested until Brandon shows up—and throws her life into chaos . . .

Visit us at www.kensingtonbooks.com

Books by Shirley Kennedy

Women of the West Series
Wagon Train Cinderella
Wagon Train Sisters
Gold Rush Bride

In Old California Series
River Queen Rose
Bay City Belle
Lucky Creek Lady

Lucky Creek Lady

In Old California Series

Shirley Kennedy

LYRICAL PRESS
Kensington Publishing Corp.
www.kensingtonbooks.com

LYRICAL PRESS BOOKS are published by
Kensington Publishing Corp.
119 West 40th Street
New York, NY 10018

All Kensington titles, imprints, and distributed lines are available at special quantity discounts for bulk purchases for sales promotion, premiums, fund-raising, educational, or institutional use.

Special book excerpts or customized printings can also be created to fit specific needs. For details, write or phone the office of the Kensington Sales Manager: Kensington Publishing Corp., 119 West 40th Street, New York, NY 10018. Attn. Sales Department. Phone: 1-800-221-2647.

Lyrical Press and Lyrical Press logo Reg. U.S. Pat. & TM Off.

First Electronic Edition: March 2019
eISBN-13: 978-1-5161-0440-6
eISBN-10: 1-5161-0440-4

First Print Edition: March 2019
ISBN-13: 978-1-5161-0443-7
ISBN-10: 1-5161-0443-9

Printed in the United States of America

To my daughter, Dianne, whose patience, support, and understanding have made those long hours I spend at my computer much more enjoyable.

Acknowledgments

Living in a modern city like Las Vegas, Nevada, I wouldn't have a clue as to what life was like during the California Gold Rush if it weren't for the countless authors who've written about that fascinating period of time in our nation's history. These are only a few of the books that sit on my shelves: *The Rush*, by Edward Dolnick; *California Gold and the Highgraders*, by F.D. Calhoon; *Eldorado*, by Dale L. Walker; *Gold Mines of California*, by Jack R. Wagner.

I use the Internet a lot, too. What a handy reference source! While writing *Lucky Creek Lady*, I was able to find that hotels had indoor plumbing in the 1850s; the California Stage Company acted as agents for the steamship lines; the use of tracheotomies in the US began around 1820; and much more.

So my many thanks go to those who contribute to the Internet, as well as those authors whose books helped me make Laurie and Darcy's 1855 world as real as possible.

Chapter 1

"I'm going home!"

If Laurie Sinclair hadn't been carrying her father's lunch pail, she would have clapped her hands as she performed a happy little skip along the narrow road that led up to the Monarch Mine.

Her younger sister, Ada, who walked beside her, laughed at her enthusiasm. "I do believe you're glad you're leaving."

"How did you guess?" Laurie couldn't keep her buoyant mood to herself. Six months ago, she'd traveled clear across the country to join her family in the mining town of Lucky Creek, high in the Sierra Nevada Mountains of California. What a horrible decision! She so hated living in a place so primitive, so remote, so foreign to anything she'd ever known that from the day she arrived, all she could think of was getting back to her beloved Philadelphia. How wonderful that at last she could and was leaving tomorrow.

Ada sighed. "I'm going to miss you. How will I know what's the latest fashion after you're gone?"

"I'll write often, I promise. I'll miss you, too." *And I'll also worry,* Laurie reflected. She loved her family and would miss them tremendously. "We can blame it all on Father, can't we?"

"Nothing would stop him."

"All he wanted was to race to California and pick up all those gold nuggets lying on the streets before they were gone. Now look what's happened." Laurie would never forget that awful day back in 1850 when

Sam Sinclair announced he was leaving for the gold rush. The whole family was dumbfounded. Why would he want to go? Unlike most men who headed west to make their fortune, he'd already made his. They lived in a mansion on Society Hill, the best neighborhood in Philadelphia, where all the rich people lived. The Sinclairs might not be among the very richest, but they were wealthy enough that they moved in all the best social circles. What could their father find in California that they didn't already have?

"What a miracle he really did find gold," Ada said.

"I wish he hadn't. Then we'd all still be living in Philadelphia."

"I never understood why you stayed behind when Father sent for us. All I could figure was you wanted to live with Aunt Florence. Wait. I'm out of breath." Gasping for air, Ada stopped and bent over, hands on knees. "Such a steep climb. I've got to rest a minute."

Laurie stopped gladly. She, too, hadn't completely adjusted to the thin mountain air. "It wasn't only Aunt Florence. You know what fun she is, but she's not the real reason I stayed behind. The truth is, I wanted to get away from Mother. I was twenty years old and tired of her bossing me around. I thought if I didn't like living with Aunt Florence, I could join the family any time I wanted. Then I met Brandon Cooper. After that, you couldn't have dragged me from Philadelphia."

"Really?" Ada gazed at her accusingly. "You never told us. You had so many suitors, I could never keep them all straight. I remember what you wrote about Brandon, though. Rich, handsome, brilliant, and catches bugs."

"Don't say 'bugs.'" How annoying that no one in the family could grasp Brandon's brilliance, his distinguished reputation in the scientific world. "I've told you before, Brandon is a renowned entomologist. He's gone on several expeditions throughout the world—the East Indian Archipelago, the Spice Islands. He's acclaimed for finding a new species of orthoptera. That's 'grasshopper' to you." She'd fallen completely, madly in love with him, and he with her. He'd asked her to marry him but said she should keep it a secret till he got back from his next expedition.

Her family thought she was having a grand time living with Aunt Florence, but she was growing more and more miserable. There was always another expedition Brandon had to go on before they could marry. He was stringing her along, so after two years, Laurie finally told him she'd waited long enough. Either marry her or she'd leave for California to be with her family. She was sure he'd be so devastated at the thought of losing her that he'd finally set the date. That didn't happen, so Laurie found herself in Lucky Creek, California. She glanced up at the snowcapped mountains surrounding them. "This must be the most lonely, most dismal place I could ever imagine."

Ada sighed patiently. They'd been through this before. "But the smell of the pine trees—those gorgeous snow-peaked mountains. There are those who find it beautiful here."

"You can have it." That was thoughtless. Ada always saw the best in everything, and Laurie wouldn't hurt her feelings for the world. "I take that back. Lucky Creek is an exciting town with plenty to offer."

"No, it's not. The truth is, I don't find it beautiful here, and neither does Mother. We're not blind to all the crime here. There's lynchings and hangings and they hate foreigners."

"I was trying to be nice, but I agree," Laurie replied. Lucky Creek had a sheriff, but he was weak and subject to corruption, and justice seldom prevailed. And like all mining towns, prejudice against all foreigners ran amazingly high. Gold prospectors whose skin wasn't white were often run off their claims, and worse.

"We'd move back to Philadelphia in a heartbeat if we could, but you know Father. He loves it here, so we're stuck." Ada eyed her accusingly. "I'm not likely to get a letter like you did."

The letter from Brandon. Laurie had it almost memorized. He'd made a terrible mistake and wanted her back. He'd gone on enough expeditions. It was time to settle down. He missed her terribly, and would she please come home and be part of his life again. Of course, she would, the sooner the better. She hated disappointing her family but hastened to make arrangements for her return east. This was her last full day in Lucky Creek. Tomorrow she'd leave by stagecoach for San Francisco. From there, she'd take a steamship bound for New York, then on to Philadelphia. Not an easy journey. Weeks on the ship, full of boredom and idleness, would pass before she got there, but she would gladly endure whatever hardship she must, just to be in the arms of Brandon Cooper again.

"Did you and he ever...?" Ada blushed easily and now her cheeks were turning red.

"Did we ever what?"

"Nothing." Her blush deepened.

"Good grief. Do you mean, did we ever make love?"

"Well, yes."

"No one else must know, especially Mother."

"Of course."

"We did it a few times, three to be exact."

Ada gasped and slapped a hand over her mouth. "You didn't!"

"We did. Three times when Aunt Florence was out, and the servants gone. It was...very nice." Actually, it hadn't been all that nice, but that was only because she couldn't relax and kept worrying someone would catch them. Of course, all that would change when they married, she was sure of it.

They'd caught their breath and started walking again. Finally arriving at the Monarch Gold Mine, Laurie again was struck by its ugliness. Long, wooden sluice boxes stood on rickety stilts over the muddy ground. They stretched from the nearby river to the mine entrance where grunting, grimy men with shovels scooped heaps of ore from iron carts into the sluice boxes. From there, gushing water washed separate pieces of ore down the boxes as they extended down the hill, all of it a muddy, unsightly mess.

The office—mine headquarters, as Father called it—consisted of nothing more than one ramshackle building with shingles missing from the roof. An unpainted barracks for the workers stood nearby. Worst of all, the entrance to the mine itself made Laurie's skin crawl whenever she looked at that yawning black hole in the side of the mountain. Heavy beams lined the sides and top and rusty iron carts ran in and out on a narrow set of tracks. Who in their right mind would want to go down that dark, dangerous place? Mining accidents happened all the time. So far, the Monarch had been spared, but you never knew.

As they walked toward the office, Ada pointed toward a wagon parked in front. A sign on the side read ATLAS MINE. "Looks like Darcy McKenna's here."

"I hope not."

"You don't like him, do you?"

"Not especially."

"Well, I do. I think he's dark, tall, lean and, well, intriguing. There's something mysterious about him. He never talks about himself or where he comes from."

"I haven't the least interest in where he's from." Laurie definitely didn't care for the owner of the Atlas Mine. She wasn't sure why. He was always polite enough. Maybe she disliked him because he always seemed so driven, as if running a profitable mine was all that mattered in his life. Or, she had to admit, maybe she disliked him because the few times she'd met him, and he looked at her with those piercing blue eyes, she had the feeling he didn't like what he saw.

Ada pointed to another wagon, marked COYOTE MINE. "That's Brock Dominick's wagon. They must be having a meeting."

Laurie had no desire to mingle with the mine owners. At least Darcy McKenna knew how to be polite, but Brock Dominick, a crude-mannered man with a powerful build, hadn't the faintest notion how to act in a civilized manner, and didn't seem to care. "We won't stay long. Just long enough to give Father his lunch, and then we'll leave."

Inside the office, Laurie's father and her brother, Hugh, appeared to be engaged in a serious discussion with the visiting mine owners. Darcy McKenna and his assistant, Tom Crain, were there, along with Brock Dominick and a few other owners. They stopped talking when Laurie and Ada walked in. "Hello, ladies," Samuel Sinclair called. Laurie's affable father had been having more than his share of problems lately, but he never let his worry show. "Ah, so you brought me my lunch. Seems I forgot again."

"Did you really forget, Pa?" Laurie's brother, Hugh, inquired, "or did you want an excuse to see more of Laurie before she leaves?"

"Never mind all that." Samuel looked slightly sheepish as he took the lunch pail. "Thank you, daughter, and Ada, too. Want to stay a while? We were just finishing up. They're claiming I'm a dangerous character." He smiled at Darcy McKenna. "Aren't you, my friend?"

Darcy didn't smile back. "What I'm saying is, you're taking a chance with all that gunpowder."

"Damn right," Brock Dominick agreed. "You'll blow yourself to kingdom come if you're not careful."

"You let me worry about that. Did you know my little girl is leaving tomorrow?" Father cast a sad eye at Laurie. "Hate to see her go, but she's hell-bent on getting back to some fellow in Philadelphia, and I can't stop her."

Brock remained stone-faced and said nothing, which didn't surprise Laurie. She expected nothing more from a man as coarse and unfeeling as the owner of the Coyote Mine.

"That's too bad, Sam." Darcy sounded genuinely sorry for his friend, but when he turned to her and inquired, "When are you leaving?" she knew he was only being polite and hadn't the least interest in what she did. Briefly she told him her travel plans.

"Have a pleasant journey, Miss Sinclair."

"Thank you, Mr. McKenna, I shall." And she certainly would. How wonderful she could at last escape this miserable mining town with its gritty men like Brock Dominic and Darcy McKenna whose talk was all about mining, who cared little for the social graces. She addressed her father and brother. "I hope you can get home early tonight for my farewell dinner."

"We might be a little late," said Hugh. "Mr. McKenna just sold us some of his gunpowder, and we're going to put it to good use. But you'd better not start without us. If you do, that precious boat ticket of yours might disappear."

"You wouldn't dare." Laurie gave her slender, sandy-haired brother a playful swipe on the arm. At twenty-seven, he hadn't got over playing the occasional practical joke. When she was little, sometimes he went too far with his joking and teasing, but she'd always tried to overcome her resentment. A hard worker, he'd become Father's indispensable assistant at the mine.

"We'd best get back to our discussion," Sam said to Laurie. "We're trying to figure what to do with those pesky high-graders."

Dominick's face clouded with rage. "I say, kill 'em all. Shoot 'em like dogs."

"Now, now, we don't want to go to extremes, Brock," Sam replied.

Laurie hadn't been in town long before she heard about the thieves who stole the high-grade ore out of the sluice boxes, always in the dead of night when no one was around. Called high-graders, they were a big problem with all the mines.

"After we've done all the hard work of mining it out of the ground," Darcy said. "I'm doubling the guards at the Atlas. What about you, Sam?"

Father's expression became tight with strain. "Looks like I've got a serious problem with it, too."

Finding the whole business of mining to be utterly boring, Laurie turned to her sister. "We're in the way. It's time to go."

She and Ada said their goodbyes, reminding Father and Hugh they'd better be home in time for Laurie's farewell dinner. As they started down the mountain, Laurie remarked, "I'll miss my family and a few people I met in church, but I certainly won't miss that Darcy McKenna."

Ada looked surprised. "Seems to me it's that awful Brock Dominick you shouldn't miss, not Darcy."

"Brock's out-and-out crude and disgusting," Laurie replied with amusement. "So, I don't have to wonder why I don't like him. But Darcy? I'm not sure. Maybe I don't like him because he doesn't like me."

"What's not to like about you? You're the beauty of the family and smart besides. Back in Philadelphia, you could have had just about any man you chose."

Laurie hated discussions about who in the family was beautiful and who was not. She'd been gifted with a wealth of auburn hair; big, velvet-brown eyes; and a fine figure. Not so, poor Ada, whose thin, mousey-colored hair, plump face, and chubby figure had so far not attracted any suitors. Her extreme shyness didn't help either. But as Laurie had pointed out countless times, Ada possessed such a compassionate heart and caring nature that someday some man was bound to see how beautiful she was but in a different way. Ada always scoffed when she said that and claimed that at her age she was well on her way to becoming an old maid. "And I really don't care. I'm happy and I feel useful. What would Mathew and Maryanne do without me?"

Laurie felt a pang of sadness remembering Hugh's wife, Maude, who had died in childbirth two years ago. Mathew, the baby, had survived. Ada had gladly taken over his care, along with his sister's, Maryanne, who had just turned three. "Hugh's lucky, Ada. You do a wonderful job."

"Let's get back to Darcy McKenna," Ada persisted. "Like I said, there's something about him that's enormously attractive. It's hard to describe exactly. Maybe it's because he has a kind of careless charm about him that he's totally unaware of."

Laurie burst into scornful laughter. "You think he's charming?"

"Absolutely I do, and wealthy besides. They say his Atlas Mine produces more gold than any mine around, except the Coyote, of course. Brock Dominick's the really rich man in this town."

"Even so..." Laurie left her sentence hang. Why should she waste her breath on a man she would never see again? "What do you suppose Hugh meant when he talked about putting some gunpowder to good use? I hope they're not planning something dangerous."

"You worry too much. You should be thinking about all the good things, like tonight we'll have a lovely celebration, and tomorrow you're off to Philadelphia and the man you love. How could you be anything but giddy with happiness?"

Ada had hit upon the perfect phrase. Laurie indeed found herself giddy with happiness. "You're right. What was I thinking of? I'm the luckiest girl in the world."

Ada burst into delighted laughter. "And may your marvelous luck continue."

"Oh, it will." Not that she needed any luck. A bright, beautiful future lay before her. That anything might go wrong would be unthinkable.

* * * *

With Darcy holding the reins, he and Tom left the Monarch Mine and headed back to his own mine. "I wish I hadn't done it," he remarked.

"Done what?" White-haired, with a weathered face and scraggly beard, Tom Crain had spent most of his fifty years in the out-of-doors, hunting, fishing, and now gold mining. He'd become Darcy's right-hand man at the Atlas Mine. "You mean selling Sinclair all that gunpowder?"

Darcy nodded. "He claims he knows what he's doing. You heard me straight-out tell him I didn't think so. I did my best to persuade him to get someone who knows about explosives, but you know how he is. Stubborn. Won't listen to advice. Thinks he can do it all himself."

"He's been successful so far, hasn't he? The Monarch has produced a lot of gold."

"Not anymore it doesn't. Their output has gone down. I can see why he wants to blow open a new vein but why he's so all-fired sure he'll find gold there, I have no idea."

"Maybe…"

"Maybe what, Tom?"

"There've been rumors. I wouldn't be surprised but what the high-graders are the reason the Monarch's profits are down."

"Maybe. I've heard them, too, but it's not our business."

Tom said no more. They rode in silence until he remarked, "That Sinclair girl is sure a pretty little thing. Too bad she's leaving."

Darcy slanted a skeptical gaze at his friend. "You think so? I don't."

Tom squinted in thought and took a long time answering. "I grant you, she's a little bit stuck-up—"

"A lot stuck-up. She doesn't belong here. She'll be happier in Philadelphia with her parties and fancy clothes."

"Maybe so, but we need more women like her in this town."

"Why?"

"She's got culture, Darcy. Well educated. Knows her manners. Knows how to dress proper, not like those gaudy women you find in the hotels." Quickly he added, "Mrs. Wagner excepted, of course."

"Of course." Darcy gave his friend an affable nod. Leave it to Tom to sense the special relationship he had with Mrs. Lucille Wagner, owner of the Gold Spike Hotel.

Tom wasn't finished. "That Miss Sinclair has a head on her shoulders and isn't silly like a lot of women. I reckon I could have a decent conversation with her if the occasion arose."

"Well, it won't because she's leaving tomorrow, and good riddance."

"I still think it's a shame. You have a lot in common, seeing as how you're both well educated and all. Plain to see you come from the same background."

"Same background? Why do you say that?"

"Well, because you talk right, use the proper grammar and all. You've got good manners. That is, when you care to use them. I never asked but just assumed you came from a fine family back east."

Darcy smiled wryly. "Guess it's time I told you. I come from West Virginia, Tom. From Mingo County, the heart of the coal mining country. Every last man in my family worked in the coal mines. I did, too, starting when I was eight years old."

Tom stared in surprise. "Eight? That's mighty young."

"Not according to my parents, it wasn't. I started as a trapper. My sole job was to sit all day waiting to open a wooden door to allow coal cars to pass through. That meant I had to open that door about twelve to fifty times a day. The rest of the time, I sat in the dark two hundred feet below the surface of the earth. Nothing to do. I just sat there."

"That don't sound very pleasant."

"It wasn't. When I turned ten, I got promoted to breaker boy. That was less monotonous but more dangerous. I worked with other boys the same age. Every day except Sunday we sat on long wooden benches picking out the bad stuff mixed with the coal—rock, slate, clay, that sort of thing—as it came down the chutes. At times, the dust from the coal was so dense we couldn't see. My face was black, and my eyes were red."

Tom shook his head with sympathy. "What about your parents? How come they let you work in the mines at so young an age?"

"That's just the way it was. I don't blame my parents. Where I grew up, children were expected to work. Otherwise, they'd be spending their time in what my parents considered sinful idleness. Not just them. That's what everybody thought. I had nine brothers and sisters. We all worked from the time we were around seven or eight."

"What about school?"

"No school. We never went to school. My parents sent the boys to the mines soon as they were able. They sent the girls out to do domestic work."

"God Almighty." Tom pondered for a while. "Then how come you got yourself educated?"

"That's a long story I'll tell you sometime."

Tom made a quick grimace and said no more. Good. Darcy rarely talked about his past, but Tom had become a good friend who deserved to know at least something about where he came from. He also didn't care to hear another word about the irritating Miss Laurie Sinclair, who'd be gone tomorrow, anyway. Why she annoyed him so much, he didn't know but wouldn't waste another moment thinking about her.

* * * *

Laurie would never forget her first shocking glimpse of the mountain town of Lucky Creek, California. She'd known better than to expect the same tree-lined streets and stately brick mansions of Philadelphia, but nothing could have prepared her for the primitive conditions of her new home. Most of the town consisted of muddy, trash-strewn streets and a collection of squalid shacks and tents scattered along the American River. At least the main street of town showed a semblance of civilization with decent boardwalks where a lady could walk without muddying her skirt. Day and night, the main street teemed with activity, what with several hotels, restaurants, and saloons that flourished alongside groceries, bakeries, a bank, saddlery, and blacksmith shop. Men in miners' clothing thronged the streets, some headed for their mining claims with their picks and shovels. Or, if they'd been lucky, they were headed for the Assay Office with their bag of gold dust, or, if they'd been really lucky, gold nuggets.

To say the Sinclair family lived in one of the finest homes in Lucky Creek wasn't saying as much as that description might imply. At least the large, two-story house Sam Sinclair built for his family was located in what could be termed the better part of town. Surrounded by similar two-story houses with wide front porches and green lawns, it stood on a tree-lined street that might have reminded Laurie of Philadelphia except the pine and fir trees stayed green the year around, unlike the dogwoods and poplars of Society Hill. *I won't miss it at all*, Laurie thought when she and Ada arrived home from the mine and walked into the usual noisy, bustling Sinclair household. The house was spotless, thanks to Mei Ling, their young Chinese maid. Delicious aromas wafted from the kitchen where Valeria, their Bolivian cook, had something in the oven and three different items cooking on the big woodstove. In the parlor, their mother, Elizabeth Sinclair, sat on the settee reading from a storybook to Mathew and Maryanne. Again, Laurie remembered Hugh's late wife, Maude. What a shame she couldn't be here to see how healthy and happy both her children were, and how adorable.

Elizabeth looked up from the storybook and sighed. "I can't believe this is your last day here. I'm going to miss you, Laurie, but I must say, I'm delighted with your reason for leaving."

"I knew you would be." Struck by the irony of it all, Laurie recalled how she'd welcomed the opportunity to stay behind when the family moved west. Finally, she could escape the smothering presence of her mother. At age twenty, she wanted to make her own choices, especially where men were concerned, but Elizabeth Sinclair knew better. In her zeal to find "just the right suitor" for her daughter, she insisted upon knowing each suitor's age, education, family background and finances before giving her approval. How ironic that when left to make her own choices, Laurie chose the perfect man to warm her mother's heart. Brandon Cooper, five years older than she, blond and handsome, came from one of the oldest and finest families in Philadelphia. A great-uncle on his father's side had signed the Constitution. Brandon himself had graduated cum laude from the University of Pennsylvania and had already distinguished himself in the elite world of entomology.

"And I'll miss you." Laurie meant what she said. She'd miss Ada, too, and Hugh and Father. Actually, words would never convey how much she'd miss her family, surprisingly her mother most of all. White-haired, with a regal posture, Elizabeth Sinclair no longer tried her daughter's patience. Since she'd moved to Lucky Creek, she found ways to look at the bright side and never lamented her fate, even though she had every right to. In Philadelphia, she'd led a privileged life: wealthy husband, plenty of servants, beautiful home in a fine neighborhood, a high standing in Philadelphia society. Now she lived in this coarse, crude, mining town, the ugliest place on earth as far as Laurie was concerned. If Mother ever uttered one word of complaint, Laurie never heard it. Of all the family, Mother was the only one who'd never rebuked Sam Sinclair for uprooting her from the life she loved. "It's something Samuel felt he had to do," she explained many a time, and had rejoiced when her unpredictable husband finally found enough gold that he was able to open his own mine, the Monarch, and she and the family could join him.

Laurie sat on the settee and placed little Maryanne on her lap. "And I'll miss the children, too. I feel guilty, leaving you and Ada to care for them."

Ada quickly spoke up. "Oh, no, you should never feel that way. You must do what makes you happy. Don't worry, Mother and I will do fine, and of course there's always Hugh who helps when he can."

Laurie suppressed a disdainful sniff. She wouldn't contradict kindhearted Ada, but their widowed brother rarely if ever lifted a finger to help with the care of his children. But wasn't that the way of things? Child-rearing was women's work. Still, Laurie didn't like the way Hugh almost completely ignored his children. Not long ago, he'd made matters worse when he moved out and took up residence in a fine suite of rooms at the Egyptian Hotel. Of course, he'd left his children behind for his family to care for. According to Father, Hugh was levelheaded, thoroughly dependable, and doing a good job at the mine, although lately he'd got some wild idea in his head about a lost lake covered in gold dust. According to the stories he'd heard, it was the greatest find of all—a golden lake high in the mountains, hidden and unimaginably rich. Those who'd seen it swore they'd seen sheets of gold dotting the lake's surface like leaves in autumn. They'd seen Indians fishing with golden fish hooks. Everyone scoffed, especially their sensible father, who had no time for such impractical dreams. Hugh claimed he'd find it someday, though. He just needed time.

By late afternoon, the tantalizing aroma of Valeria's *picante de pollo* filled the air. Hardly anyone dined fashionably late in Lucky Creek, and dinner would be ready at six o'clock. They'd invited their next-door neighbors, the Harrisons, to help them celebrate. Although a family's so-called social standing meant nothing in a place like Lucky Creek, Mother highly approved of the Harrisons, who once had lived in Boston and hobnobbed with the wealthy Brahmins of Beacon Hill. Like Sam Sinclair, Warren Harrison had caught the gold rush fever and headed west. Unlike Sam, he soon realized there were other ways to make money besides digging for gold. He now sold mining equipment throughout the Sierra Nevadas, a business that had earned him a small fortune. Warren and his wife, Agatha, had three well-behaved children. Ruthie, their little girl, was the same age as Maryanne, and they often played together.

Father and Hugh would be home any minute. The Harrisons were served refreshments while they sat visiting in the parlor and waited.

And waited.

Six o'clock came and went. Where were Father and Hugh? They should have been home by now. By six thirty, Valeria indignantly marched in from the kitchen, announced, "If I no serve dinner now, it's ruined," and marched out again.

They agreed they'd better get started. No one wanted to tangle with their fiery-tempered cook. As they all sat down at the dinner table, the crystal glasses on the table shook, accompanied by a low, rumbling sound. "That sounded like thunder," Laurie remarked. "Was it supposed to rain?"

Warren Harrison leaped to his feet. "That wasn't thunder, that was an explosion."

Elizabeth Sinclair slammed a hand to her heart. "At one of the mines, do you think?"

Warren gave the answer no one wanted to hear. "I'm afraid so. From what I could tell, it could have come from the Monarch."

Chapter 2

The dinner instantly forgotten, Warren Harrison gave Laurie, her mother and sister a fast ride in his carriage to the Monarch Mine. Laurie's stomach knotted with fear when she saw black smoke pouring from the entrance. A crowd had gathered. People were milling about, but no one was getting close or attempting to go in. Was Father still inside? Was Hugh? She started to run toward the entrance, but Tom Crain appeared before her, blocking her way. "You can't go any farther," he yelled, his voice harsh. "Get back. That smoke is deadly."

She gulped and took a deep breath, trying to control the fear rising within her. "But Father's in there, and my brother, and I must—"

He firmly grasped both her arms. "No, you can't. I don't know where your father is, but you can't look for him now. Your brother's over there." He nodded toward a small group gathered about a still body lying on the ground. "He's alive but just barely."

She rushed to her brother's side. Kneeling beside him, she couldn't hold back a cry of shock and anguish. She could hardly recognize him, his face blackened from soot, or burns, she wasn't sure which. He lay with his bloodied right arm partly bent beneath him in such an unnatural way it had to be broken.

Doc Hansen, the town's only doctor, had already arrived. After a quick examination, he declared Hugh must immediately be taken to his clinic where he would do what he could for his injuries, but the doctor didn't look hopeful.

Mother and Ada stood by crying as Hugh was carried away. "Where's Samuel?" Mother cried, looking at Laurie with pleading eyes. She'd always been a strong woman; Laurie had never seen her cry. But now she looked on the verge of hysteria. "Is he still in the mine? Is anyone else in there?"

Father had told Laurie that at one time the Monarch had employed over two hundred miners. Now the number was reduced to only a few. Had anyone else been in there besides Father and Hugh? How much worse could this be? "I'll see what I can find out." Laurie tried to keep her voice steady, not easy when her insides ached with fear. She raced toward the entrance again where a group of men stood at a distance, watching the black smoke still billowing out. They were doing nothing, just shaking their heads in a helpless sort of way. She recognized Brock Dominick of the Coyote Mine along with Tom Crain and Darcy McKenna. She ran up to them and inquired, "My father—is he still in there? Is anyone else? Can you get them out?" She'd tried to keep the panic from her voice but without complete success. It didn't matter. Nothing mattered except the fate of her beloved father.

Darcy drew her aside. "They say your brother was barely conscious when they found him. He could hardly talk, but they understood him to say he barely got out before the roof of the mine shaft collapsed and your father had been behind him."

"So, you don't think he got out?"

"It doesn't look that way."

She couldn't utter another sound and suddenly shivered from the cold. The night had turned chilly, as it always did in the mountains. In their frantic haste to get to the mine, no one had thought to put on a wrap.

Darcy removed his buckskin jacket and threw it around her shoulders. "Here, take this."

"I couldn't." She started to remove it.

"You could." He pressed the jacket into place on her shoulders and stepped away. "Will you be all right?"

He'd been so kind she'd forgotten she disliked him. "I'll be fine. I must get back to my family." She turned away, dreading to give her mother and sister the terrible news.

* * * *

The crowd had dispersed by the time Darcy and Tom left the scene of the Monarch Mine disaster and headed for home. Nothing more could be done. They'd have to wait at least a few more hours before the smoke cleared enough that they could get inside. Tom shook his head. "Poor bastard. You warned him it wasn't safe."

Nodding in agreement, Darcy flicked the reins. "Sam Sinclair was a good man. Foolish, maybe, but if ever a man could be trusted it was Sam."

"You think he's dead?"

"It would be a miracle if he's still alive."

"He died for nothing. The miracle would be if that blast opened up another vein of gold as good as the first one."

Darcy didn't speak for a while, focusing his attention on the treacherous mountain road. "He wouldn't have taken a chance like that if he wasn't about to go broke. The Monarch was close to closing down. That old vein of gold was nearly exhausted."

"What do you suppose the family's going to do? Hugh will be laid up for a while, if he lives. Then there's Sam's wife, the two grown daughters, and those little ones of Hugh's. They're not but more than two and three, aren't they?" Tom's brow furrowed with concern. "A real shame."

"We'll go back tomorrow. The smoke should have cleared by then."

"Maybe they'll be a miracle, and we'll find him alive."

Darcy threw his friend a cynical smile. "Pigs will fly before that happens. Sam's dead, Tom. No way on earth he could have survived that explosion. We'll be lucky if we find what's left of him."

* * * *

The town possessed what was optimistically called the Lucky Creek General Hospital, although it was nothing more than an oversize clinic, financed and run by the generous and compassionate Doc Hansen himself. Sickness and injuries were so common in the mining camps that from the day the unimposing, one-story wooden structure opened for business, it ran at full or near-full capacity. With rudimentary equipment, assisted by one experienced nurse and two Indian women to help her, the good doctor treated an endless stream of miners whose injuries ranged from sprained fingers to broken bones, frostbite, snake bites, grizzly bear attacks, and more. Rampant diseases took their toll, everything from colds to measles, mumps, diphtheria, cholera, and pneumonia. Bad nutrition, a common problem in the camps, led to scurvy.

While his family hovered close by, Doc Hansen examined Hugh, muttering gloomily to himself and shaking his head. "He's badly hurt. I'll set the arm, but I don't know about that head injury. And then there's those broken ribs. Not much we can do about those, other than just let them heal."

They waited while Doc set Hugh's badly broken arm. Once finished, he remarked, "Did the best job I could, but it's broken in several places, and I don't know how well it will heal. A good thing he was unconscious when I set it, so he didn't feel the pain. You all go home now. Get some rest. We'll see what happens in the morning."

Exhausted, they returned home. Elizabeth had made a valiant attempt to hold herself together, but she'd lost the only man she ever loved, and maybe her only son, and she had lapsed into kind of a dazed silence. Ada, so delicate and vulnerable, had pretty much fallen apart and couldn't stop crying. Grief for her father tore at Laurie's heart, but she did her best to remain strong for them all. She checked on the children. Mei Ling had stayed to watch them. Laurie thanked her and sent her home. She made sure her mother and sister got to bed and went to bed herself. She tried to sleep, but her mind kept jumping from one anguished thought to the next. Father dead. Hugh badly injured and maybe would die. And sometime during the night the thought struck her. *I won't be going home tomorrow.* But all that seemed unimportant now. She didn't dwell on it long, and soon her never-ending, anguished thoughts returned.

She wasn't sure how much she slept that night, if she'd slept at all. Early next morning, she got up, dressed, and went downstairs intending to put on a pot of coffee. Ordinarily, Valeria didn't arrive this early, but Laurie found her in the kitchen, the coffee already brewing. "Good morning, Valeria. How good of you to come early."

Her cook's command of the English language was sketchy at best, but Laurie understood the sympathy that filled Valeria's eyes as she gave Laurie a hug, saying, *"Lo siento por tu pérdida...*I'm sorry."

Talking slowly, Laurie replied, "I hope your husband—*tu esposo*—doesn't mind that you came early." She hadn't spoken idly. Their Bolivian cook was married to a white man, Emery Finch, a card dealer who worked at the Palace Hotel. Laurie had never met him but had heard of his reputation. Noted for his foul language and trigger temper, he was also noted for his fiery speeches demanding all foreigners be banned from the gold fields. He was said to rule his wife with an iron hand. Possessing a volatile jealousy, he never let her out of his sight except to come to work. More than once, Valeria had shown up with a bruise on her arm or face. She laughed off any suggestion her husband had beat her, but the Sinclairs suspected otherwise. The strange thing was, Valeria wasn't the kind of woman who couldn't stand up for herself. Somewhere in her forties, with a tough, weathered face, she came from a town called Sucre that nestled high in the Andes Mountains, over nine thousand feet above sea level. She never complained but once told Laurie life hadn't been easy for the *cholitas*, the women of Indian heritage, who lived in Sucre and worked mostly as lowly servants. Laurie loved the manner in which she dressed in colorful layered skirts and shawls, a bowler hat perched atop her long, black braids. Sometimes she removed her hat when she came to work. Other times, the hat sat securely on her head while she cooked dinner, a source of amusement for the Sinclairs, although they never let on how funny they thought she looked. But above all else, they highly appreciated not only her skilled cooking, but her loyalty and devotion, especially to the children.

"*Mi esposo* no mind," Valeria assured her. Laurie wasn't sure she believed her but was grateful she was there just the same.

Agatha Harrison from next door arrived shortly after, expressing her sorrow and offering to help any way she could. "You've had a hard night. Now you just sit down and I'll fetch us some coffee."

Her neighbor's kind words touched Laurie's vulnerable emotions so much she almost cried. She sat at the kitchen table and watched while Agatha poured them cups of coffee from the big pot Valeria had just brewed on the stove. "Do you think there's a chance Father could still be alive?"

"There's always that hope, of course," Agatha said carefully. "Warren knows about such things, being as he's lived around here for years. I hate to tell you this, but he says the best you can hope for is they find what's left of him, so you can give him a decent burial. Mr. McKenna said he and Mr. Crain will look for him today if the smoke's not too bad. Warren says Mr. McKenna knows all there is to know about mines. If there's anyone who'd be better at finding your father, I don't know who it would be."

"That's reassuring," Laurie replied without conviction. Darcy McKenna had been kind to her last night, but her low opinion of him hadn't changed. No need to say so, though.

Agatha slapped a hand to her chest. "Oh, dear, I just remembered. You were supposed to leave today."

"I know, but I can't go now, can I? Guess I'll have to"—Laurie's voice broke miserably as a flash of disappointment ripped through her—"cancel my ticket." She hadn't realized until this moment how deeply, desperately she'd wanted to leave Lucky Creek. If she'd been asked yesterday, she'd have said her entire future life depended on her getting back to Philadelphia, into the loving arms of Brandon Cooper, and nothing could possibly stand in the way.

"Such a shame, Laurie. I know how much you wanted to get back to the fellow who collects all those insects."

At another time, Laurie would have laughed, but today nothing was funny. "I'm afraid he'll have to wait."

"If he loves you, and I'm sure he does, he won't mind in the least. Right now, your mother needs you, and Ada, and of course poor Hugh, if he even lives."

"Of course, I'm disappointed, but it'll be a short delay, just long enough for the family to get on their feet again. A week or two at the most, I should imagine."

"Of course." Agatha sounded doubtful. "Doesn't the stagecoach company act as agents for the steamship line?" Laurie nodded. "Then you'll need to cancel your tickets and get your money back. I'll have Warren do it if you like."

How good to have a neighbor who cared. "Thanks, but I'll take care of it myself. We'll be going back to the hospital to see Hugh, and I'll return the tickets then."

Strange, how all her hopes and dreams had centered on those tickets, but now, in the space of only hours, she'd hardly given them a thought. Right now, she must focus on her family's tragedy, but that didn't mean she wouldn't get back to Philadelphia. It would just take a little longer than she'd thought.

* * * *

Eyes red from crying, Ada soon came down for breakfast, but Mother did not. When Laurie went upstairs, she found her mother lying pale and exhausted in her bed. Determined to return to the hospital, she'd tried to get up but felt dizzy and weak and had to lie down again. "I must go see Hugh," she whispered, so softly Laurie could hardly hear.

"You're not going anywhere," Laurie told her. "You've had a shock and you need to rest. Ada can stay with you, and I'll go. If he's awake, and I'd wager he will be, I'll explain you were feeling a bit ill and will visit later. I'm sure he'll understand."

She waited, prepared for further argument, but her mother breathed a weary sigh. "All right then. I'll just lie here and rest for a while."

That didn't sound like Mother at all. Laurie hid her concern. "Good. I want you to stay in bed and not lift a finger. Then I'll find a ride to the mine and see if"—hard choking the words out—"they've found Father. I'll be back soon as I can."

Ada agreed to stay with Mother. At least she'd stopped weeping and seemed resigned to the sad fact Father was gone. "Albert brought the rig back," she said, referring to the down-on-his-luck miner Father had hired as their stableman. Sometime last night he'd brought Sam's horse and carriage back from the mine. Fine with Laurie. She'd have had to walk otherwise. She caught Albert before he had a chance to unhitch the horses and had him drive her to the hospital.

At least Hugh was still alive. According to the nurse, he'd awakened, appeared to have all his senses, and had fallen asleep again. "We still don't know," Doc Hansen said when he stopped by. "There's the broken arm, the head injury, and those ribs were pretty badly crushed. If he lives, he'll need time to heal and will surely be laid up for a while. A long while, I'm afraid."

At least her brother was still alive, and for that she was grateful. She'd think of the bad news about his ribs later on when she didn't have so much else on her mind. "Have you heard anything about my father?"

The kindly doctor shook his head. "All I've heard is there are men up there looking, but I don't know if they've entered the mine yet. That smoke can be deadly. No sense taking a chance, especially when your father is likely..." He caught himself and cleared his throat. "I wouldn't get my hopes up."

The doctor's words hit her hard. She wished she could be like Ada—start to weep, let it all out—but instead she took in a deep, steadying breath. "Thank you, Doctor, I know he's likely dead, but there's always the hope."

"You should go up there yourself. I know for a fact several of the owners are there. They've brought some of their workers along, and if there's a way to get in there, they'll find it."

Laurie thanked him. "Come back later in the day," Doc Hansen said. "He should be waking up soon."

For her next stop, she had Albert drive her to the office of the California Stage Company where she cancelled her reservations and was able to return her tickets and receive the refund. At the sight of the money in her hand, she came close to choking up. Always generous, Father had given her the money for her trip home, despite his disappointment that she wasn't going to stay. He was like that. Always generous. Always willing to give her anything she wanted. She'd been his special pet, more so than Hugh or Ada, although he would never admit it, nor had Laurie ever boasted that she was.

That errand done, she had Albert drive her up the narrow mountain road to the Monarch Mine and arrived to find only a small plume of light-colored smoke arising from the mine entrance. A group of men stood not far away, talking earnestly. One, seeing her arrival, broke from the group and walked toward her. Why did it have to be Darcy McKenna? She sighed to herself and climbed from the carriage.

Darcy touched two fingers to the broad brim of his hat. "Good morning, Miss Sinclair. You're wondering if we've been in the mine. We haven't yet, but as you can see, the smoke is just about gone, and we're about to send in a search party."

He was certainly being kind, she'd give him that. "Will it take long, do you think?"

"There's no telling. Depends upon how deep we have to go. I wish I could have talked to Hugh and found out more. How's he doing?"

"The doctor doesn't know yet."

"Weren't you planning on leaving today?"

"Yes, I was." His question surprised her. Why should he care when and if she left? He was simply making polite conversation, she supposed. Considering he was about to search for her father, she owed him a decent answer. "I already got a refund for my stagecoach and ship tickets, so I'll have to stay at least another week, maybe two at the most."

"You never did like Lucky Creek, did you?"

What business was it of his whether she liked this town or not? "I hate it here and won't stay a minute more than I have to." She should stop right there, but something about this man galled her no end, and she couldn't let it go. "Not that I worry. My fiancé will completely understand why I've been delayed. Among his many fine qualities, he possesses all the patience in the world."

"That so?" Darcy's solemn expression remained the same except for a faint twinkle of amusement in the depths of his eyes. "Are you talking about the man who collects bugs?"

He was needling her, she knew he was, yet she couldn't help rising to the challenge. "Brandon Cooper is already one of the most noted entomologists in America. He's traveled the world—South Africa, the East Indian Archipelago—in search of rare specimens of orthopteroid insects."

His forehead creased. He removed his hat and scratched his forehead. "Or-thop-ter-oid? I'm impressed."

"For your information, that's grasshoppers and crickets. And furthermore, his collection of microlepidoptera is remarkable. That's moths."

"Well, now." He got serious again, as if he'd suddenly realized he shouldn't be laughing at someone who had just lost her father. He replaced his hat. "We'll be going into the mine soon. Go home. You need to be with your family. If and when we find anything you'll be the first to know."

She watched as he turned away and headed toward a group of men who stood at the mine entrance. What had she been thinking? She'd just made a fool of herself. She didn't know how much education he had, but obviously Darcy McKenna wasn't the least impressed with her fiancé's great achievements in the field of entomology. How very childish she must have sounded with her bragging, doing her best to impress him. And why? She didn't even like the man.

He'd given her good advice, though. With a sigh, she returned to the carriage.

* * * *

Idiot woman. As Darcy strode toward the mine entrance, he shook his head in disgust. Not at her but at himself. Yet again, he'd let the snobbish Miss Laurie Sinclair get under his skin. Usually if he didn't like someone, he'd simply avoid them. If by chance he had to deal with them, he did so quickly, making sure he remained detached, cool, unruffled. But that didn't happen when he talked to Laurie Sinclair. When she mentioned her fancy fiancé with the fine education, his blood shot through his veins like one of those geysers in Wyoming. Entomology? Who cared? A bug was a bug, as far as he was concerned. He'd never been to school. No shame in that. Lots of people had never been to school, yet that was a fact about himself no one needed to know. And besides, in a very real way he'd received the best education in the world, just not in a schoolhouse.

Tom and the rest stood waiting. "Think it's safe to go in now?" Tom asked.

"Safe as it will ever be." He might not know about entomology, but no one could know more about mines than he did. "Come on, men. Let's do our best for Sam's family. He was a good man, and we owe him that. I'll lead the way."

Chapter 3

In the late afternoon, Laurie asked Albert to take her back to the hospital to see how Hugh was doing. When she arrived, she discovered he'd recovered consciousness and lay in a groggy haze. The doctor wasn't there, but the hospital's only nurse stood by his bed. Laurie got her aside. "Do you know yet if he'll make it?"

The nurse nodded. "Doc Hansen says he will. He's full of laudanum for the pain, besides being in a state of shock, so don't stay too long."

Hugh would live. Laurie whispered a prayerful, "Thank you, God," as she sank to a chair by his bedside. He looked terrible with his ribs bandaged, arm in a cast, a big bandage on his head, part of his face blackened from a powder burn. He lay quietly with his eyes closed. She wouldn't disturb him, just sit here quietly and let him rest.

Memories of their childhood flooded back as she watched him. Years older than she, Hugh had once been her idol. When she was little, she used to follow him around, awestruck by his wit and superior manner. Only with the passage of time, did she realize he wasn't perfect. He liked to tease her, but often his so-called playful teasing went too far. "Can't you take a joke?" he'd ask. Only when she was older did she realize he was just being mean. He told lies, not caring if he got her into trouble. He did selfish things, and was a disappointment to their parents, especially Father. Hugh wasn't robust like Sam. Not very tall, with a slender build, he would run away when other boys confronted him. "You must stand up and fight like a man," Father often told him, but he never did. Only when he went to work at the Monarch did he finally redeem himself in his father's eyes. From what Laurie could see, he did his work well and Father was satisfied.

She loved her brother despite all the bad things. Her heart had gone out to him when Maude died and left him with the two little ones. Father had been pleased with his work in the mine, so of course, she was pleased with him, too. Besides all that, he was family. That alone would have earned her love and loyalty.

Finally, he opened his eyes. With a bewildered expression, he looked her way. It took him a while to focus. "Laurie, is that you?"

"It's me. You're in the hospital."

"Hospital," he echoed as if trying to understand.

"There was an explosion. Do you remember?"

"Explosion?" A glint of recognition lit his eyes. "Father? Did he make it?"

"I'm afraid he didn't make it out. They're looking for him now, but they don't expect…" She could not go on.

"Dear God," he whispered. He remained silent for a time before saying, "I told him not to try it."

"Try what?" Laurie bent close to hear what he was saying.

"Find a new vein of gold." Hugh closed his eyes and lapsed into silence again, as if the mere utterance of a few words had worn him out. Finally, he reopened them. "He was a proud man, Laurie. That old vein had just about played out. He was hell-bent on finding a new one, even though he knew he was taking a chance."

"You mean he was guessing?" She hadn't been long in the mine country but long enough to know wild guesses seldom paid off.

"I'm afraid so."

"But Father still had his investments, didn't he? And his savings?"

"There's plenty left. Nothing to worry about."

She remained until Hugh drifted off to sleep again. She left the hospital relieved the family still had money, despite all the rest.

* * * *

An atmosphere of gloom hung over the house when Laurie returned from the hospital. As yet, no one had hung a black wreath on the front door, but they might as well have. Donations of food from the neighbors filled the kitchen. A steady stream of solemn-faced visitors stopped by to pay their respects. Sam Sinclair had made a lot of friends in Lucky Creek, and many wanted to express their hope he might still be alive, although most looked doubtful.

At least Mother felt better. Up and dressed, she was receiving the guests in the front parlor. However, once she and Laurie were alone, she despairingly declared, "No one will come out and say so, but they're all sure Sam's gone. Even so, there's still a part of me that's hoping somehow he survived."

"I'm hoping so, too." Like Mother, Laurie clung to a glimmer of hope that her father might still be alive. But what if he was? How awful to think he could be lying in total darkness, maybe in pain, waiting for a rescue that might never come. "How did Father do it?" she burst out. "I don't see how anyone could bear to go beneath the ground, work in the dark, and you never know when a ton of rocks and dirt might fall on your head."

"It's the lure of the gold." Mother sighed with resignation. "Men have gone crazy over this gold rush, your father included. He got rich, but for what? Now it's probably cost him his life."

* * * *

Hat in hand, Darcy McKenna arrived in the early evening. Laurie answered the door and invited him to where Mother and Ada, alone at the moment, sat in the parlor. Judging from his solemn behavior, the tightness around his jaw, she already knew what he was going to say. He wasted no time in pleasantries. "I have bad news."

Laurie looked toward her mother. Would she collapse? Get hysterical? But with a steadying intake of breath, Mother said, "Sam is dead, isn't he?"

"We found his body. If it's any consolation, he must have died instantly."

Face etched in sorrow, Elizabeth took a long moment before she spoke again. "Consolation? Not much, I'm afraid, but I appreciate your efforts to find him. Surely it wasn't easy."

"I wasn't alone. It was the least we could do. I suggest..." Darcy seemed to be searching for the proper words. "I suggest you bury him soon, what with..."

Laurie finished for him. "The warm weather and all. We understand, Mr. McKenna."

"Well, then. Unless there's something else I can do, I'll be on my way."

"I'll show you to the door." Laurie accompanied him from the parlor. Not wanting to cry in front of him, she held back tears. Despite her dislike, she had to admit he'd conducted himself well, shown the proper respect, and didn't mention the number of hours he must have spent looking for her father, nor the danger involved. At the door, she thanked him. "You must have taken a lot of your valuable time to search for him."

He put on his hat and shrugged as if it was nothing at all. "I wasn't the only one searching. We all wanted to help. Sam Sinclair was a good man. He'd have done the same for me."

His answer warmed her heart. Perhaps she'd been mistaken. This was a new side to Darcy McKenna she hadn't seen before. "I haven't talked to Mother yet, but I'm sure we'll bury Father tomorrow. He would want you to be there."

"Of course. One good thing. There won't be anything keeping you here after the funeral."

Why would he care when she left? But, of course, he was just being polite. "I hadn't thought, but I'll be leaving in a few days, I should imagine. It all depends on when the next ship for New York leaves San Francisco."

"Good. You'll be a lot happier back where the streets are paved and life's a lot easier."

Something about this last remark irked her no end. "What are you implying?"

He seemed to take her evident annoyance in his stride. "I'm implying the obvious, that you're not suited for life in a rough-and-ready town like Lucky Creek. You're a lady who likes her comforts, and I can't say I blame you." He gave her a disarming smile. "No insult intended."

Really? She wasn't supposed to be insulted after he'd just informed her how soft and spoiled she was? But today wasn't a day for expressing stupid grievances. She forced a smile. "I'm not offended in the least, Mr. McKenna. Good day and thank you again for your help."

He nodded briefly. "Good day, Miss Sinclair."

Annoyed though she was, she caught herself watching as he walked to the picket fence where he'd tethered his horse. He wasn't handsome in the usual sense, not like Brandon with his six-foot-two height, golden blond hair and gorgeous smile. Yet she couldn't keep her eyes off him. Maybe it was his dark brown hair that she found attractive, even though he wore it unfashionably long, nearly to his shoulders. Maybe it was his lean, sinewy build. Not an extra ounce of fat on him, just hard muscles. Or could it be the way he walked, so effortlessly and graceful. She hadn't thought she could find anything about him attractive, but despite herself, she did. She watched until he mounted his horse with one easy swing and rode away.

* * * *

At least Mother had taken the awful news better than expected. Next morning, when Laurie came downstairs, she discovered Elizabeth dressed and putting her hat on. With a determined jaw, she announced, "You, Ada, and I are going to the hospital to tell Hugh. He's the head of the house now and will know what to do."

The three of them found Hugh lying weak and pale in bed, but at least he was conscious and aware of his surroundings. Hugh gazed up at Mother. "Father's dead, isn't he? I can tell by your long faces."

"They found his body." Mother's face twisted. She had to bow her head a moment to regain her control. She looked up dry-eyed, mouth firmly set. "Thank God you were spared."

"Barely," Hugh replied. "Father was always there for us, and now..." He bit his lip, on the verge of tears himself. "I tried to reach him. I'll never forgive myself that I couldn't."

The three spent the next few minutes trying to convince Hugh he wasn't at fault and there was no way could he have prevented the accident. At last he capitulated, agreeing no man could have done more than he had to save his father.

Up to then, Mother hadn't shown any interest in the family's finances. Now she asked, "Will we have to shut the mine down, Hugh?"

He firmly shook his head. "Of course not. Whatever gave you that idea? We'll reopen soon as the smoke clears out. Soon as I'm able, I'll get back, too. The vein isn't played out yet, and besides all that, there's always the chance we'll find another vein as good as the first one."

Mother smiled in relief. "I'm so happy to hear that."

"The Monarch's still paying off. Not like before, of course, but enough you won't want for anything."

"You're sure?"

"I'm sure. You're going to be fine." He looked at Laurie. "We're all going to be fine, so you can go back home and marry the insect fellow."

Despite her grief, Laurie couldn't help but feel relieved that soon her life would be back to the way she'd planned it. She would take her time, certainly not rush off tomorrow, but she wouldn't waste any time in finding out when the next ship left for New York and the man she adored.

* * * *

They buried Sam Sinclair on a bleak windy morning, in the small cemetery on a hill overlooking the town. Dressed in a borrowed black dress, holding tight to her hat because of the stiff breeze, Laurie drew some comfort from observing the large crowd of mourners who'd come to say their farewells to a man everyone knew and liked. How gratifying that so many of the miners had come. The mine owners, too. Darcy McKenna and Tom Crain. Brock Dominick of the Coyote Mine. The Hudson brothers who owned the huge New Cornwall Mine, and many others, some from as far away as Hangtown. Too bad Father couldn't see how many friends he had. But then, if he was looking down from Heaven, maybe he did.

Afterward, mourners filled their house to overflowing, partaking of the plentiful food and drink supplied by thoughtful neighbors. The last guest didn't depart until late afternoon, leaving the family to breathe a collective sigh of relief. Ada went to her room to rest. Sinking to the sofa, Mother declared, "I think the funeral went well, don't you? Sam would have been proud he had so many friends."

Laurie agreed that he would indeed have been proud, and furthermore the town would never forget him. She suggested that after they rested, they should go to the hospital to see Hugh. They would describe the funeral, and maybe, if he was up to it, discuss the family finances. They could bring Mathew and Maryanne along. Both had been asking after their father.

"I'm already thinking of the future," Elizabeth said. "I see no reason to stay here now, and neither does Ada. Why shouldn't we move back to Philadelphia? Hugh could stay and run the Monarch, or perhaps he'd want to sell the mine and come with us. What do you think, Laurie?"

"I can't think of anything more wonderful. I hated to leave you behind, and now I won't have to." She would have said more, but a knock sounded on the door. "I wonder who that is. Maybe one of the guests forgot something."

She hastened to answer. Of all people, Brock Dominick stood on the doorstep. Such an intimidating man, perhaps because he was so powerful, both in his looks with his thick neck and barrel chest, and his position as owner of the biggest, richest mine in the area. Always polite, she hid her distaste for the man and inquired, "Did you forget something, Mr. Dominick?"

The owner of the Coyote Mine didn't bother to smile. "I've some business I'd like to speak to Mrs. Sinclair about. Is she alone?"

Earlier, Brock had been just another guest, conducting himself with the appropriate sympathetic demeanor, but now he'd reverted to his usual iron-faced expression. Laurie swung the door wide. "All the guests have gone, if that's what you mean. Please come in."

Mother sat alone in the parlor when Laurie led their guest in and motioned him to a seat. Aware of Brock's rudeness, Laurie didn't want to leave Mother alone. "Mr. Dominick is here on some sort of business. Do you mind if I stay?"

Mother smiled wanly. "Of course, I don't mind, although"—she threw their guest a puzzled glance—"I have no idea what we might have to discuss."

"Go or stay, Miss Sinclair, it makes no difference to me."

He'd already expressed his condolences. What could this powerful man want? Laurie sat on the settee next to Mother. "Do go ahead, sir. What is there to discuss?"

The mine owner leaned back in his chair, completely at ease, lightly touching his fingers together. He regarded Mother with a curious gaze. "Were you aware that a while back, I loaned your husband a considerable amount of money?"

Mother was obviously bewildered. "Why, no, I was not. Sam didn't mention—"

"Did he tell you the Monarch was about to go broke?"

"No, I—"

"Ordinarily I'd be speaking to Hugh about this, but the doctor says he's not well enough to talk yet, given his serious injuries. So, in all fairness, I've come to you instead."

A loan? The Monarch about to go broke? Laurie could hardly grasp what he was talking about. "What are you getting at, Mr. Dominick?" She was becoming more uneasy by the second.

Bending forward intently, Dominick seemed to warm to his task. "Several weeks ago, your father came to me seeking a loan after the bank turned him down. That highly profitable vein of gold of his had just about played out. He thought he was on the verge of discovering another, though, just as good, if not better than the first. All he needed was some cash to tide him over."

Mother still had a blank look on her face, so Laurie spoke up. "So, you loaned him some money?"

"Twenty thousand dollars, to be exact. For new equipment, and he wanted to hire more men, as well."

Mother's lips moved, but nothing came out. Losing her husband was bad enough, and now this? Plainly, she couldn't handle another shock, and Laurie must speak for the family. *What do I know about loans?* she asked herself. Only what she'd heard when Father talked business back in Philadelphia. She wouldn't allow this man to see her bewilderment, though. She took her time answering, struggling not only to find the right words but also to sound confident, like she discussed loans all the time. "That's a considerable amount of money, Mr. Dominick, but if we owe the money, we will pay it. I would need to talk to my brother, of course, but possibly we might work out some sort of payment plan."

"That won't be necessary."

"It won't?" Something told her this wouldn't be good. Dominick's heretofore impassive expression had shifted into what she could best term vicious expectancy, reminding her of a large beast about to spring on its prey.

"Surely you would know I don't lend that kind of money without collateral."

"Yes, of course. So, what—"

"The collateral for your father's loan is the Monarch Mine, Miss Sinclair."

Her mind went spinning. "I know nothing about business. Tell me what that means."

A spark of—could that be enjoyment?—flashed through his eyes. "It means your father signed a note promising to repay the loan in installments. If he defaulted on a payment—that means if he didn't pay—then the whole balance of the note would come due."

"So...so..." She struggled to understand. "What you're saying is we owe the entire balance now because he missed a payment?"

"Exactly right."

"All twenty thousand?"

"Not quite. He made a few payments. All you owe now is eighteen thousand, five hundred sixty dollars." With a mocking smile, he added, "And fifty-six cents, but if you pay the rest, I'll let that slide."

"I had no idea. Father never told us about any such loan." Laurie turned to her mother. "Did he ever mention it to you?"

Wordlessly, she shook her head.

"I have the paperwork if you care to see it," said Dominick.

Laurie had no doubt but that he did. She thought fast. Clearly, Mother was in no condition to discuss business with Brock Dominick, or anything else, for that matter. *It's up to me.* "So let me see if I understand. My father borrowed some money from you, and because there's a payment overdue, you can take the Monarch Mine. Is that correct?"

"Business is business, Miss Sinclair." His voice held all the warmth of a snow-covered grave. "I'm doing you a favor by letting you know. You have two more days."

"What does that mean exactly?"

"It means you have two more days to pay the loan." A cynical smile crossed his face. "If you can come up with eighteen thousand, five hundred sixty dollars by Friday, then fine. Otherwise the Monarch is mine."

"Is there anything else?"

"That's it, Miss Sinclair."

A sick feeling hit her in the pit of her stomach, but she knew she mustn't show her distress in front of this horrible man. She'd be polite if it killed her. She rose to her feet, as did he. "I thank you for taking the trouble to inform us, Mr. Dominick. I'll need to talk with my brother and will let you know our decision as soon as possible."

She showed Dominick to the door and let him out. Breathing a sigh of relief, she hurried back to the parlor. Mother hadn't moved. She sat staring into space with a shocked look on her face. Laurie sat beside her and took her hand. "Are you all right?"

"I'm not all right. I don't know what to do, Laurie. I'm tired. Maybe I'll go lie down."

Up to now, Elizabeth Sinclair had been a strong, forceful woman who never vacillated and knew exactly what she wanted. Laurie had clashed with her often, and at times, deeply resented her mother's domineering attitude. Not now, though. She hated seeing her mother so bewildered and unsure of herself. Gently she replied, "After a day like today, who wouldn't be tired and want to lie down? Come on, I'll help you upstairs."

Without a murmur of protest, Elizabeth allowed herself to be led to her room. Sick at heart, Laurie helped her lie down and got a cold cloth to lay across her forehead. As if a cold cloth could make her problems go away.

Everything had gone horribly wrong, and Laurie couldn't think what to do. She must go see Hugh immediately. Why had he said their finances were in good shape? But surely, he'd known about the loan and how Father intended to repay it. She felt better already, sure that her brother would know what to do.

Chapter 4

"We have no money, Sis. Father spent it all."

Laurie sat at her brother's bedside, stunned. After giving her the bad news, Hugh turned his head to the wall. For a time, she remained silent, struggling to comprehend the devastating effect this awful news would have on the family. "Completely gone? But surely there must be—"

"There's nothing left." Hugh turned his head back and looked at her with anguished eyes. "I didn't want to tell you before. Couldn't face it. What Father did was terrible. The worst of it was I could do nothing to stop him."

"What did he do?" She braced herself. She couldn't imagine, but it must be something really bad.

"When Father first came out here, he did well. Found gold, started the Monarch. When he sent for the family, I came willingly. Everything went smoothly at first. I met Maude and married her. Father made me his assistant at the mine. I learned a lot, Laurie. It was all good, me working with him. I was happy. Maude was happy. I proved myself to be invaluable and was proud of my success. We were turning a huge profit, giving the family the kind of life they deserved, and I was part of it. Even when Maude died, I had no regrets. Dying in childbirth like she did—it could just as easily have happened in Philadelphia as here."

Laurie nodded in sympathetic agreement. "I've never once heard you complain about leaving your fine life in Philadelphia behind."

"Exactly. Grief-stricken though I was, I carried on, and it wasn't until I discovered the books had been doctored that I knew something was wrong."

She'd thought she was prepared for anything, but nothing like this. "What do you mean?"

"I thought the mine was doing fine, but then I discovered the truth. Unbeknownst to me, Father was having financial difficulties. When I tell you why, you won't believe it. You'll think I'm out of my mind, but I know it's true."

"Just tell me."

"Father had started to gamble. You know how it is in this town. You can't walk ten feet on Mein Street without passing a gambling saloon. I guess he got so tempted he couldn't resist. Many's the time when he claimed he had to work late, he was in some saloon on Mein Street playing faro or sometimes *vingt-et-un*. The Gold Strike was his favorite saloon. He never told me any of this, but I worked with him every day and would have been a fool not to know. What I didn't realize was his gambling had gotten out of hand. That's when he started draining the company accounts and doctoring the books. I figure he was desperate when he borrowed all that money from Brock Dominick. By then, he was counting on finding that new vein of gold, but now we know that didn't happen."

Father a gambler? "I find this hard to believe."

"You think I'm lying?"

"Of course not. But that's not our father. You must be mistaken. He would never—"

"It was Sam Sinclair, and that's not all."

"Good lord!" She'd lifted her voice, something she never did. The nurse on the other side of the room raised her head and gave her a cold stare. Barely above a whisper, she continued. "There's more?"

"Yes, there's more. I hate to tell you this, but you've got to know. You've heard of Mrs. Lucille Wagner, the widow who owns the Gold Spike?"

Silently she nodded. Somehow, she knew this was going to get worse.

"Father was seeing her. They were... I guess you could say they were carrying on."

By now, her mind had gone so numb she accepted this last revelation without protest. "So, what you're saying is our father gambled all the family's money away as well as cheated on our mother."

"That's what I'm saying, and it's true, Laurie. Do you think I'd lie about something like this?"

"It's like you're talking about a different man, not the wonderful man I knew all my life."

"At this point does it matter what you believe? Our family is completely broke. The money's gone. The Monarch's gone. So, there you have it. Believe it or don't believe it, what does it matter?"

In a fog, she asked, "But what are we going to do?"

"Damned if I know. Maybe when I'm well enough, Brock Dominick will give me a job." He moved slightly and winced from the pain of his broken ribs. "If I ever get well. I can't help the family now, Laurie. You're on your own."

* * * *

Looking back, Laurie realized how foolish she'd been to expect a visit to her brother would miraculously solve their problems. What a fantasy to believe that somehow, he'd produce the money to pay off the loan, or, better still, assure her Dominick was lying and Father had never signed such a note in the first place. Hugh had shocked her almost beyond belief. How could those terrible things he'd said about Father be true? But why would he lie? He'd told lies when he was younger, and done mean things, but that was the old Hugh. Over the years, he'd changed into the man Father always hoped he'd be. Right now, he needed to rest and recuperate, and she wouldn't burden him further. The responsibility for helping the family belonged to her now, and she'd do the best she could.

Arriving home, she decided to wait to break the bad news until after the children had been fed and put to bed. Small though they were, they would know something had gone horribly wrong, just from the sound of the adults' voices. Now, the children gone, sitting at the dinner table with Mother and Ada, she broke the bad news as gently as she could.

"As you know, I spoke to Hugh today. He says we're totally broke. We can't pay the loan to Mr. Dominick because we don't have the money." That wasn't all Hugh told her, but her mother and sister didn't need to know the rest, and she hoped to God they'd never find out.

Mother had recovered at least enough to come downstairs to dinner, but her hands trembled slightly, and her shoulders slumped as if all hope was gone. "We have no money? I cannot believe Sam would do such a thing," she near-whispered, shaking her head in despair. "What do you think, Laurie? Was Mr. Dominick trying to trick us?"

"I don't want to believe it, but what else can we think? Brock Dominick's a despicable man, but why would he lie? And besides, he offered to show us the paperwork. We'd recognize Father's signature." She wished she could sound more hopeful, but what else could she say?

Her face pale, eyes red from crying, Ada appeared to be nearly as bad off as Mother. She looked at her sister with pleading eyes. "What will we do, Laurie? What about the children? Are we going to starve to death?"

Laurie had no idea what they were going to do. The trouble was, of the three of them, she appeared to be the only one who hadn't fallen apart. Someone had to hold this family together—give them some sort of hope—and apparently it would have to be her. "Well, let's see now…" Her mind raced. She must find something positive to say. "We still own the house. We could sell it and go back to Philadelphia."

"No." Mother spoke with an intensity that didn't invite argument. "I could never go back like this. How could I face my friends knowing I'm a charity case?"

Ada spoke up. "She's right, Laurie. Go back now? I'd die of humiliation."

"But Aunt Florence would take you in, wouldn't she?" Laurie was baffled. "She's always been wonderful to me, and I'm sure—"

"Absolutely no." Mother clenched her jaw with determination. "I love my sister. It's fine that she invited you to live with her, but hadn't you noticed how bossy she is? How she likes to run everything? Believe you me, if I allowed her to support me, I'd be living at her beck and call, and frankly, I'd rather die first."

At least Mother had roused herself out of her deep grief and shown a spark of her usual self. Laurie smiled and remarked, "Then I guess we can forget Aunt Florence."

"I think you better had."

Laurie racked her brain for ideas. Unsure and desperate, she plunged ahead. "I haven't been in Lucky Creek long, but I see there are things we could do here we could never do back east. Maybe we could start a business of some sort. Take laundry, for instance. There's always a need for that. In fact, I heard in some cases the miners are sending their dirty clothes clear to places like China to get it done. I'd venture to say we could make a tidy profit with a laundry."

"Are you out of your mind?" normally timid Ada exclaimed. "You want us to scrub clothes and iron them and…and…" She fell back in her chair, apparently so overwhelmed she couldn't continue.

Mother bit her lip in bewilderment. "I just don't know…all that scrubbing? How could we dry things in the wintertime? We'd need a lot of clothesline…and soap? Wouldn't we need a lot of soap?"

"All right, forget that idea. I didn't think it through." How foolish to believe that after lifetimes of privilege, her mother and sister could bring themselves to perform manual labor. Not that they were spoiled, it wasn't that. Mother wasn't coping well and seemed confused. Small, delicate Ada could never handle so much as a day of hard labor, and Laurie wouldn't want her to. "Don't worry, I'll think of something."

Something, but what? Absolutely nothing came to mind, but she mustn't give up. A heavy weight pressed against her chest. If they didn't have any money what would happen to Mathew and Maryanne? Those two adorable children shouldn't want for anything. What would happen to Hugh, Mother, and Ada? Not a one able to fend for themselves, at least for the moment. *That leaves me.* Hard to believe that she, Laurie Sinclair, former devotee of parties and the social life, had suddenly become the only hope this family had to save them from poverty and worse.

* * * *

The weight still pressed against her chest when she woke up the next morning. If she'd thought some brilliant idea would strike her during the night, she'd been sadly mistaken. But at least she had errands to run today. They'd keep her busy and her mind occupied. Getting dressed, she decided not to wear the borrowed black dress again. In Philadelphia she'd have worn mourning for at least six months. In their house on Society Hill, all curtains and blinds would have been drawn tightly, and a black wreath placed on the door. Not in Lucky Creek, though, where everyone came from somewhere else and nobody cared about old traditions. She chose her full-skirted dark blue bombazine with the high collar. Along with white gloves and her plain grey bonnet, she'd look mournful enough. That is, if anyone in this rough-and-ready town cared, or even noticed.

She'd written a letter to Brandon, telling him the tragic news, and how, because of it, her return had been delayed. Not for long, though, she promised, and again mentioned her eagerness to rejoin him. She hated how slow the mail was. Probably by the time his answer reached Lucky Creek, she'd be on her way back.

Early in the afternoon, she walked into town, to Mein Street, and mailed her letter. She dreaded her next errand, but it had to be done. Over her arm, she carried Darcy McKenna's jacket, the one he'd lent her the night of the explosion. Until now, she hadn't had a chance to return it but was anxious to do so. He lived at the Gold Spike, the very same hotel where Hugh said her father… No. She would not allow herself to think about the awful things Hugh had told her. Too hurtful. Too dreadful. She would drop off the jacket at the front desk. At this time of day, he'd be up at his mine, which was fine with her. This way, she would avoid another encounter with the irritating mine owner.

A sprawling wooden structure three stories high, the Gold Spike Hotel covered over half a block on Mein Street. Walking along the wooden boardwalk in front, Laurie approached the swinging doors, wishing she could close her ears to the tinny piano music blasting from within. Like all respectable ladies of the town, she picked up her pace as she passed, hoping to avoid the occasional drunk staggering out. God forbid she should encounter one of the saloon's painted ladies.

"Miss Sinclair? Is that you?"

She allowed herself a muttered "Dammit!" and turned around. There stood Darcy McKenna, sweeping his hat off as a gentleman should, and regarding her quizzically. Today a leather-tooled gun belt rested at a jaunty angle around his slim hips. The handle of what looked a very large pistol jutted from the holster.

"Good afternoon," he said. "Planning on visiting the saloon?"

"Good afternoon, Mr. McKenna." She flicked a glance at his pistol and couldn't resist. "Planning on shooting someone?"

He broke into hearty laughter. It was the first time she'd ever seen him laugh like that. "Not today, I hope."

"I didn't think you'd be in town this time of day.'

He jerked his head toward the nearby Wells-Fargo Bank. "Getting money from the bank. That's what the gun's for." He noticed the jacket she was carrying. "Is that mine?"

She held it out to him. "Yes, I was returning it. You were most kind. Good day, Mr. McKenna." That was polite enough and all she need say. In her current mood, she didn't care to talk to anyone. She started to turn away.

"You don't have to rush off." His gaze raked over her. "Is everything all right? You look… Is everything all right aside from the obvious?"

"The obvious being I just lost my father and my brother's lying in the hospital with six of his ribs and an arm broken. Isn't that enough?"

"More than enough."

Maybe it was because he was being nice, and his eyes had filled with sympathy, but whatever the reason, the words slipped out before she could stop them. "There's something more."

He immediately asked, "Were you on your way home?" She nodded. "Walking?" She nodded again. "Then come with me. I'll drive you home in the wagon, and you can tell me about 'something more.'" He got that amused look in his eye again and jerked his head toward the saloon. "Or I could buy you a beer if you like. Give the boys a thrill. They don't often see a lady like you in the Gold Spike Saloon."

Was he sincere or being sarcastic? It didn't matter. He'd made her smile, and she didn't feel like being standoffish. "I'll take that beer some other time, if you don't mind. If you could just drive me home, I'd appreciate it."

Before she knew it, she was sitting next to Darcy McKenna in his big wagon with ATLAS MINES painted on the side. He gave her a questioning glance as he flicked the reins and the two horses took off at a fast pace up Mein Street. "So what else is wrong?"

Gloved hands properly folded in her lap, she sat silent a moment. She didn't want him to think she was complaining or, even worse, asking for help. "If I tell you, don't get the wrong idea. I'm only telling you because you asked, and because you're a mine owner, and I'd appreciate your knowledge of the subject."

"Of course."

"We're a proud family. We solve our own problems."

"Of course."

As they rolled along the muddy, not-so-beautiful streets of Lucky Creek, she proceeded to tell him about Brock Dominick's visit of the night before. "Needless to say, we were totally shocked. Father never said a word about such a loan. I admit I was skeptical, but when I talked to Hugh, he said we owe the money." She stopped herself from adding they hadn't the means to repay the loan. None of his business, and besides, she had too much pride and too much loyalty to Father to admit he'd left his family penniless.

They reached the house, and Darcy pulled the wagon to a stop in front. He dropped the reins and turned to her. "So, what will you do?"

"We have two more days to decide. I'm not sure yet, but we'll probably let Mr. Dominick take the Monarch. I guess it wasn't paying off anyway, so no great loss. Beyond that, we might stay, or we might return to Philadelphia. Personally, I'll be returning soon as I can."

"I wouldn't expect otherwise since you hate Lucky Creek."

"Doesn't everyone? You don't actually like it here, do you?"

"You'll find this hard to believe, but I do like it here. Sure, there's too many saloons, muddy streets, and nothing close to what you would call culture, but I wouldn't return east if my life depended on it."

The fervor in his voice surprised her. "I suppose I can understand. After all, you own a successful mine, but think of the thousands of others who've failed to find gold. They've wasted their time and money and can't get home fast enough."

"Perhaps, but there are thousands of others who would never go back. Think about it. California offers opportunities these men would never have if they'd stayed home. They won't find gold. That's over. But here a man can be as independent as he likes, not like back east where the status of a man's family, the class he's in, determines his success." Finished, Darcy raised an eyebrow. "I made a speech, didn't I? Need help getting down?"

"I can manage." Feeling his gaze upon her, she climbed from the wagon concentrating on looking as graceful as she could. She turned and looked up at him. "Thank you for the ride and for listening to me."

"You're welcome. Thanks for returning the jacket. And sorry about Dominick. He's a scoundrel if ever there was one. Anything I can help you with, let me know."

As he drove away, she looked after him. He'd surprised her with his insight concerning the advantages of living in the West. Up to now, she'd thought of him as just another mine owner who never thought beyond the daily yield of high-grade ore and the current price of an ounce of gold. Plainly he was more than that and more of a deep thinker than she'd thought. He'd been polite, too, and thoughtful. A harmless man, doing his best to be kind and courteous.

But wait. Something about him—maybe it was those sharp blue eyes— told her he wasn't so harmless.

And he wasn't a man to be trifled with.

Not that she intended to trifle with Darcy McKenna. Why would she do such a thing when Brandon Cooper awaited her with open arms? A sudden fear stabbed at her heart. How long would he wait? All the ladies loved Brandon. His wealth and dashing good looks made him a most desirable catch.

She *must* get back to Philadelphia, soon as she possibly could.

Chapter 5

After dropping Laurie Sinclair off at her home, Darcy continued on to the Atlas Mine. His mind should have been on practical matters, but his conversation with Laurie Sinclair dominated his thoughts to the point he could think of nothing else. When he walked into the office, Tom took one look and remarked, "Something eatin' you? Your face looks like a thundercloud."

"Wait till you hear what that bastard, Dominick has done now..."

Darcy described how he'd run into Laurie and what she'd told him about the mine owner's visit. "Makes my blood boil. The day of Sam's funeral, he visits the family to tell them he's taking their one source of income away. Has the man no shame?"

"You know the answer to that. I've been here since forty-nine, seen all kinds of mischief and skullduggery, and Dominick's done more than his share. He's ruthless. You know as well as I he's responsible for half the high-grade thefts around here, maybe more. You think he gives a damn that he visits a widow before her husband's cold in his grave and tells her there's a loan due?"

Darcy sat at his desk and slung his legs up, resting his boots on the top. "What bothers me..." He frowned in thought. "Everyone knows that gold vein at the Monarch was just about played out."

Tom nodded. "Sam was about to close down. He so much as said so himself. I reckon the explosion that done him in was his last hope. I figured he had other irons in the fire, but maybe he didn't. Maybe he was broke, else why would he have any dealings with that crook, Dominick?"

"You're missing the point." Darcy swung his legs to the floor and sat straight. "Why would Brock go to all that trouble to get hold of a played-out mine?"

"You got me. In these parts, there's many a shut-down mine that would pay off better than the Monarch, but nobody wants 'em. Say now..." Tom's eyes lit with sudden awareness. "You don't think...?"

"Maybe Dominick knows something we don't?" Darcy got out of his chair and reached for his hat. "Come on, Tom. It's time we took another look at that mine shaft."

* * * *

Five hundred feet beneath the surface, lanterns held high, Darcy and Tom edged their way through the jumble of rocks, fallen timbers, and other debris strewn along the main shaft of the Monarch Mine. "Isn't this the spot where we found Sam?" Tom asked.

"It is, and we didn't go any farther." *And should have*, Darcy thought. "We'll go as far as we can." He raised the lantern above his head. "See there? The shaft's not timbered from here on, so watch out." They were taking a chance, but after the years he'd spent belowground, Darcy had no fear. He knew when to be extra careful, though, like now, in an unsupported tunnel that could easily collapse and bury them. They crept forward, crawling over huge boulders, until they came to a solid wall of rock that marked the end of the area opened by the explosion.

"Well, shoot," said Tom, shaking his head. "Looks like we've hit a dead end and nothing to show for it."

"I think I see something. Hold your lantern up."

Halfway up the wall, embedded in the rock, the flickering rays from two lanterns caught a mass of something gleaming. "Holy jumping Jehoshaphat, look at that." Tom crouched closer. "It looks like a huge crab, don't it? A big, solid glob of gold with gold legs spreading all over the rocks."

Darcy pulled out a knife, stabbed it into one of the thicker legs and worked it around. He pulled it out and peered at it closely. "At least seven inches wide and an inch deep, all solid gold."

"Wonder how far it goes."

"Maybe it goes halfway to China. Maybe we dig another two feet and it's gone."

"What do you think?"

In a rare moment of exuberance, Darcy tossed down the knife and clapped his friend on the shoulder. "I think the Monarch Mine won't be closing any time soon."

"That's great news for the Sinclairs." Tom paused to think a moment. "Or is it? Dominick had to know about this. Now he'll be the new owner of the Monarch whether they know about the new vein or not."

"We'll see about that," Darcy said.

* * * *

After Darcy brought her home from town, Laurie walked in the door and was met by her distressed-looking sister. "Mother's gone insane," Ada cried. "She's dismissed Mei Ling and Albert."

"Oh, my lord, she didn't need to do that." Laurie hastened upstairs to her mother's bedroom and found her lying flat on the bed, a wet cloth over her eyes. She took a moment to calm herself before she softly asked, "Why did you dismiss the servants, Mother?"

Elizabeth pulled the cloth from her eyes. "Because we're poor now," she answered in a piteous voice. "Because we have no money to pay them. I couldn't let Valeria go, though. Who would do the cooking?"

Laurie laughed with relief. "Thank God for that, although we could have kept Mei Ling and Albert for a while. We're not that poor yet, and besides…" An old mEmery came back to her. "Didn't Father once say he'd hidden some money somewhere?"

After a moment's contemplation, Elizabeth sat up and swung her legs to the floor. "Yes, he did. Now where did he say he put it?"

She spent the next two hours searching for the cash she insisted her husband had left somewhere around the house. Laurie and Ada helped search but soon gave up. "We couldn't be that lucky," Ada said, and Laurie agreed. Both were surprised when, late in the afternoon, Mother cried, "I found it."

Deep in his closet, stuck in an old boot, Sam Sinclair had secreted a roll of twenty-dollar notes. After they counted it out, Laurie gleefully addressed her mother and sister. "That's enough to keep us going in Lucky Creek for a while. Here's another thought. It's also enough to pay our passage back to Philadelphia. What do you think?"

A long and somewhat heated discussion followed. Again, Mother described her intense dislike of living on her sister's charity. Ada hated the thought of it, too. So did Laurie, but she'd soon be married, and, as both her mother and sister pointed out, she wasn't the one who'd suffer the humiliation and embarrassment of being poor. And no, they wouldn't be accepting any help from Brandon Cooper, even after he and Laurie were married. It was a matter of pride.

But the problem was, what would happen if they stayed in Lucky Creek? Where would they get the money to survive? Take in laundry? Was Laurie insane? They could not possibly engage in any sort of manual labor, and that was that.

After endless wrangling, Mother threw up her hands. "I give in. I can see now we don't have a choice. We shall go back to Philadelphia and"—her face screwed up in distaste—"live with my sister."

Ada smiled bravely. "Maybe it won't be so bad. Just think, we'll be living in civilization again and...and..." The smile faded quickly. "It'll be awful, but what else can we do?"

Laurie hid her relief at her mother's decision. Now she could return to Philadelphia with a clear conscience, knowing she hadn't left her family to eke out their existence in a wild and lawless mining town. Still, her heart went out to them. They might not love Lucky Creek, but the thought of returning to Philadelphia as paupers dismayed them both. The world as they knew it had come to an end. She couldn't blame them for looking so sad and dejected. "Then it looks like you've made up your minds. I'll see about booking our return passage tomorrow."

They spent the rest of the afternoon in a gloomy discussion concerning how they would sell the house, what to take and what to leave. At least servants were in great demand. Mei Ling and Albert would easily find work elsewhere, and Valeria, too, when the time came.

That evening Laurie was doubly glad Mother hadn't dismissed Valeria. In the past, their cook had revealed a bit of a fiery temper, but today she'd remained in good humor and said nothing about the other servants being gone. When Laurie peeked in the kitchen, Valeria muttered something in broken English that sounded like, "I cook you something extra special." A pot of what she called *camarão no leite de coco* sat on the stove. How delightful. Nothing could raise their spirits more than shrimp in coconut sauce, a dish they loved.

Later, they were settled in the parlor when Laurie answered a knock on the door. Darcy McKenna stood on the doorstep, hat in hand but no smile.

"Mr. McKenna? I didn't expect to see you again so soon."

"May I come in? I have some business to discuss."

Silently she opened the door wide and waved him in, refraining from giving her usual warm welcome. Why should she? This afternoon, he'd been reasonably congenial and well mannered, but tonight he'd returned to being his brusque, strictly business self. Wordlessly, she led him to the parlor. Other than a quick greeting to Mother and Ada, he wasted no time on idle chitchat and immediately launched into the explanation for his visit. It began, he said, when he and his assistant, Tom Crain, became suspicious as to why Brock Dominick was so eager to get hold of the Monarch Mine. Did he know something they didn't? They returned for another look at the shaft where Sam had set off the gunpowder. What they found prompted this visit. "Sam was right. There's a new vein of gold right where he thought it would be."

Laurie was the first to recover from the shock of this latest news. "How big is it, do you think?"

"Like I told Tom, it could go halfway to China or end a few feet away. You never know. Looks like Dominick found it first. I can see why he wanted to get his hands on it."

"So that's why he showed up the very night of Father's funeral."

"Looks that way." A wry smile crossed Darcy's face. "This never-ending search for gold brings out the worst in people. Some rise above it, but not Dominick. No wonder he was so anxious to foreclose on your loan. I'm surprised Sam agreed to those terms. Either he was desperate or..." Darcy paused in order to choose his next words carefully. "Brock's a thief and a conniver. I wouldn't put a bit of forgery past him, if the need arose. The trouble is, Sam's gone, and it's nothing you could prove. Brock's a big force in this town."

Laurie frowned. "That loan is due in two days. If we don't pay it, we lose the Monarch, new gold vein or no. I'm glad you told us, Mr. McKenna, but what can we do about it?"

"That's why I'm here. I'm willing to pay off the entire loan."

"You are?" Laurie could hardly keep her mouth from dropping open. "But how could we ever pay you back? I'm presuming you'd want something in return."

"In return, I will become a partner and own fifty-one percent of the Monarch."

Mother looked bewildered. "But it's closed now, Mr. McKenna. The miners are gone."

"We'll hire them back. I'll invest whatever it takes to explore the new vein. That includes the hiring of new miners, buying new equipment, and all that goes with it. Of course, I'm counting on Hugh to come back soon. I'd need his help." He went on to explain in detail what was needed to open the Monarch again. He used words like hoists and bulkheads, which Laurie didn't understand but had heard Father use. When Darcy finished, he spoke directly to Mother. "Right now, Hugh's in no condition to conduct business, and there's no time to waste. It's up to you. So, what do you think, Mrs. Sinclair? I don't want to rush you, but time is short."

"I...I..." Mother stuttered. In confusion, she turned to Laurie. "What do you think?"

So, it's up to me. Laurie cleared her throat and sat straight, attempting to look as businesslike as possible. "So, let me make sure I understand, Mr. McKenna. You are willing to pay off the entire loan we owe Mr. Dominick. Is that correct?" He nodded. "And in return, you will become a partner and own fifty-one percent of the Monarch. Further, you will invest whatever it takes to explore the new vein. That includes the hiring of new miners, buying new equipment and all that."

"In the mining business, new partnerships come and go, Miss Sinclair. What I've suggested is common practice."

"But what about...?" Laurie was finding it hard to stay businesslike when she knew so little about the mining industry. "Won't this take time? I mean, we won't be getting rich overnight, will we?" She hated to reveal the family's dire financial situation but could see no way out. "If you want the truth, my father left us with practically nothing. Mother has already dismissed our maid and stableman. How will we live until the mine starts paying again, if it ever does?"

"How's Hugh doing?"

Startled by his question, she took a moment to answer. "As I'm sure you know, he'll live, but he's still in a lot of pain, still in the hospital."

"So, it'll be a while before he's able to work again."

"If he ever can, Mr. McKenna." If he noticed the reproachful note in her voice, so be it. She didn't care for his apparent lack of sympathy.

He ignored her implied disapproval. "Here's the problem. The Monarch is closed, every last miner gone. We'll be starting from scratch to get her open again, and that requires a lot of work. Hiring new miners, buying new equipment, updating the books, on and on. I can't do it all—got my own mine to run—and right now, what with all the thieves around here I can't think of a man I'd trust to take over and run it. I was counting on Hugh. If he can't do it, we may have to wait until he can."

"Do exactly what?" An idea was forming in Laurie's head. Impossible, of course, but she'd at least ask. "I mean, what needs doing at the mine, other than actually working below the ground with a pick and shovel?"

He cocked his head and looked at her oddly. "You're not thinking..."

"I'm just asking."

"I can give you a general idea. At the Monarch, your father did the hiring and firing, made the big decisions, such as which shafts would remain open and which would close. Hugh pretty much ran the office. He kept the books and was responsible for the payroll. That's a big job, handling the money. Sam was lucky he had someone he could trust. Not all mine owners do."

She could be getting in way over her head but couldn't stop now. "So maybe... If you had someone to run the office, you could start work on the new vein right away?" A vision of that dark, menacing entrance to the mine popped in her head. "Nothing underground, of course."

He sat back, folded his arms across his chest, and looked at her long and hard. "I believe we all agree you weren't cut out to be a miner, Miss Sinclair. So, what you're saying is, you could run the office and do the payroll, despite the fact you've had no experience and—"

"I'm a woman? I'm good with numbers. In school, arithmetic was my best subject. Just show me what to do and I'll do it."

"Laurie!" Mother looked at her aghast. "What are you saying?"

"What I'm saying"—she looked directly at McKenna—"is that I could handle the work at the Monarch, as long as I don't have to lift anything heavy and most certainly not go underground. Also, what I'm saying is, I don't particularly want to do this, but it would only be temporary, would it not?"

He nodded warily.

"Then for the convenience of my family, I'm willing to do it until such time as either Hugh returns to work, or the new vein starts to pay off and you can hire someone else. It shouldn't take long, do you think?" She sat back, the picture of composure, and looked him in the eye. For once, he seemed to have lost that maddening self-control of his and was doing a poor job of hiding his astonishment. Good. For some perverse reason, she was enjoying the sight of the always-so-sure-of-himself Darcy McKenna at a loss for words. "Well, Mr. McKenna?"

For a long moment, he remained silent, then got an amused look in his eye. "I've never hired a woman before."

"There's a first time for everything, isn't there?" Someone else must be talking. She couldn't believe what she'd just said, but the bare facts gave her no alternative. Unless the Monarch stayed open, the Sinclairs would be living on charity, and that would happen over her dead body. Mother couldn't help. Neither could Ada. It was all up to her. She held her breath while she waited for his decision.

Finally, after a long, silent moment, he shrugged and nodded. "As long as you know what you're getting yourself into."

"I'm not sure that I do, but I'll soon find out, won't I?"

"It's only until Hugh comes back."

"Of course."

"Any time you regret your decision, you have only to tell me."

"Fine. I assume you agree."

Except for the slight raise of an eyebrow, he'd shown no surprise, but he must be astounded that he'd actually hired a woman. She smiled at him pleasantly, so he could see how at ease she was. "You won't regret it."

He rose to leave. "I'll have the papers drawn up tomorrow."

He bid Mother and Ada good night. Laurie accompanied him to the door. Maybe the truth would dawn on her later as to what a reckless, foolhardy thing she'd just done, but for the moment she brimmed with confidence and a touch of satisfaction that for once Darcy hadn't seemed quite so sure of himself. "Good night, sir. My family and I are grateful for your generosity in paying off our loan."

"I'm not a generous man, and you needn't thank me. I wouldn't have made the offer had I not expected a handsome return from that gold mine of yours."

"When should I start?"

"You're sure?" Disbelief still lingered in his eyes.

"Very sure."

"Why don't I show you around first? Give you an idea of what you'll be doing."

"Fine with me."

"In that case, I'll meet you at the Monarch at seven o'clock tomorrow morning."

"That's awfully early."

"We don't work banker's hours in a mine."

"Could you make it eight o'clock instead? I'm asking because it will take me a while to walk up there."

"But why can't you—" Realization lit his face. "Your stableman's been dismissed, and you don't know how to hitch the horses, do you?"

She opened her mouth to defend herself, but why should she? Since when was a lady supposed to know how to perform such a task? Even so, she'd better explain. "I never had the need to hitch my own horses. That's what we had a stableman for. If he wasn't around, my father and brother took care of such things."

He broke into a knowing, absolutely maddening smile, as if he'd been right, that she, spoiled and pampered all her life, wasn't capable of doing anything remotely resembling actual labor and considered herself too good to try. "Understandable. That's why I'm wondering if you might wish to reconsider your decision to work at the mine."

"Absolutely not."

"Then would you care to learn how to hitch the horses?"

He had her trapped. Cornered. Only one response could she give. "I suppose…why not? We have the wagon, the landau, and the curricle. If I could just learn how to hitch up the curricle, I suppose I could manage. All I need is to find someone to show me how it's done." Whom she could find, she had no idea but would worry about that later. Right now, all she cared about was not letting this annoying man get the best of her.

"I'll be here at seven in the morning to show you. Good night." He gave her a quick salute and turned away.

He'd spoken in such a commanding manner she didn't think to argue. "Goodnight, McKenna," she called after him and watched as he returned to his horse and swung into the saddle in that fluid, graceful manner of his. The truth struck hard as she watched him ride away. What had possessed her? She'd been born and raised in a genteel world where only persons of the lower class performed manual labor. How could she have ever considered working at an ugly, muddy mine far removed from civilization? Worst of all, she'd be forced to deal with Darcy McKenna, one of the most irritating men she'd ever met. Or so she kept telling herself.

There was something about him she found… What was the right word? Intriguing? Fascinating? Oh, surely not. Brandon Cooper was intriguing and fascinating. Darcy McKenna? A complete mystery. Tough and unfriendly. Never opened up. Kept all his feelings to himself. If he liked her, she wouldn't even know. Good lord, how could she even wonder such a thing, especially about a man she had no interest in, whatsoever?

A gloomy atmosphere awaited when she returned to the parlor. Despite the good news concerning the loan, her mother and sister were engaged in a grim discussion concerning money. The notes they'd found in the boot would stretch only so far, and they must conserve it. At least for the time being they'd have to cut expenses to the bone. That meant Valeria, too, must go. "How can we do without her?" Mother bleakly inquired. "I've never cooked in my life, and neither have you girls."

"I've never so much as boiled water," Ada said. "I've never put wood in the stove."

Laurie reminded them how lucky they were that thanks to Darcy McKenna, the loan to Dominick would be paid in full. "As for the rest, lots of people manage without servants. Remember, it's only temporary. That new vein will soon make us rich again. It's only a matter of time."

Laurie's optimism didn't impress Mother in the least. She still looked grim. "I dread telling Valeria we're letting her go. You know how she is."

"I'll take care of it." Laurie, too, dreaded telling their cook she'd been dismissed, but she'd do whatever had to be done.

"And what about you, Laurie?" Mother inquired. "Whatever possessed you to say you'd work at the mine? It's most unseemly for a lady like you to be engaged in that type of activity."

"We're not in Philadelphia anymore," Laurie replied with a gentle smile. "Before this is over, I predict we'll be doing lots of unseemly activities. We'll manage, though. I'm sure of it." She'd given herself the perfect opening to give them her latest news. "Speaking of activities, here's a new one. Mr. McKenna will be here at seven tomorrow morning. He's going to show me how to hitch up the curricle."

"You?" Ada burst into laughter. "However will you manage? You don't know the front of a horse from the rear."

Laurie picked up a pillow from the couch and tossed it at her sister. "Never fear, I'll manage all right."

"And what about Mr. Darcy McKenna? Do you think you can manage him, too?" Ada asked.

Sometimes her sister was wiser than she thought. "He's the least of my problems. I'll be dealing with him only because I have to."

And that, of course, was very, very true.

Chapter 6

Laurie awoke in the morning finding herself eager to start the day. How odd. Instead of dreading the very thought of spending long hours in a place she detested, she was actually looking forward to this new turn her life had taken, kind of like a new adventure. Only temporary, of course. Darcy McKenna wasn't a man who easily showed his emotions, but when he talked about the new vein of gold they'd found, excitement sparked in those extraordinary eyes of his. He couldn't hide it. With any luck, the mine would soon start paying off again—maybe better than before—and she'd soon be heading for Philadelphia.

As for learning how to hitch up the horses, this was all part of the new and necessary path she'd chosen. Of course, she could do it. Lots of women knew how to hitch a horse and carriage, and soon so would she. So, what was the proper attire for working at a mine? Nothing frivolous. After careful consideration, she chose the plainest dress she owned, the dark blue bombazine that buttoned nearly to her throat. She fixed her hair in a bun, foregoing the usual curly tendrils she usually arranged to dangle around her face. Confident she'd dressed appropriately she went downstairs.

Where was Valeria? Laurie had hoped to find her already there, but she hadn't arrived yet. Too bad. Laurie hadn't looked forward to telling her she'd been dismissed and was eager to get it over with. She fixed her own breakfast. By the time she finished, it was nearly seven o'clock. She threw on a light wrap and walked to the small stable that stood behind the house. The heavy wagon Hugh and Father used for their work stood inside, along with the six-seater landau, used when the entire family went for an outing, and the light, two-wheel curricle. The sight of the landau brought her nearly to tears, remembering Father sitting tall and proud in the driver's high seat as he drove his family to church on Sundays. Who would drive them now? Perhaps she'd better learn to hitch up the landau and wagon, not just the curricle. Not today, though. One would be all she could handle.

The stable had always been the exclusive domain of the men in the family and she'd never paid much attention to the family's two horses, Brownie and Prancer. During these past few days, the servants had seen to it that the horses were fed and the stable cleaned, but now? Dear Lord, she hadn't thought it through. With the servants gone, not only would the three women of the household be doing the cooking and cleaning, they'd also be feeding the horses and shoveling out the stable. Problems she would deal with later.

Darcy had already arrived and was busily laying out the gear he'd collected from inside the stable. He looked up when he saw her. Unsmiling, all businesslike, he gave her a nod, obviously his version of a friendly greeting. "You want the curricle, right?" She nodded. "Watch carefully."

Dutifully, she stood and watched while he led the horses from the stable, tied them to a post, and picked up a brush. "What are their names?" he asked.

"That's Brownie and that's Prancer."

"First you always want to brush the horse."

She watched as he gave Brownie a thorough brushing, complete with commentary as he went along. "You don't want a piece of dirt left that might irritate the horse," he muttered as he brushed. "Make sure you don't miss anything." When he finished, he stepped back, held out the brush to her, and declared, "Now it's your turn. Let's see how you do with Prancer."

For the first time ever, she was about to handle a horse all by herself. The whole idea of it scared her, to put it mildly. What if this animal suddenly bucked? What if he kicked her? Never mind. Look confident, like she hadn't a care in the world. She took the brush. "Don't help me. I must learn how to do this alone."

"Fine."

At least he wasn't laughing at her. Mustn't make a mistake. Concentrating on everything he'd told her, she brushed Prancer and found that despite her fears, the horse remained docile, not seeming to notice she was there. She made doubly sure she'd brushed every inch of that horse before she stepped back and asked, "How's that?"

"Fine."

"What's next?"

"Next, you hitch the horses to the carriage. First we'll go over the name of each piece of gear." He pointed at and described the various parts of the horse gear she'd seen all her life and never paid the least attention to.

As he described each piece, she listened carefully, silently repeating each name, making a point to remember it. When he was done, he said, "All right, now you're going to harness the horses."

God help her, she would do this right if it killed her. Under his direction, acutely aware of his sharp eyes upon her, she began to harness Brownie and Prancer. Harness, traces, straps, cinches, head stalls. The collar, bridle, and bit. Never had she been so intent on anything in her life. When she'd got to the breast plate, she circled it around Prancer's chest with exquisite care. "Not so high it would cut into his windpipe," he said. "Nor so low it obstructs the horse's movement." There, she'd done it just right, she knew she had.

When she finished, he awarded her a quick "Good enough," and pointed to the curricle in the stable. "Time to roll it out."

She entered the stable. Facing the curricle, she picked up the shafts. Stepping backward, she gave a hefty tug. The thing wouldn't budge.

"Need some help?" he called.

"No, I do not." Bracing herself, she tried again but still no movement.

"Are you sure?"

"Positive." By God, she'd move this buggy or die in the attempt. Taking a deep breath, gathering every bit of strength she possessed, she pulled with all her might. Her hands slipped. Before she even knew what happened, she had fallen backward and now sat plopped on the ground, her skirt hiked up to her knees.

He stepped forward, frowning with concern. "Are you all right?"

"I'm fine." She burst out laughing and held out her hand. "Help me up, please, and I hope you enjoyed the view."

Blank-faced and without comment, he pulled her to her feet. Had the man no sense of humor? "Stand back. I can do this." She got a firm grasp on the shafts again. The wheels moved! Only a few inches, but enough that with another tremendous tug, they started to roll. Grasping the shafts firmly, she backed out of the stable, teeth clamped to contain an unladylike grunt. She didn't stop until she reached the proper spot behind the horses. She dropped the shafts, caught her breath, and in a miraculously steady voice remarked, "You said the shafts go through the tugs on both sides, if I remember correctly."

"Right."

The heartless man showed not the least appreciation for the tremendous effort she'd just made. No applause, no "good work," no nothing, and that included his stony-faced reaction at her generous display of leg when she fell backward. Actually, she hadn't wanted him to notice how mightily she'd struggled, but that was beside the point. She finished without a problem. Success! Surely, he must see what a capable person she was, even if he didn't care to admit it. That she'd hitched two horses to a carriage all by herself was a major achievement in her life. Inside, she glowed with pride. Outside, she gave a careless shrug. "So, is that all there is to it?"

"Just about. Of course, hitching a wagon is different, but you managed the curricle all right, so you won't have any trouble."

That was about as close to a compliment the man could give, so she'd better not expect anything more. "Then shall we proceed to the mine?"

"Want to do the driving?"

Just when she was savoring her success at harnessing the horses, hitching the carriage, now she was supposed to drive, too? Her heart sank. Only one answer could she give, though. "I've never done it before, but how hard could it be? Of course, I shall drive."

After a slight hesitation, he came close to actually smiling. "That won't be necessary. You've had enough lessons for one day." He nodded toward his horse. "I'll tie Champ to the curricle and do the driving. That is, unless you object?"

"Either way is fine with me." She accompanied her remark with an uncaring flip of her hand. Vastly relieved, she climbed to the high-perched seat and waited as Darcy tethered his horse behind and settled beside her. He would never know how unsure of herself she'd been, how she'd nearly given up, coming close as a gnat's leg to admitting she wasn't capable of doing a simple task performed by thousands of people every day. Only her pride had saved her from complete humiliation, but he didn't need to know any of that.

When they started for the mine, Darcy gave her the reins, told her how to use them and taught her a few simple commands. Then he took over, and they chatted the rest of the way. He did most of the talking, describing what he needed to start up the Monarch again, and how he would go about it. She could tell from the excitement in his voice that here was a project that sparked his interest. "I want to hire as many Cornish miners as I can," he told her.

"That's fine, but I hear they're a crude lot."

"Yes, they are, but they're the best there is. If you're going to work at the mine, you'll have to get used to them. You think you can manage?"

"Why would you think I couldn't?"

"The way you were raised. That fiancé of yours, for instance. Fine manners, I'd wager. Smart. Well educated. No doubt a paragon of virtues rolled into one." He slanted an inquiring glance. "Isn't he?"

How odd that a man who in many ways seemed rough and unpolished would use a word like "paragon." Sometimes he surprised her. Even more surprising, why was he so interested in what Brandon was like? If she didn't know better, she'd think he was jealous. "How did you guess?" she asked, feigning great surprise. "Brandon is all of that and more." That wasn't enough. She couldn't resist one more little jab. "He's a wonderful man in every respect. I can hardly wait to get back to him."

Darcy said no more, and they rode the rest of the way in silence.

The Monarch Mine had looked ugly enough to begin with. Now that it was muddy, trash-strewn and deserted, it looked even more depressing. Laurie had paid little attention before, but when she walked into the ramshackle office, she looked around with new interest. This was where she would work, if only for a short time, and she'd better pay attention. Darcy followed her in. After a quick look around, she inquired, "So what am I supposed to do?"

"This isn't my own mine or my own office," he began. "But they're basically the same, so I'm assuming Hugh mainly took care of the payroll. That's a big job. Wasn't that Hugh's desk over there?" He walked to a large, battered desk and opened a few drawers. "Here we are." He pulled a big blue ledger from one of the drawers. "Here's what we call the time book. Sit down and I'll show you."

Laurie sat beside him at the desk. He was looking at her strangely, as if he wasn't sure she could understand. "Go ahead. I'm listening."

"It's a bit complicated."

Did he think she was an idiot? "Keep going."

"All right then." He opened the ledger. "This is your basic book for payroll, or you can call it a ledger. There's also a cash book and books for accounting, but this is the one you'll mostly be dealing with." He went on to explain how she was to write the name of each employee in the ledger. Then the foreman, or foremen, as the case might be, would insert the time in days, or proportions of a day, each person has worked, and the particular work he has been engaged in. "It makes a difference, you see. Men who work underground are paid more than those who work on the surface."

"I can certainly see why," she said.

"Yes, it's a dangerous business. Payday comes once a week. Ordinarily the payroll master goes to the bank to get the money, but being as it's you, we'll get somebody else to—"

"I am perfectly capable of going to the bank myself." She'd come close to snapping at him.

"Fine." He sounded a little annoyed himself. "You will have an armed guard. That's standard practice, whether the paymaster is a big, burly six feet two or…you."

What did he almost say? Something insulting, no doubt. *Or a weak, insignificant female like you.* "That makes sense, Mr. McKenna. Of course, I'll need a guard. So, I take the money up to the mine and pay each miner what he's earned. Sounds simple to me and nothing I can't handle."

"I'm not so sure." He leaned back in his chair and eyed her up and down, as if he felt the need to assess her carefully. "Some of those miners are rough characters, not the type of man you're accustomed to. I mentioned the Cornish miners. They're from the coal mines of Cornwall. That's in England."

"I know where it is." Good lord, did he think she was some kind of ignoramus who didn't even know where Cornwall was?

Blank-faced, he continued on. "They're considered some of the best hard rock miners in the world. A rough bunch, though. They speak English, but they're hard to understand. You might find—"

"I shall cope, Mr. McKenna. Shall we move on?"

"Fine, then. I've a few more things to show you, but if you think you've mastered the payroll, then after that we're done."

"So, when should I start?"

"Any time you want. There's plenty to do, even though I'll have to wait until the paperwork is complete before I can actually get underway."

Laurie looked around the office with a critical eye. Dirty, bare windows. Shabby furniture. Dust everywhere. "I'll start tomorrow. If nothing else, I'll get some curtains up before you even start."

His lips twitched with suppressed laughter. "Curtains are not at the top of my priority list, Miss Sinclair."

So, he found her amusing? Fine; she didn't care. Curtains were on top of her list whether he liked it or not.

Soon after, they closed up the office and returned to the curricle. "Do you think you can manage by yourself on the way home?" he asked.

"I don't know why not. It wasn't nearly as difficult as I expected."

On the way back, she drove the curricle herself. This time, he rode his horse behind her after making some remark about "just in case." She did just fine. "Just in case" didn't happen, and she remembered how to hold the reins and the simple commands he'd taught her. All in all, the day had gone well, and when she pulled the curricle to a stop outside the stable in back of the house, she announced. "You don't have to stay. I can do the rest myself."

"I'm sure you can but allow me to assist anyway." At least he wasn't smirking and seemed sincere enough as he helped her unhitch the horses. He instructed her on how she should rub them down and give them their oats. While she was doing that, she watched, silently grateful when he turned the curricle around and backed it into the stable.

As he swung back on his horse, he called down to her. "There are times when you'll need the wagon. In a few days I'll show you how to hitch it up, too."

"Fine, then." She waved a quick goodbye and in a buoyant mood walked into the house. The day had gone better than expected. How silly she'd been to fear she couldn't manage something as simple as hitching two horses to a buggy. Maybe she could do a lot of things she'd thought she couldn't, and this was just the beginning.

Once inside the house, her spirits fell. The problems she hadn't thought about all day began to surface. Had Mother gotten up nerve enough to dismiss Valeria? Probably not, and she, Laurie, would have to do it. How was Hugh doing? She hadn't had the chance to visit today, and she must do so. And if by chance Mother had dismissed Valeria, who was going to cook dinner, clean the house?

She looked forward to tomorrow, although she wasn't sure why. Darcy McKenna didn't like her. Plain to see he was only tolerating her because he had to. Although... She wished now she hadn't been so snappish. Today, to her surprise, there were times when she'd actually enjoyed his company.

* * * *

That evening, Darcy sank into the one comfortable chair in his room at the Gold Spike Hotel. With a sigh of satisfaction, he gazed around at what had been his home for the past five years. Slightly on the shabby side, the room contained the one chair, a bed, plain wooden dresser and washstand. He might live in less than luxurious surroundings, but even so, he had no intention of moving. His good friend, Tom, recently remarked, "That place is a dump. Maybe you couldn't find anything better when you first came to Lucky Creek, but there's far better places now. Why don't you move?"

"What's wrong with it?" Darcy had asked.

"Your bed squeaks. That noise from below is so bad I don't know how you sleep, what with the drunks and fancy ladies whooping it up every night."

Tom would never understand. Darcy himself hardly understood why, unlike his rich colleagues, he had no desire to live any differently than he had before he opened the Atlas. He'd wasted little time, if any, examining why this was so, but suspected his lack of interest in the luxuries of life had something to do with the fact he'd spent his entire boyhood in a coal mine. Twelve hours a day in total darkness. Sitting on a hard bench with nothing to do but listen for the next car coming so he could open the door and let it through. Except Sunday. God, how he'd looked forward to the one day a week he could see the sun, white clouds, the beautiful, blessed blue sky. When he was eleven, they promoted him to breaker boy. My God, how had he stood it? Hour after hour in the dim light, at least not alone but with other boys, their miserable faces black with soot, their spirits bitter and crushed. He was lucky he hadn't lost a hand or a finger. Many did.

Darcy pulled off his boots and dropped them on the floor. He looked around and smiled to himself. A dump? This room was a palace compared to eight hundred feet belowground in a West Virginia coal mine. He wasn't like other men, never would be. Let them have their fancy mansions, fine carriages, and beautiful wives to show off. Marriage wasn't for him, nor was flaunting his wealth in any way, whatsoever. For him, the luxuries in his life lay in the satisfaction he received from making a success of his mine, seeing his investments grow, although what he'd do with the money he didn't much care. His room might be shabby, but its big window that faced east made up for it. As long he could see the sun rise over the mountains each morning, look up to a blue sky, he had everything in life he'd ever need.

A light knock sounded on his door. A soft, female voice whispered, "Darcy? Are you there?"

He went to the door and opened it wide. "Come in. Haven't seen you for a while."

Lucille Wagner, widow of hotel owner Lucius Wagner, stepped inside. Her salt-and-pepper hair piled in a knot atop her head indicated that she'd been in the world longer than he had, maybe by quite a few years. He'd never asked her age because it didn't matter. At first glance, she looked like just another middle-aged woman in her high-buttoned, white shirtwaist and plain black skirt. Still attractive, though. She might have lost her girlish figure, but her comfortable curves and liveliness in bed made her all the woman he needed. Their relationship consisted of a lot more than just the sex, though. His words flowed easily when he talked to her. As she listened, those big grey-green eyes—her best feature—brimmed with humor and friendliness. Smart and insightful, she could hold her own on any subject they cared to discuss.

He greatly admired her but didn't love her, and she was fine with that. She didn't love him either, although he sensed her warm fondness for him. Her husband had owned and operated the Gold Spike. When he died suddenly of a heart attack, everyone thought his modest, self-effacing little wife would sell. After all, she was only a woman, so how could she possibly run a successful business? But Lucille surprised them. She kept the hotel, and with a shrewd business sense that maybe even she didn't know she had, took over the operation herself. With the improvements she made, and was still making, profits grew each year. Darcy had been friends with Lucius, but after his death, he and Lucille had drifted into more than just an ordinary friendship. She lived in a suite of rooms at the other end of the second floor, so what could be handier? They hadn't planned it this way, but their special arrangement suited them both. Neither ever made demands on the other, nor expected anything of the other.

Once inside, Lucille shut the door and inquired, "Where have you been?"

He waved her to his one good chair and sat on the bed. "Here and there. Been busy."

She settled into the chair. "You haven't been sick?"

"No."

"You haven't visited for a while."

What she meant was, he hadn't come to her bed for a while. "Like I said—"

"You've been busy." A hint of a smile played on her lips. "I've missed you."

He owed her an explanation, but how could he explain when he himself wasn't sure why he hadn't paid a visit to one of the most understanding, sympathetic women he'd ever known. Sometimes when he went to her room, they just talked. He didn't drink much, but once, when he'd had one too many beers, he'd let his barriers down and told her about his miserable childhood. She'd listened with such compassion that for once he held nothing back. Reached deep inside himself to a place he'd never visited before, to his agonized memories of the heartless greed of the mine owners, the cruelty of his parents, his desperate yearning just to look up and see the sun anytime he wanted. Yes, he could do that now, but even so, there were days when the world closed in on him, and he was still that young boy, helpless, trapped in the desolate darkness of a coal mine and there was no way out.

She'd held him tight in her arms that night and whispered, "You must put it all behind you."

"I pretty much have," he'd said.

"No, you haven't," she told him. "The world sees you as a successful mine owner without a care in the world, but on the inside, you're still a lost boy looking for the sunlight. If you don't find it soon, it will ruin your life."

Silently he'd scoffed at her idea, and still did. Now there she sat waiting for an answer to her very reasonable question. Why hadn't he been to see her? He'd be honest, like he always was. Never would he lie to Lucille Wagner. "I honestly don't know why I haven't been to see you. Busy, I guess. That's all I can tell you."

"You're always busy. It's something else." She thought a moment. "You've met a woman."

He burst into laughter. "I talk to women all the time, but I assure you, I haven't suddenly lost my heart to one, nor is that likely to happen."

"Really?" The skeptical expression on her face clearly indicated he hadn't convinced her. "Name some of the women you've had dealings with lately."

She had the wrong idea, but he'd humor her, despite her wrongheaded thinking. "Well, let's see now… I've mostly been dealing with the Sinclair women. They've needed some help after Sam died."

Lucille nodded agreeably. "What a sad business that was. I'm glad you're helping them. Mrs. Sinclair's a fine woman. So's Ada, such a likable girl, although it's a shame she's so shy. I don't know Laurie that well, although I've seen her in church a few times. She hasn't been here that long, but she seems a lovely person, quite beautiful, and I get the impression she's settling into her new home quite nicely."

His head jerked back in surprise. "Where did you get that idea? Laurie Sinclair doesn't belong in a place like Lucky Creek. She can hardly wait to get back to Philadelphia where life will be a hell of a lot easier than it is here. She likes her comforts and doesn't want to stay in what she considers this hellhole a minute longer than she has to."

"My goodness, it seems you've taken quite an interest in that young lady." Lucille regarded him through half-lowered eyelids. "Perhaps you have a special interest in her?"

"Good God, no." He explained how he was going to pay off Dominick's loan. How he would own fifty-one percent interest in the Monarch Mine, and despite his preference to the contrary, was committed to working with Laurie Sinclair for a while. "At least she's volunteered to help, I'll give her that. She'll leave soon as she can, though. The day her brother is well enough to take over, she'll be hightailing it back to Philadelphia and that bug catcher fiancé of hers."

"Why don't you like her?"

Leave it to Lucille to ask one of those piercing questions that made him think. "It's not that I don't like her. It's hard to explain. Laurie lived on Society Hill in Philadelphia. She grew up in a world centered on class and privilege. Lucky Creek is the last place on earth she'd pick to live. Like I said, she'll head home at the first opportunity, which is fine with me."

"Really?"

Lucille had that perceptive look on her face. He'd seen it before when she saw right through him. "Yes, really. She can't help it, but she's a bit of snob and she hates it here."

"Even though her mother and sister are staying?"

"They want to move back, too. It's a matter of money. At least they've made an effort to like it here, unlike Miss High-and-Mighty Laurie Sinclair."

Lucille chuckled. "My, my, Darcy, I hardly ever hear you make a derogatory remark, yet here you are, making no bones concerning your dislike of the young lady. But is it dislike? Are you sure about that?"

"Very sure." Was he lying? All day he'd been thinking about this morning and how she'd bravely undertook to harness the horses, despite her obvious fear. And then, when she'd fallen backward, and her skirt flew up? Seeing those long, slim legs, those slender ankles, caused an unexpected spike in his heartbeat. His breath had caught, and he'd barely managed to conceal the unexpected, and certainly unwelcome, effect she'd had on him.

Lucille got up to leave. With a pleasant smile, she remarked, "I must go. Lots to do. I'll not trouble you further. Remember, my door is always open."

After she left, Darcy sat staring into space. Whether he wanted to or not, he'd just hurt a woman he loved and respected. Of course, she was too much of a lady to show it, and had her pride, but he knew. What he didn't know was why he hadn't visited her room lately. She seemed to have this crazy idea that he had another woman on his mind, and in particular, Laurie Sinclair.

Maybe there was some truth in that. Maybe more than he realized, especially after this morning, but what good would it do him? Laurie Sinclair loved some guy in Philadelphia who studied bugs. Holy hell, he couldn't begin to deal with that.

If he was smart, he'd be showing up at Lucille's door later tonight.

But somehow, he knew he wouldn't.

Chapter 7

Next morning, Laurie found Valeria already in the kitchen. Wearing her bowler hat and bright skirt and shawl, she stood at the stove scrambling eggs with a big wooden spoon. Laurie had no idea how their Bolivian cook would take the bad news, but she could avoid the dreaded moment no longer. "Can I speak to you a moment?"

Valeria turned to Laurie and inquired, "Yes?" in her usual blunt fashion. She wasn't much of a one to dwell on the niceties of conversation.

Laurie had to clear her throat twice before she could speak. "I'm so sorry about this, but we're going to have to let you go. I'm sure you understand, what with our tragic loss of Mr. Sinclair. Of course, you'll receive your pay and a week's extra. I'd give you more if I could. You've always done an excellent job for us, and I can only hope you understand. And of course, I'll give you a glowing reference should anyone ask." There. The unpleasant deed was done. Not an easy task, but she'd done the best job she could and could only hope the cook would take the news well and not get too upset.

Valeria dropped the spoon, crossed her sturdy brown arms, and glared at Laurie. "I'm not going."

For a moment Laurie could only sputter, unable to grasp what she'd just heard. "What do you mean you're not going? I just dismissed you. Did you not understand? Like I said, you'll receive all your pay and a week's extra."

True to form, the fiery-eyed cook threw her head back and glared in defiance. Her broad face settled into uncompromising lines. "I stay here and work. You pay me what you can."

"You don't want to go? There must be a reason."

"I don't need a reason. I'm not going."

What should she do now? Laurie waved toward the kitchen table. "Let's sit down. You need to explain."

Valeria removed the pan of eggs from the stove. They sat facing each other at the table, Laurie so flabbergasted she hardly knew what to say next. "I just dismissed you. I don't understand why you'd want to stay."

Eyeing her defiantly, speaking in her broken, hard-to-understand English, Valeria began, "Not much to explain. It's my husband. He's jealous all the time. If I work in a place where there are men, he thinks I flirt with them, and he beats me. Here there are no men around anymore except Mr. Hugh, and Emery not worry about him now. He told me so this morning. I wouldn't dare leave now."

Again, Laurie recalled the awful stories she'd heard about hot-tempered Emery Finch. How her brash and very independent cook could put up with such brutal treatment, she didn't know. Maybe now was a good time to bring up the forbidden subject. "If you don't mind my asking, if your husband treats you so poorly, why don't you leave him? You don't need him. You could easily support yourself."

Valeria seemed to wilt before her eyes. "I can't," she whispered. "If I leave, he'll kill me."

"You could call the sheriff, have him arrested."

"My skin is brown. I come from below the border. You think the sheriff would take my word over a white man's?"

"Of course not. I wasn't thinking." Laurie didn't know how else to answer. She hadn't been in Lucky Creek long before she recognized the deep-seated prejudice that existed against foreigners, especially those who were nonwhite and came from any continent except Europe, and even then, resentments simmered. Lucky Creek had a sheriff, but from what she'd heard, he was weak and not beyond accepting bribes. In her own life, she had nothing to compare with Valeria's predicament. In Philadelphia, all the men she knew were gentlemen, at least on the surface, although the older she got, the more she realized life wasn't all polite talk and drawing room manners no matter where she lived. "I want to help, Valeria. I suppose we could pay you half wages—I can promise that much—and more if we can."

"Fine. I'll take what you can give me." Valeria rose from the table and went back to scrambling her eggs. Obviously, their conversation was over, and had ended on Valeria's terms—certainly not Laurie's.

Shortly after, Ada and Mother appeared. Valeria had left the kitchen. "Well, did you tell her?" Elizabeth asked.

"Yes, I did, and she paid no attention. She's not leaving. I'm a failure. I can't even dismiss the cook."

Elizabeth cocked her head and gave her an I-told-you-so look. "Let's hope you have better luck at the mine today. If anything goes wrong, and it very well might, you come straight home."

A sudden fear clutched Laurie's heart. Today was a day of firsts. Like thousands of others, she was going to drive herself to a place where she'd put in a full day's work. She would set up the payroll book and God knew what other account books, all for the first time in her life. And also, if that weren't enough, she'd be working alongside Darcy McKenna, a man like no other she'd ever known. He made her angry with his bluntness, and yet?

In some perverse way, she was actually looking forward to her first full day at the Monarch mine, although she wasn't sure why. Her mother didn't think she'd last the day, maybe with good reason.

After breakfast, Laurie headed for the stable. Ada soon followed. Looking skeptical, she declared, "I've got to see this. I can't believe my elegant sister is actually going to hitch up the curricle all by herself."

"Just watch." Laurie led Brownie and Prancer from the stable. She still harbored a fear that one of the animals might kick her, but she harnessed them with ease, thank goodness, managing to appear as if she did this every day. She rolled the curricle from the stable, making that look easy, too, and actually completed the job without one single hesitation or slip. When finished, she gave each horse a friendly pat and casually remarked, "See how easy it is? I should have learned how to do this years ago."

"No, you shouldn't have. You're just being brave." Ada wrapped her arms around herself and shivered as a cool, late-summer breeze brushed over them. "Things are so different now. Father's gone. Hugh might never be the same. Mother's not well, and we have no money." Tears glistened on her pale cheeks. "What if the new gold vein turns out to be nothing? What's to become of us? What if Mathew and Maryanne don't have enough to eat?"

Until that moment, Laurie hadn't recognized the depths of Ada's concern for their future. She should have, considering her sister's fears were real. The once affluent Sinclair family could best be described as having fallen into desperate straits. Laurie felt like voicing her own wail of despair, just like her sister, but of course she couldn't. Whether she liked it or not, she'd become the only Sinclair left who could claim being both healthy and levelheaded. That made her head of the family, at least temporarily. If they were going to survive, it was up to her.

Her admission to herself didn't come easily. Even though she'd volunteered to work at the mine, somehow, she'd assumed there'd be someone she could fall back on. All her life, someone had watched over her, someone she could turn to for guidance and advice. Now she herself was that someone. Head of the family. Maker of decisions. And maybe, above all else, person responsible for keeping spirits high. She had no idea what the future held, but more than anything else, her mother and sister mustn't worry. With a casual toss of her head she replied, "Don't be silly, Ada. Mr. McKenna wouldn't be investing in the Monarch if he thought that new vein wouldn't pay off."

Her sister wiped a tear away. "I can't believe you're actually going to work there. It's such an ugly place. How will you cope with all those rough miners? They can hardly speak English, some of them, and don't know their manners."

"I shall cope. There's other things in the world besides good manners."

Ada wrinkled her nose. "Well, I don't know what. Promise me you'll be careful, working up there with God knows what kind of men."

"I promise I will be." Ada needed something to distract her, Laurie thought. Something to keep her from worrying so much. An idea struck her. Outlandish, but it might work. "Actually, I was hoping you could help. You've seen the office and how bare and ugly it is. I had thought you might lend a hand and put up some curtains. I could do it, but you have an artistic flair that I lack. You could do some decorating. Brighten the place up. That sort of thing."

"Oh, I couldn't."

Ada's response was no more than what Laurie expected. Full of fears, she resisted new ideas and always said no to begin with. "Think about it. You might change your mind."

"No, I won't. You know me, Laurie. If I had my way, I'd never leave the house. I still don't know how you'll be able to work up there."

"I consider it a challenge. Maybe it'll be fun, and I'll make new friends." Such a lie. She hoped she sounded convincing considering the doubts she had.

Ada didn't look at all convinced. "But you said you don't even like Mr. McKenna, and now you've got to work with him."

"He's not all bad."

"But you were going to go home. You were going to marry Brandon Cooper. What if he doesn't wait?"

At her sister's words, a sudden fear knifed through Laurie's heart. "He loves me. Of course he'll wait." She put on a cheerful face and threw an arm around Ada's shoulders. "We're going to be fine. Maybe we'll be a little bit poor, but it's only temporary. And remember, Valeria's not leaving. We won't have to cook after all."

Ada returned a brave smile, just as Laurie expected sooner or later she would. "Of course, I'll try, and I'll do my best to look on the bright side. Why should I worry as long as we have a roof over our heads, food on the table, and the children are happy?"

"Why indeed?" Laurie spoke with new confidence. She wasn't sure what the future held, but in reassuring Ada, she'd also reassured herself. The events of the past few days had filled her with grave misgivings and a gnawing fear of what the future would hold. But at least for today she knew what she had to do and where she was going. She'd let tomorrow take care of itself.

* * * *

Before going to the mine, Laurie stopped off at the hospital to visit Hugh. He still lay flat in bed, had gained full consciousness but was still in a lot of pain. At least he was well enough to voice his complaints. "They won't tell me when I can get out of here. I want to go home."

She remembered where he'd been staying the past few months. "Back to your fancy suite at the Egyptian?"

He started to laugh, then winced in pain. "Forget the Egyptian. You know what I mean."

She told him she'd be working at the mine, but of course Mother and Ada would be there to help him when he did get home.

He stared at her in amazement. "You're working at the mine? Am I hearing you correctly?"

His negative reaction didn't surprise her. Hugh firmly believed men should be the moneymakers in the family and make all the important decisions. Women, because of their fragility and frivolous nature, should stay at home and meekly follow instructions. "It's only until you're well enough to come back."

He eyed her suspiciously. "And it's all right with McKenna?"

"Perfectly all right. He's delighted he has someone to do the timekeeping." A bit of a lie. If anything, Darcy McKenna was only tolerating her because he had to. But Hugh didn't need to know that. "And while I'm there, I might even dig out your accounting books and see if I can work on those, too. That is, if I learn enough."

"Absolutely not. I forbid it. You leave those accounting books alone."

Her brother's fierce reaction surprised her but shouldn't have. After what he'd been through, he didn't want to hear someone else could do his job just as well. "Then I won't," she said with a smile. "I couldn't do the accounting books half as well as you and can't imagine why I thought to try."

Hugh accepted her explanation with an irritated grunt, but after that, his good humor returned, and he seemed in fine spirits by the time she left. A touch of apprehension hit her as she climbed to the high seat of the curricle and picked up the reins. Driving along the wide main street of Lucky Creek was one thing. Driving the steep, narrow road to the mine was quite another. She'd always been a passenger. Now she alone was in command. That meant she had no one to turn to, no one to advise her if something went wrong. Had she been foolish? Should she never have attempted such a bold, unladylike endeavor? Firmly grasping the reins, she started up the narrow road to the Monarch Mine. The sun warmed her face. The steady clip-clop of horse hooves boosted her confidence by the minute. A heady feeling gripped her. *I'm in charge. I can make this curricle go to any place I choose, at any pace I choose.* Really, nothing she couldn't handle. What a carefree, enjoyable feeling. Why hadn't she done this sooner?

At the mine, after unhitching the horses and making sure they got their oats, she entered the dilapidated headquarters of the Monarch Mine Company. Not to her surprise, Darcy had already arrived, along with Tom. Judging from the line of men extending from the door, they'd begun hiring miners. When she walked in, Darcy gave her a quick nod, remarked, "If you need any help, ask Tom," and turned back to the man he was interviewing.

So obviously, she'd be working on her own today. Fine with her. She would not ask Tom and must figure out what to do by herself. The less she had to do with Darcy, the better.

She sat at Hugh's desk and pulled out the time ledger. She recognized Hugh's fine, cursive handwriting filling the first few pages. Maybe she should rip them out and start anew? But no, best to keep a record. Despite what he'd told her, she scanned the pages anyway. Nothing made sense, but she kept on scanning, trying to look busy. Along about lunchtime, Darcy appeared at her desk. "I've done some hiring. I'll have a list for you tomorrow. If you need any help getting started—"

"I can manage just fine, thank you," she said with a friendly smile. He'd deliberately ignored her all morning, but he wasn't going to know she'd even noticed.

"There's nothing to do until tomorrow. You may as well go home."

Was that sympathy in his eyes? Apparently, he'd seen through her pitiful attempts to act busy. How humiliating. She'd like to crawl under a rock but wouldn't give him the satisfaction. "Fine then. I have much to do at home."

She picked up her reticule, waved a breezy goodbye, and headed toward the stable. Was he perhaps standing at the window looking after her? She wished she could turn around and see if he was but wouldn't give him the satisfaction. Besides, he might not be looking, and that was the strange part. From the time she was fourteen and got her figure, she was accustomed to men's lustful gazes and found them annoying. So why should she care whether Darcy McKenna's gaze rested upon her? Of course, she didn't care in the least. Even so, despite herself, she cast a quick glance over her shoulder. Silly girl. No one stood in the window.

She had hitched up the horses and was on her way home before she thought of the answer to her own question. She didn't care whether or not Darcy was looking at her because she loved Brandon Cooper. How could she have forgotten?

* * * *

When Laurie arrived home, she found Ada in the parlor reading a story to Mathew and Maryanne. Ada looked up from her book and frowned when she saw her. "Have you heard the latest? Little Ruthie next door has diphtheria."

"Oh, no, what awful news." Laurie would never forget the deadly epidemics that swept through Philadelphia when she was a child. She vividly recalled her mother's helpless panic at outbreaks of scarlet fever, whooping cough, smallpox, or sometimes diphtheria, a horrible disease that started with a mild sore throat and often ended with the patient unable to swallow, unable to breathe. Many, especially young children, didn't survive. Ruthie and Maryanne were the same age and often played together. As casually as Laurie could manage, she asked, "Has Maryanne played with Ruthie lately?"

"Just yesterday. Ruthie seemed all right. Now her mother says she's got a fever and sore throat. Doctor Hansen came by. He says it's definitely diphtheria." Ada's face clouded. "Hasn't this family had enough sorrow? I don't know what I'd do if either of these darling children gets sick and… and…" She choked up and couldn't go on.

"We will just have to have faith that it's not going to happen." What next? Laurie had done her best to sound optimistic, but she, too, couldn't bear the thought of her little niece or nephew contracting that deadly disease. Both children were so special. Each had been a delight to care for from the day they were born. They simply could not get sick. Not chubby, rosy-cheeked Mathew, who squealed with delight every time he saw a horse. Not blonde, blue-eyed Maryanne, who loved to cuddle on Laurie's lap and be read to. No, they would not, could not, get sick. God couldn't be that cruel.

That night at dinner, Valeria served *feijoada*, another family favorite, a sort of Bolivian stew with black beans, beef, and pork. It took a lot of work to make, and she'd cooked it all day in a thick clay pot. "Yum, good," Ada remarked after her first bite. "Valeria's on her good behavior. This must be her idea of a peace offering after she refused to leave this morning."

"Fine with me." Laurie's day hadn't been the best, but now, at dinner, her spirits had lifted, and she was looking at the bright side. During the day, they'd brought Hugh home on a stretcher and carried him up to his room. He might be unable to come down for dinner yet, but surely, he soon would be. She'd managed to get through her first day of work at the mine. Maybe she hadn't done much, but at least she'd survived, and would return tomorrow, determined more than ever to do the job right. But before long, she wouldn't have to worry. Hugh would soon be back to work, and that meant she could soon return to Philadelphia.

A dark cloud still lurked, but only in the deepest corner of her mind. This family had suffered enough. Nothing more could possibly go wrong.

Chapter 8

The first thing Laurie did next morning was tiptoe into the children's room to see how they were doing. Mathew was sleeping soundly, his forehead cool to the touch. Which was not the case with Maryanne. Her face looked flushed. When Laurie laid her palm on the little girl's forehead, she whispered, "Oh, no."

She immediately summoned Mother and Ada. Fearfully they gathered around Maryanne's bed. "It's diphtheria," Elizabeth said in a bitter voice. "My worst fear come true."

Laurie tried to sound hopeful. "Maybe it's not, and even if it is, lots of children survive it."

Mother remained silent, gloomily shaking her head.

During the next two days, Maryanne's condition gradually worsened. Her fever remained high. She'd developed a hacking cough. Her tonsils were swollen. She started wheezing and was having trouble catching her breath. They gave her spoonsful of honey for her throat, but she still kept coughing. Mother made a mustard plaster to put on her chest for the congestion, but it did no good. Laurie wanted to stay home, but both her mother and sister assured her she wasn't needed.

By the third day after she got sick, Maryanne was no better but not any worse, either. Laurie didn't want to leave her. "I think I should stay home today."

"Ada and I can take care of her," Mother firmly told her. "Go to work. She'll be fine."

Worried but hopeful, Laurie hitched up the curricle and drove to the mine. Until today it had been closed, but this morning she found a lively scene awaiting her. Water gushed down the sluice boxes. A group of miners, picks and shovels in hand, were gathered around the mine entrance. What a nice surprise. The Monarch Mine no longer sat idle. Darcy hadn't been around the last two days, but when she entered the office, she found him and Tom already hard at work. She said good morning to them both. Tom smiled and returned her greeting. After a curt nod, Darcy said, "You can get started on the time ledger now. I'll be needing time sheets for each miner. Tom can help you get them set up. We need hours worked, what kind of task, and so on." He turned back to the miner he'd been talking with.

How rude. Couldn't he at least have given her a friendly hello? But then, what had she expected? She was a working girl now, not a fine lady whom all gentlemen must cater to. She had come here to work, not for some trivial visit. At the moment, Darcy McKenna was in charge, and whatever he said to do, she would do. She sat at her desk and tucked her reticule in a drawer. Tom came over with a handful of blank time sheets and sat next to her. She directed her attention to her work. With Tom helping, she soon became so immersed in the intricacies of timekeeping that the time flew by.

Before she knew it, Tom had left. She was working on her own, and to her immense satisfaction, knew what she was doing. While she worked, a never-ending stream of miners entered the office, stayed for a quick interview and left. She'd paid no attention until a burst of especially loud laughter caused her to raise her eyes. A group of boisterous Cornish miners had entered. They all looked alike to her. Big, burly men, some with beards, wearing sturdy boots and rough working clothes. She felt nothing in common with them, especially when she heard them talk in a strange dialect she couldn't understand. One of them laughed a lot. Young, maybe twenty-two or so, clean-shaven, tall and broad shouldered with a thick head of curly black hair. He was standing in front of Darcy's desk and apparently had just been hired. When he caught her looking at him, he jovially called what sounded like "Allycumpooster, ma'am."

Allycumpooster? She frowned, trying to understand what the man just said. Darcy spoke up. "He's from Cornwall, Miss Sinclair. That's how they talk. What he means is all is in order and he's happy I hired him."

She smiled at the man and wiggled her fingers at him. "Congratulations."

The man immediately strode to her desk and stuck out his hand. "Kenvern Trenowden's the name, Miss. Those be my brothers over there. That's Petrok, and that's Steren."

Laurie looked to where the Cornishman pointed. Two men who looked remarkably like Kenvern, although older, appeared to be distressed at their brother's boldness and were trying to wave him back. "Pay him no never mind," one of them called. "Kenvern be not knowing his place sometimes."

"Quite all right," she called. Rather than offending her, the Cornishman had brought a bit of cheer to her otherwise unexciting day. She offered her hand, watching as it totally disappeared into the Cornishman's large, rough one. "I'm Laurie Sinclair, and I'm delighted to meet you."

Kenvern Trenowden beamed. "Likewise, and pardon me manners. I'm learning, you know. I won't speak this way forever. The day will come when you understand me." He stepped away, joined his brothers, and they hustled him out of the office in a hurry.

Darcy called over to her, "Those Cornish miners are the best in the world. We're lucky to have them. Don't be offended by their rough manners."

Did he think she was a complete snob? "I don't mind at all. He was only being friendly."

She'd hardly got back to work before the door to the office burst open, and one of the Cornish miners poked his head in, the one called Steren, she thought but wasn't sure. Peering in her direction, he asked, "You're Laurie?"

The alarm in his voice caused her to rise quickly from her chair. "I'm Laurie."

"Then you'd best come quick. There's a lassie outside. Said your name and fainted dead away."

What could he mean? Laurie rushed outside. A group of miners had gathered around the man who'd just introduced himself as Kenvern Trenowden. A limp, unconscious woman lay in his arms. Who...? Laurie drew closer. A soft gasp escaped her. "Ada!" She rushed to where the miner stood holding her. "What happened? What's wrong with her?"

"Don't rightly know, ma'am. She come running up the road toward us. We could see she be anxious. Breathing hard she was, and when she got here, she cried out your name and fainted dead away."

Ada had never fainted before. Seeing her white-faced sister draped like a rag doll in the Cornishman's arms was such a shock that Laurie needed a moment to find her voice. Darcy appeared, his mere presence bringing an air of command. He took one look and said, "Bring her inside." He addressed the group of miners who'd gathered around. "The rest of you wait here."

Laurie followed Darcy and the miner into the office. She must think clearly. Must find a place where the miner could lay her sister down. Ahead of her, Darcy strode to the dilapidated sofa that stood unused in the corner, piled high with boxes of old ledgers and junk of all descriptions. With no regard to neatness, he began clearing it off. She joined him, frantically tossing items to the floor. Kenvern stood by, calmly holding Ada as if he might be holding a bundle of thistles in his arms. When they'd cleared the sofa, he laid Ada gently on the cushions and stepped back, shaking his head with concern. "Caught her just in time, I did, else she'd have landed in the mud."

Laurie knelt by Ada's side. "Sister, are you all right? Please answer me."

Ada's eyelids fluttered. She groaned and opened her eyes wide. For a moment she stared wildly around, as if she didn't know where she was. Her lips moved, just barely at first, then in a barely audible voice, "Couldn't find the doctor. Ran all the way."

"I want to hear all of it, but you must rest a minute."

"There's no time to rest," Ada cried in a desperate voice and struggled to sit up. "Little Ruthie died this morning."

"Oh, no," Laurie cried out. Her heart wrenched in sympathy, not only for Ruthie but for her parents. What could be worse than losing a child?

"That's not all," Ada continued. "Maryanne's worse. Her fever's gone up and she's struggling to breathe."

"Did you send for the doctor?"

"I knew I had to get the doctor, but how? You were gone and had taken the carriage. None of the neighbors were around except Ruthie's parents next door, but how could I bother them when their child just died? Of course, Hugh couldn't help, and neither could Mother. You know how she is—just so very helpless these days. That's when Valeria said she'd go get the doctor herself. I was so grateful, Laurie. By then I didn't want to leave Maryanne's side."

"Of course, you didn't." Hearing the near-hysteria in her sister's voice, Laurie spoke softly. "So, did Valeria find the doctor?"

Ada shook her head. "I waited for what seemed like forever. Finally, Valeria came back empty-handed. No Doc Hansen. He's at the hospital and can't leave. There's an epidemic going on. Every bed is full and then some. The doctor said I should bring Maryanne to the hospital, but is that the right thing to do? What can they do for her that we can't do at home? I would have had to carry her, jostling and bouncing her about, and I didn't think that was a good idea because she's having trouble breathing." Ada shook her head in dismay. "I couldn't think what to do, so that's when I decided to run and get you. Valeria had to leave. That awful husband of hers came and got her. The best I could do was ask Mother to sit by Maryanne's side until we got back. So, then all I had to do was run up the mountain to the mine to get you."

Laurie regarded her sister with surprise. Ada hardly ever took a long walk, let alone ran up a steep mountainside. "You mean you ran all the way? I don't know how you did it."

Ada's broke into hysteria-edged laughter. "I don't know how I did it either. Then I fainted, didn't I?"

"Dead away, and a big, burly miner caught you before you fell in the mud." Laurie got to her feet. "We've got to get back to Maryanne. Rest here while I get the carriage."

Ada took a deep breath as if to steady herself. "I'll be all right. We must get back fast as we can."

Laurie's mind raced. First, she must catch Brownie and Prancer, who'd been turned out to graze. Then she'd have to hitch up the curricle, which would take extra time because she was so new at it. She'd hurry fast as she could.

Darcy had been quietly standing by. He stepped up and declared, "I'll take care of it. Wait here with your sister." Without giving her the chance to answer, he hurried from the office. Minutes later, he returned and announced, "I've rounded up your horses and hitched them to the carriage. Are we ready to go?"

"We?"

"I'm driving."

"But you have a mine to run. I wouldn't have thought—"

His eyes slightly narrowed. "You're wasting time. If you want to drive, fine, but if you want to get back fast as you can, I'll drive, not you."

"Let's go." Whether she liked him or not, he was right. She wouldn't waste time arguing.

Darcy drove the three of them down the mountain at a speed Laurie would never have attempted. The pine trees became a blur of green as they raced by, but somehow, she wasn't terrified. Darcy's calm bearing and sure grip on the reins gave assurance he knew what he was doing. When they arrived, Darcy told them he wasn't leaving. He'd wait in the carriage, and if they needed to take Maryanne to the hospital he'd be there to take her.

Laurie had held out hope that her niece would be better by now, but the truth hit hard the moment she stepped into the children's room. Maryanne lay limp and still, eyelids half closed, cheeks flushed with fever. When Laurie sat next to her and laid a palm on her feverish forehead, she started to cough, a rough, hacking kind of cough that sounded horrible. She started struggling for breath.

Mother had been sitting by the bed, her face lined with worry and fatigue. She rose and declared, "The mustard plasters aren't helping. Nothing is. I'll tell Hugh you've returned, but he can't do anything either."

Ada stood wringing her hands. "See how Maryanne's throat is swollen? What if it swells completely shut? What shall we do then?"

For a moment, Laurie closed her eyes. The weight of the world had just descended on her shoulders, and she wasn't sure she could bear it. Her little niece had contracted a deadly disease and could very well die, as so many did, especially little children. But many pulled through, and if she had anything to say about it, Maryanne would be among the survivors. "We must do all we can to save her."

"But how?" Ada pleaded in a desperate voice. "Should we keep her here and give her another mustard plaster? Should we take her to the hospital? What do you think, Laurie? You're the one who's got to decide."

And just like that, she was the one in charge now. She, Laurie Sinclair, former free-from-care debutante, would be making the decisions. Up to now, reliability and responsibility had never been her strong points, but whether she liked it or not, she was in charge. Maryanne's life lay in her hands. A decision must be made, and she would make it. Nothing to be gained from waiting around. "No more mustard plasters. I'm taking Maryanne to the hospital. You must stay here, Ada. Mother and Hugh need you, and you must keep an eye on Mathew. God forbid he might come down with it, too."

With Ada's help, she bundled Maryanne in blankets, carried her downstairs and out to the front where Darcy sat waiting in the carriage. He'd brought his horse, tied behind the carriage, and could leave any time. She stopped short and looked up at him. "Ada was right. Maryanne needs to get to the hospital. Should I drive so you can get back to the mine? It's a deadly disease, Mr. McKenna. It's only fair I tell you in case you don't want to be exposed to it."

Darcy fairly sprang from the carriage and took the little girl in his arms. "I'll do the driving. You climb in, and I'll hand her up to you."

"Then you don't mind? It's diphtheria, after all, and—"

"For God's sakes, just get in."

* * * *

When they entered the hospital, Darcy carrying Maryanne in his arms, they found the place packed to overflowing. The nurse greeted them briefly. "No more beds, just the floor." She pressed some blankets into Laurie's arms. "The doctor will see her when he can." She scurried off before they could ask anything.

They found an empty spot on the floor between two other children who looked feverish and had that awful hacking cough and laid Maryanne between them. By now she lay listless and burning with fever. Her neck had swollen, and the bouts of coughing were ever more frequent. She was having trouble breathing, at times struggling for every breath. Laurie sat on the floor beside her. "I'll get her some water," Darcy said. As he walked away, Laurie wondered if he would take the time to stay.

When he returned with the water, he sat next to Maryanne on the other side. With the greatest of care, he held her head up slightly and tipped a bit of water into her mouth. He dipped a clean handkerchief in the water in the glass and gently brushed it against her lips. "She needs liquids," he said. "Mustn't let her get too dry."

"It looks as if you've done this before."

"I had eleven brothers and sisters. Once when there was an epidemic, four of them came down with scarlet fever. It's a different disease but just as nasty. Some of the symptoms are the same."

Funny, she'd never thought that he might have a family, but of course he did. She hesitated to ask but had to know. "Did they live?"

"Two died. We couldn't afford a doctor, but I doubt we could have saved them anyway." He suddenly frowned, as if realizing how discouraging he sounded. "Doc Hansen's an excellent doctor. I've heard nothing but good things about him."

So, he had brothers and sisters? Where did he come from? What sort of childhood did he have? She'd never thought to inquire before, never had the least interest in the life of a man who constantly annoyed her. But now wasn't the time to ask. She was grateful, and more than a little surprised he'd gone to all this trouble for a little girl he hardly knew. "It's awfully kind of you to take the time. I mean, I know how busy you are at the mine."

He took his time answering. "There are times when you have to figure what's important in this life and what isn't. I'm not going anywhere."

So, he would stay, thank goodness. She didn't want to be alone. She accepted his answer and argued no further. After all, she couldn't expect more from a man so closemouthed. Clearly any further expressions of gratitude wouldn't be appreciated. They sat waiting. Occasionally she could see the doctor moving from patient to patient, besieged by family members, so overwhelmingly in demand that as anxious as she was that he get to Maryanne, she sat quietly, patiently awaiting her turn. When at last Doc Hansen arrived and knelt by Maryanne's side, Laurie gave him a quick greeting and lapsed into silence. No need to describe her niece's symptoms. What could she say that he couldn't see for himself? In an agony of suspense, she watched while he listened to her chest with his stethoscope, laid his hand for a few seconds on her forehead, peered into her mouth. Finally, he stood and motioned to her and Darcy to step away from where Maryanne could hear.

"It's diphtheria. I can tell from the grey patch at the back of her throat."

Oh no, oh, no. Somehow, she'd clung to the possibility that maybe Maryanne was suffering from a bad cold or the influenza, but the doctor's pronouncement shattered her last hope. "What can we do?" she asked, her voice rising to a near-hysterical level. But she mustn't lose control, must remain calm for Maryanne's sake. More softly, she continued, "I mean there must be something we can do."

"She's burning up with fever. Best you take her home and put cool cloths on her forehead."

Darcy asked, "Is there some kind of cough syrup she should take?"

"You could try, but I doubt it would do any good."

Laurie flung out her hands in simple despair. "That's all?"

Doc Hansen nodded gravely. "I wish we had a cure, but there isn't one. If she continues to have trouble breathing, and she very well might, you could try the treatment for croup. Boil some water in a kettle and get the steam up. Put a towel over her head and have her breathe the steam. Sometimes it helps."

"Sometimes?" She heard the desperation in her voice and didn't care.

The doctor heaved a deep sigh. "Sometimes."

She remembered Ruthie, and how she died. "But what if her breathing gets worse? What if she can't breathe at all?"

"Well…" Head bowed, Doc Hansen lapsed into silence, as if in deep thought, weighing a decision he must make.

When would he speak? Losing her last shred of patience, she burst out, "Please tell me, Doctor. There must be something we can do."

"There is, but it's highly unlikely you could use such a method. I only mention it because you're insisting."

"I understand. What is it? Tell me."

"Mind you, this can only be used as a last resort. It's a procedure known as a tracheotomy. It's recognized as a legitimate means of treating a severe airway obstruction."

"I never heard of it."

"Neither have most people, and that includes many doctors. Obviously, I've heard of it, but I've never done one, nor do I intend to. It's a surgical procedure that involves using a scalpel to make an incision on the anterior aspect of the neck. That's the front of the neck. It opens a direct airway to the trachea, which is the windpipe. The resulting stoma, or what you would call a hole, serves independently as an airway. Then a tube is inserted so the patient can breathe without the use of the nose or mouth."

"It sounds risky."

The doctor nodded grimly. "It's much too risky for me to try. Actually, I couldn't if I wanted to because I'm not equipped for such a procedure. Aside from the scalpel, I'd need a tenaculum, two aneurysm needles to use as retractors, a pair of artery forceps, on and on, and of course the tubing. I simply don't have all that equipment."

It was useless to ask, but in the interest of exhausting all possibilities, she'd ask anyway. "Is there a doctor around here who could perform it?"

"Actually, there is. Doctor Grover Scott has a clinic over in Hangtown. He's done a few tracheotomies, and successfully, I might add." He frowned in thought. "But the problem is, Hangtown is a four-hour drive from here. Maybe more, if the weather's bad. I don't know if the child could endure having to travel twenty miles over a rough road. Better to take her home. Use the steam…"

"Doctor, help!" came a man's desperate call from the other side of the room.

"Must go," Doc Hansen muttered. Shoulders slumped, he wearily turned away and left them standing.

They returned to Maryanne. As Laurie sank beside her, a wave of hopelessness nearly overcame her. She looked up at Darcy. "We may as well take her home. Try the steam. Maybe…" She was going to say, "Maybe the steam will help," but choked on the words. No sense deluding herself. Nothing was going to help. Her precious little niece was fighting for her life and could very well lose the battle.

Darcy knelt beside her. "Let's take her home," he said quietly.

"I feel so helpless."

"I know. We'll try the steam."

His calm presence gave her strength. Saying she felt helpless made her look weak and inadequate, and she would not say it again. "Yes, we'll try the steam. Let's hurry and get her home."

Chapter 9

By the time they reached the house, and Darcy had carried Maryanne to her bed, Laurie knew the doctor's advice wouldn't work. Maryanne was so sick that draping a towel over her head, making her breathe hot steam, would not only have been cruel, it wouldn't have helped. By now her neck had swollen so much she was hardly recognizable. She breathed with increasing difficulty, sometimes gasping for every breath. Laurie, Mother, and Ada hovered over her bed. "It's like she's choking to death," Ada cried.

"She's getting worse, our poor little girl." Elizabeth sank to a chair beside the bed and dropped her face in her hands. "I can hardly bear it."

Darcy had stood by watching but not intruding. "She needs the tracheotomy, Mrs. Sinclair. It could be her only chance."

"She needs a *what*?" Ada asked.

Using the doctor's words, he explained what a tracheotomy was. As he spoke, both Mother and Ada grew wide eyed. "Cut her throat open?" Mother asked in an incredulous voice. "Mr. McKenna, are you out of your mind?"

Laurie gazed at Darcy in surprise. "Not for a moment did I take the doctor seriously. The whole idea of a trach...trach...whatever it's called is just too horrifying. Besides that, you heard what he said. We'd have to go to that doctor in Hangtown, and that's much too far."

"No, it's not. The road's not bad. I could get us there in give or take four hours." Darcy had chosen his words carefully, and spoke softly, as if trying not to force his opinion upon them.

"But just look at her," Ada exclaimed. "She can hardly breathe. A trip like that would probably kill her."

"It might, but then again, it might be her only hope."

Darcy's words hit Laurie hard. "So, what you're saying is, the trip might kill her, but what chance does she have if we keep her home?"

"It's for you to decide. I'll wait downstairs."

After he left, the three stared at each other in shocked silence, not wanting to make what could be a fatal decision but knowing they must. Elizabeth was the first to speak up. "I think Hugh should be the one to decide. He is, after all, Maryanne's father."

Laurie vigorously shook her head. She wouldn't say it aloud, but her brother had shown little interest in his children. He loved them, she supposed, but if they left the decision to him, would he have his daughter's best interest at heart or decide what was best for himself? "Let's not inflict him with a decision like this. He's still in so much pain he's not thinking clearly. It's up to us to decide."

Ada spoke up. "Laurie, this tracheotomy… Did Doc Hansen think it might really work?"

"He seemed to think so. He said this doctor in Hangtown has performed several and they've been successful."

Elizabeth still looked horrified. "But cutting into her throat? How could she survive such a thing?"

Maryanne fell into another fit of coughing that went on and on. Weak and exhausted, she finally stopped but still fought for breath. Her face had taken on a slightly bluish color. Finally, she managed to draw enough air in her lungs that the blue color receded.

"She's better, I think," Elizabeth said.

"For the moment," Laurie answered grimly. She felt Maryanne's forehead. "She's as hot as ever, if not worse. Did you see how blue she just got?"

Elizabeth spoke again. "Bad enough you took her to the hospital, but clear to Hangtown? That's way too far. This is too much for me. It's for you to decide, Laurie, but you know what I think. She needs to stay right where she is in her bed."

"I think so, too," Ada said. "It would be foolish to move her. Sick as she is, how could she stand such a trip?"

Maryanne was beyond talking but looked up at Laurie with such pleading eyes that Laurie's heart wrenched at the sight of her suffering. She loved this little girl as she would her own. If she were to die… No, she couldn't bear the thought of it. But little Ruthie had died, hadn't she? The threat was real. So how could she not seize upon anything that might save Maryanne? But taking her clear to Hangtown seemed an outrageous idea. What if she died along the way? What if they couldn't find the doctor?

And if they did find him, what if he refused to do the tracheotomy? What if he did do it and she died anyway?

But what if Dr. Grover Scott performed the procedure and it was successful?

Maryanne started gasping for breath again, eyes wide with fright, her little chest heaving laboriously as she desperately fought for air. Laurie's mind raced. Mother was wrong. Ada was wrong. Clearly if something wasn't done, her little niece could not hold on much longer. Like little Ruthie, she would go through the agony of fighting for air until she lost the battle and died. Only one thing to do. It had to be done and damn the consequences. "I've decided. She's going to have the tracheotomy."

Mother placed a hand over her heart. "Are you sure? How could you even think of taking that child on such a journey?"

"She'll never make it," Ada cried.

Ignoring them, Laurie sped from the bedroom and called down the stairs. "Mr. McKenna? Can you come quick? We're taking her to Hangtown."

* * * *

During the short time Laurie had lived in Lucky Creek, she'd become accustomed to the terrible roads. All unpaved, they were either a muddy mess from rain or snow or filled with choking dust. But awful though they were, she hadn't known what a bad road looked like until she and Darcy began their journey to Hangtown, the larger, more established mining town that lay a few miles to the north. Sitting close to Darcy, holding Maryanne in her arms, she didn't think the road looked too bad as they started out, even though it wasn't much more than two well-worn tracks in the dirt.

Had she not been so concerned about Maryanne, she would have enjoyed the beauty of the snow-covered peaks towering above them; the awesome height of the trees in the conifer forest through which they drove. Early on, they passed a spectacular waterfall that sent rainbows of color into the mist. With a deafening roar, water plunged from at least a hundred feet above into a raging stream. A crude wooden bridge passed over it. Laurie closed her eyes and held on tight as they crossed only inches above white-foamed water cascading over huge boulders directly beneath.

But that was the easy part of the journey. They soon came to a spot where the road cut along the side of a mountain. To Laurie's right, a steep wall of dirt and rocks loomed so close she could reach out and touch it. To her left, a ravine so deep she couldn't see clear to the bottom lay perilously close. Darcy kept a tight hold on the reins, intent on his driving. Clutching Maryanne tighter, Laurie tried to control the shake in her voice as she remarked, "I wish there was another way to get there."

He cut her a quick glance. "Don't look down."

"You never told me about this part."

"You never asked."

"What if we meet someone coming the other way?"

"Then we'd have a problem, wouldn't we?"

Thank God, they soon left the ravine behind without encountering anyone. Their luck didn't hold. Farther along, when they were traveling up a hilly section of a road wide enough for one, they encountered a large wagon carrying a group of miners coming down. Both came to a halt. What a blessing the hill wasn't too steep, but even so, either the carriage or the wagon must back to a spot wide enough to pull off and let the other by. Darcy uttered a curse under his breath and said quietly, "It's easier to back down than to back up. There's an old, unwritten rule about it. We're headed up, so we're the ones who should back down, only I hate to take the time." He gave the other driver a quick salute and called, "We have a sick child here, and we're trying to get to a doctor. Will you let us through?"

The driver, a burly-looking man with a full beard, took a close look at Laurie just as Maryanne had another coughing spell. He turned to his companions behind him and said something she couldn't hear. They looked like a rough bunch who could easily have their way if they wanted. Every minute counted. Laurie could only hope they'd have enough pity in their hearts to let them by.

The man with the beard turned back and called, "Come ahead."

Darcy snapped the reins. Slowly they followed as the wagon driver performed the difficult task of backing four horses and a wagon up the hill. Finally, when the bearded driver came to a wide spot and pulled off the road, Darcy drove slowly by, nodding a salute and calling, "Thank you, sir."

"God be with you," the burly driver called.

From the back came more voices.

"Bless you."

"Hope the little tyke's all right, ma'am."

"I'll say a prayer for you."

So far, Laurie had managed to hold on, but now sudden tears blinded her eyes. The kindness of those miners had touched her heart so deeply that whatever happened, she would know she wasn't alone and there were good people in this world. She would never forget this moment.

"That was very kind of them," she said as they continued on.

"Yes, it was."

Darcy's words were simple, yet she could tell from the slightest of quivers in his voice the miners' simple act of kindness had affected him, too.

Maryanne got over her latest coughing spell but still fought for every breath. She couldn't last much longer. She began to cough again. Deeper now, her breathing sounding even more desperate. Laurie hugged her tighter. "How much longer?"

"Less than an hour." Darcy flicked the reins, urging the horses to a faster pace.

* * * *

Laurie needn't have worried about finding the doctor. When they reached the main street of Hangtown, the first passerby they asked knew the exact location of Doctor Grover Scott's clinic. Luck stayed with them as they easily found it. By now, Maryanne was fighting for breath even more desperately. They hastened inside. What a relief to find the doctor there, seeing patients. The nurse took one look and directed them to an examining room. As Darcy lay Maryanne on the table, Doctor Scott appeared. The child was fighting for breath and turning blue again. "Please help us," Laurie cried in a panic. "Doc Hansen sent us. He said you can do an operation that could save her."

The doctor, a young man with kindly eyes, took one close look and snapped, "There's no time to lose. I can't guarantee I can save her at this late date, but I'll do a tracheotomy. Best you wait outside."

Laurie and Darcy left quickly and settled in the waiting room. For a time, she sat in silence. What could she say? This was no time for pleasantries, not when her little niece lay helpless, close to death, and the doctor was cutting into her throat. *Please God, let Maryanne live.* What if she died? Laurie tried not to picture that moment when she'd have to inform her family the sweet little girl they loved was gone. They would hold her responsible. Maybe they wouldn't say so, but she'd see the condemnation in their eyes. Why didn't Laurie leave the poor child where she was? Look what happened when she insisted upon taking her on that foolish journey to Hangtown.

Darcy must have sensed her reluctance to talk because he remained silent for a time. Finally, he inquired, "Are you doing all right?"

"Not really." Realizing how pessimistic she sounded, she tried to smile and failed but managed to lift her chin. "Hoping for the best, of course."

"Don't give up. There's a good chance we got her here in time."

The day had been so filled with anxiety and stress she'd hardly given a thought to Darcy McKenna. Since she met him, he'd been brusque and aloof, and she hadn't liked him at all. Today was different. His thoughtfulness and generosity were making her think twice. Who else would have taken the time to drive them clear to Hangtown on that awful road? He was a busy man with a business to run, yet here he sat, patiently waiting, lending his support to a woman he wasn't obligated to in any way. She'd already told him how kind he'd been. Clearly, he didn't expect or want her gratitude. Even so, she needed to tell him again. "I very much appreciate your doing this."

He shrugged. "Like I said…"

The door to the examining room opened wide. Laurie leaped to her feet. The doctor came out *and he was smiling.* "Your little girl's mighty sick, but I got the tube in her throat, and she can breathe now. Can't say for sure but looks like she'll be all right."

Laurie clapped a hand to her heart. "That's wonderful news, Doctor. I can't begin to tell you how much this means."

Darcy was smiling. "When can we take her home?"

"Not tonight. Mind you, she has a tube in her throat, and I'm not sure when it should come out. She'll be staying in the clinic overnight and maybe longer."

"Can we see her?" Laurie asked.

"Of course, you can. Then I suggest you get some rest. The nurses will keep an eye on her the rest of the night."

"I can get us hotel rooms," Darcy said.

He'd made a point to say rooms, not room, and Laurie was grateful for that, even though at the moment, she didn't care where she slept. "I don't want to be away from her too long. Can I spend the night here?"

The doctor nodded sympathetically. "Of course, you can."

Maryanne lay sleeping, breathing softly. A tube protruded from her throat through a heavy bandage. Such an ugly thing, but she'd have died without it, and Laurie gave silent thanks, not only to Doctor Scott, but also Doc Hansen who'd told them about the surgery. Also, thanks to Darcy because without him Maryanne would still be home and probably wouldn't have survived. When Laurie placed a hand on her niece's forehead, it didn't feel as warm. "I think her fever's broken." She turned to Darcy and smiled. "I think she's going to be all right."

He smiled back. "I think so, too. Are you hungry?"

"I just realized I haven't eaten all day."

"Then let's get something to eat, shall we? Unless you feel the need to stay."

How thoughtful of him. "She's in good hands. Let's go. I'm starving."

With its plush carpeting, fine linens, and crystal, the Gold Room at Hangtown's El Dorado Hotel rivaled Philadelphia's most luxurious dining rooms. Ordinarily, Laurie would have dressed in a manner more befitting a place so elegant, but in her ebullient mood, she didn't mind that her everyday grey muslin looked much too plain and wilted for a place like this. She'd done what she could with her hair, but after such a grueling day, she couldn't do much with the wispy strands that had escaped from the bun she'd so carefully arranged atop her head this morning.

In his dark suit of brushed cotton, white shirt, and string tie, Darcy fit much better in such elegant surroundings. Now, sitting across from him, she noticed he wasn't bad looking at all, a fact that had somehow escaped her attention before. Both in the happiest of moods, they gave their orders to an impeccably dressed waiter in a tuxedo, then sat chatting about Maryanne and the miracle of her recovery. Their dinners arrived—filet mignon for him, oysters for her. She took her first forkful of the oysters, covered with a rich sauce. "Mm, this tastes wonderful." She felt wonderful, too, and it was all thanks to this man who sat across from her. For the first time, she was curious to know more about him. She took a sip of the French champagne he'd ordered, set it down and smiled across the table at him. "Tell me about yourself, Mr. McKenna. You told me how you had to work when you were a boy. That must have been exciting, working in a coal mine."

For the fleetest of moments, Darcy shut his eyes, as if her words had struck a vulnerable spot within him. He quickly recovered and smiled pleasantly. "Very exciting. A world of fun."

The faint thread of irony in his voice told her she'd made a mistake. How callous she must have sounded. He must think her utterly frivolous and empty headed. She continued on, hoping she wouldn't make another blunder. "So, what did you do after you left the coal mine?"

"Well now..." He sat back relaxed. "I left home at a young age. Didn't have much money, but I managed to make my way to Wyoming Territory where I worked on a cattle ranch."

"My, how exciting. Did you lasso cows and that sort of thing?"

"I learned a lot about lassoing cows," he replied with a touch of amusement. At least he didn't look disturbed like he had when she mentioned the coal mine. "I learned a lot about a lot of things."

He didn't elaborate, and she wisely chose not to pursue the subject. When he asked about her life in Philadelphia, she spent little time describing it. He'd be little impressed with the party-filled, frivolous life she'd led. And of course, she didn't care to discuss her romance with Brandon Cooper.

Darcy had already made clear he wasn't much impressed with a man who collected insects for a living, whether they were rare or not.

After dinner, as they arose from the table, he remarked, "Are you sure you want to return to the clinic? I'd be happy to get you a room here. Your own room, of course."

He'd made her feel so comfortable, she hadn't given a thought that he'd attempt anything improper. "That's very kind of you, but I want to get back to Maryanne."

"Of course, I understand."

Under a bright moon, he drove her back the clinic. After bringing the carriage to a halt, he sprang down, went around the carriage, and offered his hand. How gentlemanly. A courteous and thoughtful gesture, even though she was quite capable of climbing from the carriage by herself. Her opinion of Darcy McKenna had risen to a height she never thought possible, but how could it not? He'd saved Maryanne. Without him, her niece could very well be dead by now. On that perilous drive to Hangtown he'd displayed such skill and good judgment she couldn't help but be impressed. And on top of all that, he'd just bought her one of the best dinners she'd ever eaten. Gratitude overwhelmed her. Words wouldn't be enough. In a gesture so spontaneous she surprised herself, she raised to her tiptoes and firmly placed her hands on either side of his head. Pulling him toward her, she firmly planted a kiss full on his lips. Not just a quick kiss but longer, several seconds at least. "Thank you, Mr. McKenna," she said when she finally broke away. "Words alone wouldn't do. I'm so truly grateful for all you did that I had to kiss you. I hope you don't mind."

At first, he displayed no reaction, just stood there and let her kiss him. Was he stunned? Displeased at such an intimacy? She'd never done such a thing before, had never been so forward. Maybe now he'd think she was some sort of wanton woman. How embarrassing. From now on, she must control all such impulses.

In the moonlight, she saw he was smiling, and before she could quite comprehend what was happening, his big hands clamped her face and he'd bent forward, capturing her mouth in a kiss that seemed like he wanted to devour her. A slow burn of desire curled through her as slowly he slid his hands down her arms, around to her back, and pulled her hard against his body, the warm pressure of his lips pressing against hers all the while. She was just settling closer into his embrace when, with a shuddering gasp, he pulled away, stepped back, and drew in a shaking breath. "I don't mind at all, Miss Sinclair. My pleasure."

He'd released her so suddenly that for one stunning moment, she hardly knew what hit her. One minute she'd been expressing her gratitude; the next, Darcy McKenna, the man she'd intensely disliked, had stirred such heat within her she hadn't wanted him to stop. For one insane second she considered flinging herself into his arms again. But not a good idea. This was neither the time, nor the place, nor, God help her, the man. She steadied herself and took a deep breath. "Well, Mr. McKenna, I had better get inside. I assume you'll be back in the morning?" Her voice came out normal, and for that she was grateful.

"I will indeed be back in the morning," he replied in a serious voice. "And by the way, you might want to consider calling me Darcy, considering we've just got better acquainted."

She wasn't sure if he was teasing her or not, but at any rate he had a good idea. "I shall do that, and you might consider calling me Laurie, considering, as you say, we know each other better now."

"I'll do that. Good night, Laurie."

"Good night, Darcy." She turned and walked into the clinic, head held high, and at a dignified pace. Not easy to do when her knees still slightly wobbled and her pulse had yet to return to normal. *Don't forget, you love Brandon Cooper,* she reminded herself as she walked through the clinic's front door.

Chapter 10

Darcy had always prided himself on not only being well organized but on being a straight-thinking man with a purpose, a man who always knew exactly where he was going and what he was going to do.

So, what had happened tonight? Driving back to the hotel, he kept asking himself why he had kissed Laurie Sinclair, and it wasn't because she'd kissed him first. That was nothing more than a gratitude kiss. He could easily have returned it with a polite thank you and let it go at that. So, what had possessed him to go for that second kiss? Maybe the time to be honest with himself had arrived. No more pretending he didn't know the answer and hadn't noticed the spike of heat that caught him low in the gut, set off by the mere touch of her hands on his cheeks. The trouble was, she might be vain, shallow, frivolous, and more, but every time he saw her, his pulse leaped, and he'd had to be extra careful to keep a laid-back expression on his face.

Sam Sinclair had been a good friend, a man he admired and respected. After Sam's death, Darcy had gone out of his way to help the family. Of course, he had done so in honor of his good friend, but that wasn't the only reason, and it was time he stopped fooling himself. He'd been finding excuses to see more of Laurie. Like today. At least a dozen pressing matters awaited him at the Monarch and his own mine, the Atlas, yet he'd chosen to drive over that god-awful road to save a little girl who otherwise would surely have died. Yeah, noble and all that, but the truth was he'd jumped at the chance to spend time with Laurie Sinclair.

Why? He already had a woman in his life. Lucille Wagner filled his needs in more ways than one. A lovely woman, and yet… She wasn't Laurie. Only she could have caused that rush of desire that clawed and clutched at his insides and drove him to take her into his arms and kiss her back. How he'd managed to break away, he didn't know, except—he chuckled to himself—maybe deep in his brain he'd figured out that ravishing Miss Laurie Sinclair on the main street of Hangtown might not be such a good idea.

She made him laugh without trying to be funny. Lasso cows? She'd lived such a sheltered existence she could have no way of knowing the kind of life he'd led. He'd told her about the coal mine but not the rest of it. Not how he'd left home when he was twelve. He couldn't say he'd run away because that would give the impression his parents would have searched for him and wanted him back. Nobody gave a damn when he left. He'd never seen his parents again, but he'd wager they'd rejoiced upon finding they had one less mouth to feed.

He pretty much lived off the land as he made his way across the country, not sure where he was going or what he would do. By the time he got to Wyoming, he was barely surviving, a skinny, half-starved kid, ragged, dirty, too weary to go on, and wondering why he would want to. And thinking he was worthless and had no future. What did he know other than to sit deep in a mine and pick off bad pieces of coal? He'd never been to school. Didn't know how to read, write, or add two numbers together. Had no idea what it was like to love and be loved. Not that he blamed Mum and Dad. It was all they could do to feed their family and stay alive.

He was sitting in an alley in Jeffrey City, Wyoming, starving and shivering from the cold when an old rancher found him and changed his life. Ned Grimes owned a cattle ranch close to the Sweetwater River. That day in the alley, his first words to Darcy were, "Why are you sitting in this alley, son?"

Darcy looked up to see a wrinkled old face, leathered from the sun, and two faded grey eyes peering down at him. "Why do you think I'm sitting in this alley?" was his smart-aleck answer. Back then he said what he pleased and had never heard of good manners.

"Because you're cold and you're hungry." The old man didn't leave. He regarded Darcy intently. His eyes might be aged and faded but they brimmed with kindness and sharp curiosity. "Come along, you need to get out of the cold. I'll buy you a meal."

And that was the start of a life Darcy had never known before. Never even knew it existed. The rancher took Darcy home to his ranch and put him to work. But that wasn't all he did. Ned Grimes might look like just another rancher, nothing more on his mind than the price of feed or birthing a calf. He'd been married once, but his beloved Nellie had died five years before, and he never gave a thought to replacing her. Instead, he had more than enough to keep him busy. Aside from running his cattle ranch, he maintained a garden and a glass greenhouse where he grew orchids and citrus trees. He read a lot and had more books in his house than Darcy had seen in his lifetime. Books everywhere, not only in the shelf-lined library, but stacked in Ned's bedroom, piled in the dining room and every corner of his sprawling ranch house.

"What do you have so many books for?" Darcy asked the day he arrived.

"Knowledge is books and books are knowledge," Ned had replied, adding, "You're welcome to read any of 'em."

"Thanks. I just might." He was lying. All his life Darcy had been ashamed he couldn't read. He couldn't bring himself to admit it until one day Ned squinted while trying to read a label. "Dang, but the print's too small. Read it for me, boy."

Only then was Darcy forced to admit he'd never learned to read. Sensing his shame, Ned made light of it. "There's nothing to learning your letters. I'll have you reading in no time."

Ned stayed true to his word, and once Darcy got the hang of it, if he wasn't working, he had his nose in a book. He devoured books on history, astronomy, economics, botany, as well as the works of Shakespeare, Charles Dickens, and pretty much everything he could get his hands on. Learning to read was like entering a world he'd never known before. Delighted, Ned urged him on. "A man can never get too much knowledge in his head."

Ned taught him other things, too, like manners, of which Darcy had none.

"You don't cram food in your mouth like you haven't eaten for a month, and you don't gulp your milk down, neither. And you don't just dig in. You've got to look casual, like you're really not hungry and don't care if you eat or not."

He was relentless. "Put that fork down. You wait till everyone's seated at the table afore you start to eat, and then you can begin."

There were times when Darcy resented all the nagging and thought he'd run away, but never for long. He'd grown to love that old man, the only person in the world who'd ever given a damn about him. By the time he reached eighteen, he could ride a horse like he was glued to the saddle. He knew as much as Ned about the year-round care of cows and bulls, and the best way to produce calves to raise and sell. That wasn't all. Thanks to Ned, he'd learned running a cattle ranch involved much more. "Ranchers have got to be stewards of the land, son. They've got to care for soils, grasses, plants, water and wildlife. A successful rancher doesn't just herd cattle. He's wears many hats. Cowboy, herdsman, businessman, land manager, financial manager and a heap more."

Ned's ranch bordered the Sweetwater River. Not long after Darcy turned twenty, word came that gold had been discovered higher up along the Sweetwater. "By golly, we'd better go take a look," Ned said when he heard. Bringing wide, shallow pans, he and Darcy rode to the river, waded in knee deep, and started panning. Within an hour, Darcy caught sight of something gleaming in the bottom of his pan. Gold! They later found it had washed downstream from the Wind River Mountain Range. After that, they found gold whenever they panned for it. They weren't making a fortune, but enough that they returned to the river whenever they could.

One sunny afternoon in May, Darcy and Ned were panning for gold in the river when Ned stood straight and cocked his head. "What's wrong?" Darcy asked.

"Dunno." Ned stood listening a few seconds more. "Let's get out of here."

Quickly they waded from the water. Darcy had just put a foot on the shore when at least a dozen Indians on horseback came at them through a thick grove of trees with blood-curdling shrieks, lances held high, war paint on their faces.

"Arapahos!" Ned yelled. "Run, Darcy, run!"

Darcy didn't need to be told twice. Stories had already reached them about parties of gold prospectors being attacked and robbed farther up the river. The Sioux were mostly responsible, but the Arapaho also had a hand in it. They were the worst, murdering their victims and scalping them, too. He sprinted to his horse, leaped on, got away, and headed for home. Once, looking back, he expected a dozen Indians to be hot on his tail, but they hadn't followed. When he got to the ranch house, he ran inside and grabbed Ned's rifle. Back outside, he recruited two of the ranch hands, making sure they were armed.

What had happened to Ned? Darcy wasn't much for praying, but starting back to the river, he sent up a prayer that he'd got away. The feeling in his gut told him he hadn't, though. All was silent as they approached the river. Ned's horse still stood tethered to a tree. The Indians had gone. To his dying day, Darcy would never forget the sight of Ned's lifeless body lying by the river, a lance piercing his chest. And he'd been scalped.

In his will, Ned left everything to Darcy. For a while, Darcy tried to convince himself he should stay on, which was what Ned, in his thoughtful generosity, had intended. The ranch was his. If he stayed, he'd be set for life. Only he couldn't stay. When the Arapaho took Ned Grimes's life, they took the only person in the world he'd ever loved, and who loved him. Every time he walked through the ranch house, memories of his friend sent an agonizing wave of grief coursing through him. He knew there was no changing the past, and he also knew as long as he stayed in the ranch house, he'd never get over his grief for the only man in the world who ever gave a damn about him.

It was time to move on. He sold the ranch and headed west. Later on, he realized he'd made the right decision. Not a day went by that he didn't think of Ned Grimes, but at least he'd got past the terrible grief, and when he thought of Ned, he thought of all the good times they'd had, and all the good things that old man had done for him.

* * * *

Laurie spent the night at her niece's bedside. By morning, Maryanne's fever had broken, and the swelling in her neck had gone down. She made a fuss over the strange tube protruding from her throat and kept trying to pull it out. Seeing how much better she was, the doctor removed it, remarking, "She doesn't need it now, but she'll always have a little scar, I'm afraid."

"A small price to pay," Laurie replied gratefully. The doctor said they could go home. Laurie could hardly wait. With a joyful heart, she held her little niece in her arms as Darcy drove them back to Lucky Creek. Even when they crossed the rickety bridge beneath the waterfall, she felt no fear but pointed to a grassy spot by the stream and remarked, "That would be a lovely spot for a picnic."

When Darcy pulled to a stop in front of the house, Mother and Ada burst through the front door. Expressions of astonishment, soon followed by vast relief, covered their faces when they saw Maryanne breathing normally again, the desperation gone from her eyes. Seeing her bandaged throat, Mother asked, "So she had the tracheotomy?"

"She did, and it saved her life," Laurie replied.

Mother bit her lip in chagrin. "I was wrong, and I apologize. You saved Maryanne's life, and I'm eternally grateful. I'll never question your judgment again."

"We were wrong," Ada chimed in. "I'm so glad you didn't listen to us."

While Darcy took care of the horse and carriage, Laurie carried Maryanne upstairs to Hugh's room. Still in bed, he beamed when he saw them. "So, she's going to be all right then?"

"Yes, thanks to Darcy McKenna. Wait till you hear what we went through." Laurie described the urgent trip to Hangtown and how fortunate they were that everything had gone so right. That meant everything from not having a mishap on the perilous road to Hangtown, to their luck that the doctor had been in the clinic when they arrived. "The doctor performed the surgery without delay. She'll always have a little scar on her throat, but the important thing is she's beaten that awful diphtheria and is going to live."

After a thoughtful moment, Hugh replied, "It was more than just luck. Maryanne wouldn't still be with us if it weren't for you and your bravery. Mother and Ada thought you were crazy to take my daughter clear to Hangtown, and so did I. We were wrong, and you were right." He regarded her with new respect. "What a woman you've become. That silly little twit from Philadelphia has finally grown up."

"Thanks, Hugh, but if you could have, you'd have done the same." Her modest reply concealed her delight at receiving rare praise from her older brother. Without realizing it till now, she'd crossed a new threshold in her life, a new level of respect. How immensely gratifying that her family no longer regarded her as a frivolous young woman in need of guidance.

They chatted for a while. Hugh told her how much better he felt. His ribs didn't hurt as much and soon he'd be going downstairs for the first time since the accident. "And I'll also be returning to the mine, Laurie. You'll be back with Brandon again before you know it."

Brandon Cooper. Strange, from the day they met, he'd constantly been on her mind but not so much these past few days. Understandable, of course, considering all the excitement going on.

Hoping Darcy hadn't left, she headed for the stable. She'd thanked him at least once, maybe twice, but she very much wanted to thank him again.

She found him in the stable feeding the horses. "Before you go, I wanted to thank you again."

"Again, you're welcome." Darcy was closely examining Prancer's left front hoof and appeared to have only halfway heard her. "He's gone lame," he said.

"I didn't notice he was limping."

"Sometimes they don't limp even though something's wrong. You can tell by the way his head bobs and how he tenses the muscles in his shoulder."

"Then should I use him tomorrow?"

He frowned and shook his head. "Could be it's just a stone bruising on the sole of his hoof, but we won't take any chances. Leave the horses home tomorrow. I'll come by and pick you up, say seven thirty?"

"That'll be fine." She accompanied her commonplace answer with an indifferent wave of her hand, as if she couldn't care less one way or the other. But the funny part was she found herself glad she could spend more time alone with Darcy McKenna.

* * * *

After getting dressed the next morning, Laurie tiptoed into the children's room, pleased to find Maryanne and Mathew sleeping soundly, rosy cheeked and breathing normally. In the kitchen, she found Ada fixing a pot of coffee. "Valeria's not here this morning," she said. "I guess we'll have to fix our own breakfast."

How surprising. Valeria had her faults, but rarely did she not show up for work, and on time. Best to make light of it. "We'll be lucky if she comes back, considering what we're paying her."

"I suppose." Ada heaved a discouraged sigh. "The way things are going, maybe we ought to return to Philadelphia now."

"You mustn't be discouraged. They've already started digging on the new shaft."

Ada opened her mouth to say something. She closed it, then appeared to change her mind. "What was the name of that man who carried me into the office?"

"Kenvern Trenowden."

"Such a weird name, and he talked funny, too."

"That's because he comes from Cornwall. They all talk funny."

"Did he get hired?"

"He did." Laurie carefully hid her surprise that her bashful, retiring sister had actually shown an interest in a man. So unlike her. "Kenvern's brothers were hired, too. Mr. McKenna says Cornish miners are the best."

"Hmm..." Ada bit her lip in thought. "They're quite crude. Noisy and crude."

"They weren't hired for their manners."

Ada said no more on the subject, but she didn't have to. Laurie knew her sister well and easily recognized her attraction for the young Cornishman. Too bad he was totally unsuitable. Mother, Aunt Florence—all their friends and family in Philadelphia—would be appalled at such an alliance. And yet...? How wonderful it would be if Ada could actually find someone to love, someone who loved her. What would it hurt to see what might happen if they saw each other again?

Later, when Laurie was leaving the house, she went out of her way to remark, "Don't forget, Ada, the office needs some sprucing up, to say the least. Curtains alone would be a big improvement. You're so good at decorating. I wish you'd come to the mine again and see what you can do."

"I just might. When would be a good time to come?"

Astounding. Ada had actually shown an interest in doing something outside the house. Plain to see why. "Toward the end of the shift would be the best time to come. Then you could see me in action, checking the men's time sheets and that sort of thing." *And you could also see Kenvern again.* "If you don't mind walking up, you could go home with me."

"I just might do that," Ada replied.

Laurie was standing out front waiting when Darcy picked her up. "Good morning," she called brightly, giving him a big smile. The mEmery of their kiss still lingered in her mind, as well as yesterday's congenial trip back from Hangtown, and she'd especially looked forward to seeing him again.

He returned a brief smile. "Good morning. You'll have lots to do today. We've opened the shaft, and you'll have to be ready with the time sheets."

So that's the way it was. The lack of warmth in his greeting made it clear he'd returned to being the man she worked with and nothing more. The whole way up the mountain, he remained solemn-faced while giving her a lecture on what she should know about time sheets and payrolls. She dutifully gave him her sober attention, not for a moment revealing the tumble of confused thoughts in her head. Had he ever taken her in his arms and passionately kissed her? If she didn't know better, she'd think it was something she'd dreamed.

But why should she care when Brandon Cooper awaited her? If Darcy wanted everything to be strictly business, then fine with her.

A bustling scene awaited them when they arrived at the mine. The first shift had already gone down the new shaft. Water gushed down all four sluice boxes while aboveground, a group of men stood by as a steady stream of ore-filled iron carts rolled through the entrance. Grunting and sweating, they shoveled the ore into the boxes, while lower down, other men made sure the ore slid down the hill. In the office, Laurie wasted no time getting to work. With no help from Tom, she set up the general time book plus specialized time books for different sorts of employees. Not to her surprise, late in the afternoon, Ada appeared, measuring tape in hand. She'd walked up the mountain and had arrived rosy cheeked and breathless. She must have taken extra time to fix herself up because she looked especially attractive in her favorite sprigged violet cotton gown. She measured the windows, enthusiastically declaring a light-colored chintz would be best with maybe even some tassels. She'd see to it that they were made and hung. Looking around, she shook her head at the decrepit condition of the office. "There's lots more I can do, but the curtains come first."

Fine with Laurie. She'd never been especially gifted in the art of decoration and welcomed Ada's unexpected help. At the end of the shift, she asked Ada if she'd like to accompany her to the mine entrance and stand by her side while the workmen filed out. Ordinarily, she wouldn't have even asked. Her timid sister would never do anything so bold, but because of Kenvern, she wasn't surprised when Ada said yes. They walked to the entrance to the mine, Ada giving a shudder as they drew close to the intimidating black hole. "How deep does it go?"

"Right now, they're down to six hundred feet, but they expect to go a lot lower, maybe clear down to a thousand."

"How can they work so far beneath the surface? I'd be scared to death there'd be a cave-in, and I'd be trapped down there in the darkness."

Laurie sometimes thought the same, but such fears were best ignored, and she tried not to think about it. "The miners don't worry about things like that. They earn a good wage, and that's all they care about." She doubted that was true, but with Ada it was best not to dwell on matters unpleasant or frightening.

Notebook in hand, Laurie greeted each miner as he came through the entrance, asked how he'd spent his time, and meticulously recorded it. If nothing else, Darcy would see her records were perfect. The miners reacted to a female timekeeper with varying degrees of hilarity and skepticism.

"Say now, we got a lady keeping track of us now."

"Watch out, boys, next thing you know the ladies will be down at the bottom servin' tea and such."

Such remarks brought a great deal of laughter. By the time Kenvern emerged, his brothers trailing behind him, both sisters were relaxed and laughing. Laurie noticed how Ada's cheeks flushed pink at the sight of him, and no wonder. At least six feet three, all solid muscle, he couldn't have looked more handsome. He broke into a wide grin at the sight of Ada. "*Mygar!*" he exclaimed in his booming voice. "Here's the little lassie what fainted. I hope you be all right now."

Ada blushed a deeper red than Laurie had ever seen. "Why, yes, I...I..." She could go no further. Stood with her mouth agape, overcome by Kenvern's mere, extremely masculine, presence. Gulping, she made an obvious effort to pull herself together. "How kind of you to inquire. I must go now." She turned abruptly and fled toward the office at a pace close to running.

Kenvern watched after her, frowning with concern. "I hope I didn't scare her off."

Laurie stifled her urge to laugh. Above all, she must be loyal to Ada. "Not at all. My sister had business to attend to."

At the end of the day, Darcy brought Laurie and Ada home. His stand-offish attitude hadn't let up a moment. He'd been polite enough, but Laurie felt uncomfortable riding with him and would do so no longer. Climbing from the carriage, she remarked, "I'm sure Prancer is fine now, so I won't need a ride tomorrow."

"What if he's not?"

"Then I'll find another way. I can always walk. Good night." She darted away, not giving him a chance to answer. He might still be willing to give her a ride every day, but she'd have none of it and surely didn't need his charity.

Inside, she found her mother in the kitchen. Valeria had never shown up. As a result, they would have beef sandwiches for dinner. "And you're lucky to get them," Mother complained as she awkwardly sliced the beef roast Valeria had prepared the day before. "I hope she comes back tomorrow. Otherwise, when this roast is gone, I don't know what we'll do."

After what passed for dinner, Laurie waited until she found Ada alone. "Today at the mine, why did you run off like that? Kenvern was only being nice."

Ada hung her head. "I acted like an idiot, didn't I?"

Yes, she had. While Laurie searched for something tactful to say, Ada continued, "There's something about that man that draws me to him. Am I crazy? How could I possibly have an interest in a person who can't speak proper English? Even his name's all wrong. Whoever heard of a man called Kenvern?"

"I'd wager the Cornish people think we're the ones with the funny names."

"That's not the point. I might find him attractive, but he's just not suitable. Mother would call him a lowlife. According to her, all men who work in the mines are lowlifes. How can I argue? Can you picture him at some fancy affair in Philadelphia? He'd be nothing but an embarrassment. On the other hand, he's the first and only man I've ever truly thought twice about. Ever thought about kissing"—she started blushing again—"and maybe more."

Laurie couldn't think what to say. Ada had never been so honest. Clearly, Kenvern Trenowden had awakened feelings within her she'd never had before. Her sister was right, though. Charming though he might be in his unrefined way, his lack of education and peculiar manner of speech would make him a laughingstock in Philadelphia.

A sudden pounding sounded on the door. Someone was shouting. "What on earth?" Laurie fairly leaped from her chair and hastened to open it. Her neighbor, Agatha Harrison, stood wide eyed and breathless on the doorstep.

"What is it?" Laurie asked.

"Something terrible has happened."

Chapter 11

Not in the best of moods, Darcy went straight to his hotel room after he dropped the sisters off. So he wasn't to bother picking Laurie up again? Fine with him. Maybe he'd been too standoffish, but what was he supposed to do? Among Ned Grimes's many words of wisdom, one particular piece of advice stuck firmly in his head. *No man of honor would steal another man's woman. It just ain't done.*

The trouble was, sometimes being a man of honor wasn't the easiest thing to do. Laurie belonged to the bug man back east, and he'd better not forget that. The trouble was, his mind told him one thing, his body another. Each time he thought of that kiss, which was far more often than he cared to admit, a kind of hunger grabbed at his insides. He wanted her in his bed, and in his life, too. He'd remind himself how frivolous she was, how self-centered and artificial, but no, she wasn't. She had courage. On that god-awful trip to Hangtown she never complained, and her only thought was for her little niece. She was smart, too, had done well in the office, and learned her job quickly. The miners all liked her because they knew she liked them and didn't consider herself above them in any way.

All of which would do him no good, of course. She'd be leaving for Philadelphia soon as she could, and that was that.

He hadn't been in his room five minutes when Lucille knocked on his door and invited him to dinner downstairs. "You've got to eat, and it may as well be with me." She raised a meaningful eyebrow. "We're friends now, Darcy. No hassle."

They ate in the Bonanza, Gold Spike's best restaurant. True to her word, she kept the conversation light. Not the slightest reproach as to how he'd been ignoring her. Nothing but easy chitchat until she looked him in the eye and asked, "So how are you doing, Darcy? I mean really."

Clearly, she asked because she cared, not out of idle curiosity, and he was happy to oblige. She gave him her full attention as he described his new mining venture at the Monarch. And what else had he done? Before he knew it, he'd launched into a detailed recounting of the harrowing trip to Hangtown, the little girl whose life had been saved in the nick of time. He made a point to mention Laurie as little as possible, but when he finished, Lucille softly inquired, "You care about her, don't you?"

He seldom lied and wasn't going to start now. "There's a man back in Philadelphia she's dying to marry, so it doesn't matter how I feel."

"Well, I care how you feel." Her eyes got all warm and tender. "Any time you want a shoulder to cry on, you know where I am."

What a fine woman. He was about to tell her so when a sort of rumble coming from the street caused a sudden silence in the dining room. People stopped eating and sat listening. The sound grew louder. Soon Darcy could distinguish men shouting, shots ringing out. He jumped to his feet and shoved his chair back. "Wait here, Lucille. I'll see what's going on."

Joined by other hotel guests who'd heard the commotion, he hastened to the street. Chaos awaited. People running in all directions—shots fired—a milling crowd slowly approaching up the street. Not a happy crowd but an enraged crowd. Faces distorted in anger. Men yelling, hollering, shooting their guns in the air. Seeing one of his miners come striding by, almost at a run, he yelled, "What's going on, Harry?"

Harry Peske stopped when he saw who was calling. "It's bad, Mr. McKenna. This crowd's nearly out of control, and it looks like there's going to be a lynching. I'm getting out of here, and if you don't mind my saying so, so should you."

Darcy considered level-headed Harry Peske one of his best employees. If Harry said he should leave, then he probably should, but not before he found out what had happened and who was getting lynched. "Where's the sheriff? Does he know what's going on here?"

Harry snorted. "He damn well does. He's in the middle of the mob trying to get her to the jailhouse before the mob tears her apart."

Her? "Did I hear you right? You can't mean it's a woman."

"It surely is, Mr. McKenna. You know Emery Finch, the card dealer over at the Palace?"

Everybody knew Emery, a loud, foul-mouthed man who'd made a name for himself with his crude humor and outspoken stance against all foreigners. Many cheered his fiery speeches demanding only true white Americans should be allowed to search for gold. The rest, and that included Mexicans, Chinese, and practically everyone without a white skin, should be sent back where they came from. "I've never met Emery, but I know who he is."

"He's dead, Mr. McKenna. Knifed straight through the heart by that wife of his, although I don't know if they were even legally married. Valeria, they call her. Latina from below the border, Mexico, Bolivia, or some such place."

"They want to lynch a woman? Are you sure?"

"She's Latina and she killed a white man. What more reason do you want?"

The crowd edged closer, growing uglier by the minute. Like a pack of coyotes closing in on their prey, men swarmed around, appearing to direct their seething fury at something, or someone, in the center of the crowd.

"Get a rope!"

"String her up!"

"Hang her!"

For a brief moment, the crowd parted, revealing a dark-skinned woman with a bowler hat and braids down her back. Hands bound in front of her, she walked with her head held high, mouth clamped, eyes fixed straight ahead, as if she couldn't hear the violent threats or see the menacing gestures. She had a bruise on her face and what looked like a black eye. Sheriff Selwyn Gibbs, a middle-aged man with a big pot belly, held onto her arm with one hand, his Colt revolver held at a threatening angle in the other. Darcy had never liked the man. Considered him weak, cowardly, and prone to probable corruption. Even so, Gibbs appeared to be doing his job like he was supposed to, holding firm to the woman's arm, continually yelling, "Get back! Get back! Let's have some law and order here." Two of his deputies, guns drawn, walked close behind him.

A man dressed all in black, including his wide-brimmed hat, appeared out of nowhere, carrying a large coil of rope, holding it up for all to see. The crowd roared its approval when they saw him, many shaking their fists, yelling, "Hang her high."

Harry pointed in alarm. "Look at them. They're like animals. If this keeps up, the sheriff will never get her to the jail. They're ready to hang that poor woman right here, and there's nothing we can do." He edged away. "I've got to get out of here, Mr. McKenna."

"Get home to your family." Darcy had to yell over the deafening noise. He watched his employee scurry off. He'd like to leave, too, but how could he walk away? Valeria wasn't some nameless stranger. She cooked for the Sinclairs. Laurie had fondly described her colorful clothes, her loyalty, what a great cook she was. Ned Grimes's words came back to him. *This is America. No man should be lynched. Every man deserves a fair trial.* Nor woman, either, by God.

Something had to be done, and fast. He glanced around. Not everyone had joined the frenzied mob. Bystanders lined the wooden sidewalk, faces revealing their shock and disbelief. Among them, Darcy spotted the three brawny Trenowden brothers, the ones he'd just hired. Just who he needed. He walked to where they were standing. "I need your help, boys. This isn't right. We've got to stop them. Will you help?"

Kenvern recognized him immediately. "You're the boss." He turned to his brothers. "Petrok, Steren, Mr. McKenna needs our help."

Steren nodded with respect. "What do you want us to do?"

"Follow me." Darcy plunged into the crowd, the Trenowden brothers close behind. He didn't have much of a plan, but he didn't need one. The Lucky Creek jail lay a short two blocks away. All he had to do was get the woman to the jail before the crowd overpowered the sheriff and his deputies. But considering the mob's ever-increasing fury, that might not be easy. The brothers still close behind him, he battled his way through the ever-shifting, screaming throng, at times having to push bodies roughly aside. Finally breaking through, he found Sheriff Gibbs still shouting, "Get back! Get back!" The grim look on his face revealed his desperation. The small group had come to a near stop. Valeria's fixed expression hadn't changed. Either she was being incredibly brave, or she was in some sort of trance and didn't know what was going on.

"Don't stop," Darcy yelled to the sheriff over the roar of the crowd. "You've got to keep moving or we're done for." He turned to the brothers. "Petrok, you get on this side, Steren on the other. Kenvern, you and I will go ahead."

The brothers quickly took their places, Darcy and Kenvern close in front of the sheriff and the woman. "Out of the way," Darcy began to yell. He took one step forward, then another. Would they get through? Maybe so, maybe not. This was a crowd made up of ordinary men gone mad. Crazy-eyed men fueled by vengeance, out for blood with murder in their hearts. Only the slightest thread of restraint held them back, and it could break at any moment. One thing in his favor: most of these men knew him or knew of him. As a mine owner, he'd gained a lot of respect in this town, but was it enough that they'd let him through? "Make way for the sheriff," he called again.

The small group progressed at a snail's pace, but at least they kept moving forward. Each step seemed a miracle. Any moment a crowd like this could break its last restraints and go totally berserk. Despite the turmoil, the three big, strapping Cornishmen looked as if they did this every day. If they knew any fear, they didn't show it. Their boss had given them a job to do, and they were going to do it, no questions necessary. As they inched along, the crowd seemed bent on tormenting the poor woman with constant threats and vile curses. An occasional member of the crowd, wild-eyed and snarling, would leap forward, fists clenched, trying to reach her, but her protectors easily shoved him away, never allowing even one of the lunatics close enough to touch her.

They continued on, battling every step of the way until at last they reached the jail. The crowd grew even more enraged as the sheriff hauled the woman up the four steps to the wide porch in front. At the top, he turned to face the crowd. Darcy and the brothers stood by as he yelled, "This is as far as you go, everyone. This woman is under my protection, and she's going inside."

Howls of protest went up. Darcy stepped forward, raising his arms to quiet the crowd. He wasn't sure the mob wouldn't overwhelm the small group standing on the porch at any moment, but he kept his arms raised until the noise faded enough that he could be heard. "Listen to the sheriff," he yelled. "He's only doing his job. This woman deserves a fair trial."

Hoots and hollers went up with renewed fury. Darcy called over his shoulder, "Get her inside quick." As he watched, the solid oak door swung open just enough that the deputies, gripping Valeria, squeezed inside before the door slammed shut. As Darcy turned back, something struck him on the back of his head. The crowd surged forward. Stunned, he fell to his knees. Strong hands grabbed hold and pulled him up. The Trenowden brothers hovered around him. "*Leebm lawn*," Kenvern called, which made no sense to him, but whatever he said, it worked, and the crowd backed off.

"Let's get him out of here," Severn called. Hauling Darcy between them, with a mighty effort the brothers pushed their way through the raging mob until they broke through the edge and found a comparatively quiet spot in the side street next to the jail.

Darcy stood straight, fighting to get air in his lungs. Feeling something wet on the back of his head, he reached to touch the spot and held up blood-covered fingers. "Somebody had a good aim."

The brothers overlooked his feeble attempt at humor. They gathered around, faces drawn with concern. Kenvern spoke up. "They be throwing rocks, sir. You're cut bad. You need a doctor."

"I'll be fine." His cut hurt like hell. He reached for a handkerchief, dabbed at his head, and regarded the blood-soaked cloth. Pretty bad, but he'd take care of it later. The wound was nothing compared to the horror that poor woman was going through, and it wasn't over yet. Mankind at its worst. He'd seen more than his share of violence in this world, but nothing compared to the brutality and ugliness of a lynching.

* * * *

Laurie and her family were shocked and dismayed by Agatha Harrison's news about the lynching. Valeria had been a faithful employee, a bit eccentric, perhaps, but a fine cook, and she'd always been wonderful to the children. An argument soon ensued when they got around to discussing what they should do. When Laurie declared she should go see if she could help Valeria, Mother gasped in alarm. "You can't. My daughter at a lynching? I am horrified."

Laurie wasn't surprised at her mother's fervent opposition. In Elizabeth's genteel world, she'd never experienced violence of any sort. Laurie hadn't either, for that matter, but this was Valeria, their faithful cook, and she couldn't let it go. "But, Mother, we can't just let her die. Valeria has been good to us. She loves us."

Elizabeth didn't waver. "We mustn't let our feelings get in the way of our common sense. A sensible young lady wouldn't dream of getting herself involved in anything even close to such brutality. Besides, there's nothing you can do for the poor woman. Even if we could help in some way, since when is it our responsibility?"

Ada echoed their mother's sentiment. Laurie went upstairs and talked to Hugh. He'd always thought highly of Valeria and greatly enjoyed her cooking but regarded Laurie as if she'd lost her mind. "Stay out of it, Sis. I've heard about lynch mobs, enough to know there's nothing you could do even if you did go. Emery Finch was a no-good drunkard and a bully, but what does it matter? Valeria's skin is brown, and they say she killed a white man. There's no chance in hell that mob will let her go."

The family agreed they would stay home, lock the doors, and not come out until the whole appalling affair was over. Everyone but Laurie. After listening to all the sensible advice, she threw on a light wrap, jammed her bonnet on her head, and announced, "All the wise advice in the world won't change me. I'm going. I can't even imagine what Valeria is going through right now, but it must be horrible. I'd never forgive myself if I didn't at least try to help in some way."

No one spoke. They stared at her in astonishment. She was almost as surprised as they were at her words of defiance. Not like her to be so rebellious, but she was looking at things differently these days and meant what she said.

She left without another word and headed, practically at a run, toward Mein Street, arriving just as the mob was passing the Gold Spike Hotel. Met with a deafening, frightening din of angry shouts and curses, she darted into a doorway, huddled in a corner, and gazed out at a mob gone mad. The family was right. This was far more dangerous than she had imagined. She'd been crazy to think she could somehow help, and at this point, she'd better hope she could save herself. Why hadn't she listened to Mother, Ada and Hugh? But even they couldn't begin to understand the cruelty and mindless violence of a lynch mob, the ugly taunts, the sight of a man grinning viciously, a rope in his hand, eager to hang her poor cook.

As she watched, the crowd parted briefly, long enough for her to catch a glimpse of Valeria, hands bound, staring straight ahead while men cursed and raged around her. Was that Darcy? The Trenowden brothers? She could have sworn she caught a glimpse of them but couldn't be sure. The crowd moved slowly by. She followed at a safe distance behind. They reached their destination shortly and came to a halt in front of the jailhouse. She slipped into a side street and watched as the sheriff hauled Valeria up the steps.

She'd been right when she thought she saw Darcy. He was there, standing at the top of the steps next to the sheriff. She held her breath as he raised a restraining arm, trying to calm the crowd. When the jailhouse door opened, and the deputies shoved Valeria through, she breathed a huge sigh of relief. Valeria was safe now, and so was Darcy. When the rock hit him, she gasped and cried out, "Oh, no." She tried to get to him but couldn't get through the dense crowd. As best she could, she followed as the Trenowden brothers carried him away.

* * * *

Still on the side street, Darcy held his bloodied handkerchief to the cut on his head again. It was still bleeding. The crowd still milled about, still angry. "They're not leaving."

Kenvern asked, "What should we do now?"

Before Darcy could answer he heard a woman's voice calling. "Darcy, Darcy!"

He could barely hear over the noise, but he'd swear that was Laurie's voice. He turned to look. Here she came, running, holding her skirt so she wouldn't stumble, eyes wide with alarm. When she got to him, she clutched his arms like she was drowning, and he was her only hope. She tried to talk, but what with having to take big gulps of air, she couldn't get the words out. Finally, she gasped, "Is Valeria safe now?"

He broke from her grasp and gripped her shoulders. "You shouldn't be here."

"Is she safe?"

"They got her in the jail."

"I know, but will she be all right?"

Darcy cocked his head to listen. The roar of the crowd still blasted his ears. The sound of glass shattering signaled the worst was about to happen. They were trying to break into the jail now, and they'd probably succeed. He gripped Laurie's shoulders tighter still. "I don't know if she'll be all right, but there's nothing you can do. Hear that crowd? They're like animals now—totally out of control. You're not safe here. I'll have one of my men take you home."

Her eyes suddenly widened. "Your head's all bloody. I saw when the rock hit you. You're still bleeding."

"It's nothing. It's you I'm worried about. This is no place for a woman. I'd take you home myself, but there's more I've got to do here."

"How could I leave now?" She reached for the lace hanky in her reticule and handed it to him. "Here, this might help. I saw how you faced that awful mob. I've never seen anything so brave. You saved Valeria's life."

"All I did was give her another day on this earth, and maybe not even that."

"There must be something we can do."

"You won't go home?"

Her jaw set in a stubborn line. "No."

She meant it. He had no time to argue. "Stay here. Don't even think of getting closer to that mob." He motioned to Kenvern. "Take care of her, will you? I've got to go back." He left before she could answer and shoved his way through the crowd again. Sheriff Gibbs remained outside. "Listen to me," he was yelling over the continuing noise. "I promise she'll have a trial."

He kept repeating his promise until finally the noise died down, and someone in the crowd yelled, "When?"

"Tomorrow morning, nine o'clock."

"Where?"

"Well..." Lucky Creek had no courthouse. The sheriff looked stuck for an answer.

Darcy stepped up and spoke to him. "How about right here in front of the jail? Out in the open, so everyone can see. They can't complain about that."

Sheriff Gibbs nodded in agreement. "As good a place as any." More protests went up when he announced the location of the trial. More calls rang out.

"Hang her now!"

A ripple of rebellion rolled through the crowd. For the second time, Darcy raised his arms and kept them up until he got their attention. "California's a state now," he yelled. "This is America, and in America everyone deserves a fair trial."

"Not the Latina," the man in black hollered back. He still held a rope in his hands and thrust it high. "Burn the jail down!"

Would they never listen? Through some of sort of miracle, they'd managed to get Valeria inside, but the jail wasn't all that strongly built. A mob like this could easily break the windows, smash through the doors. Or, like the genius in black suggested, they could set the whole place on fire. Darcy blew out his breath and threw his hands wide, ready to make one last desperate plea. Before he could open his mouth, two men came up the steps and joined him. He knew them both. The appearance of the Reverend Davies, popular pastor of the Baptist church, didn't surprise him. But the other? Since when would ruthless Brock Dominick gave a damn about anyone who came from below the border, and a woman at that?

Looking his usual splendid self in his frock coat and derby hat, Brock faced the crowd with an arrogant casualness that must have taken a lot of guts. "You all know me," he said, and the crowd instantly quieted down. No wonder. Brock owned the biggest mine around. Doubtless many men in the crowd worked at the Coyote Mine. In his usual blunt manner, he started to speak, and the crowd listened. "My friend, Darcy McKenna, knows whereof he speaks. Are we savages? No! We're a civilized nation now. Go home. Come back tomorrow. That woman has a right to a trial, so let her have one. What do you say?"

Amidst irate howls, some in the crowd cheered. The Reverend Davies stepped forward and spoke, echoing Brock Dominick's sentiments. At last, cries of dissension began to fade, and the crowd started to drift away. Someone raised his fist and yelled, "She'll have her trial all right. Then we'll hang her."

With a heavy heart, Darcy realized that was true.

Brock Dominick slapped him on the shoulder. "Good job, McKenna."

"Same to you," Darcy said, and added, "You surprised me." He'd been more than surprised that a man so ruthless had spoken with such eloquence and vision.

With a self-deprecating smile, Brock answered, "Sometimes I surprise myself. Justice makes strange bedfellows. These lynchings have got to stop, and it's up to us, the men who love this town and want to see it grow."

Darcy nodded and turned away. He'd learned a lot tonight. Like Brock, he loved this town. He'd found his true home here, and he'd never leave. *Laurie.* Was she all right? He must get back to her.

* * * *

Laurie watched as the crowd dispersed. At least Darcy had escaped further harm, but what about Valeria? When Darcy made his way back to the side street where she stood, she asked, "Will she have a fair trial, do you think? If she killed Emery Finch, she must have had a good reason. Maybe they'll find her not guilty and let her go."

"Not a chance."

His answer hit like a sharp blow to her stomach. "You can't mean—"

"They'll give her a trial all right, but it'll be a sham. You heard it a while ago. 'She'll have her trial all right. Then we'll hang her.' That's about the size of it, Laurie. I wish it could be otherwise, but we live in a lawless town, and there's nothing we can do."

"But the sheriff—"

"He's done what he can. Better than I expected, but he's weak, and he can only do so much. Besides, he's pretty much done his job. The trial is out of his hands, and it'll be a mockery."

"Oh." She bowed her head, shaken beyond words. She would like to cry in frustration, but what good would that do? Only seconds passed before she looked up again. A trickle of blood coursed down his cheek from the wound, reminding her how brave he'd been. "You could have been killed."

"But I wasn't."

"You need that wound cleaned."

"I'll take care of it." He looked toward Kenvern who stood nearby. "It's still not safe here. I'll have one of the brothers take you home."

Home? She hadn't thought ahead, but she did now. "I can't go home."

"Why not?"

How to explain? "My family thought I was crazy to come here."

"You were."

She ignored his comment. "Maybe I can't visit the jail, but whatever else happens, I'll be at Valeria's trial tomorrow. It'll help if she knows there's someone there who cares about her. That's the least I can do."

"Fine, but why can't you go home now and come back in the morning?"

"Because…" How could she explain? "If I go home now, they'll all be after me not to come back. They mean well, but they're relentless, and I just can't talk to them right now. I'll get a hotel room." Thank God, she had money enough in her reticule.

"Won't they worry about you?"

"Of course, they will." She frowned in thought. "I'll try to get word to them somehow."

"Don't worry, I'll have one of the brothers take a message. Where do you want to stay? I'll get you a room at the Gold Spike if you want."

Somewhere in the dim corner of her mind, a little voice was telling her that maybe what she was about to do wasn't wise. Darcy lived at the Gold Spike. Going to a hotel with a man not her husband was definitely not a good idea, even though she would have a separate room. That was especially true now, considering her feelings for him had definitely changed. There'd been a time when she thought him despicable, but not anymore. That trip to Hangtown had totally changed her opinion. Maryanne wouldn't be alive if not for the kindness and caring of Darcy McKenna. Now this latest. Seeing him defy that mob made her even more aware of how brave he'd been, with not a thought to the danger. No man could be more fearless and heroic, and besides all that, how had she not noticed before how very attractive he was? He even looked good with that trickle of blood down his face.

Obviously, she wasn't thinking clearly. She had better pull herself together. She should be thinking of poor Valeria, not her ridiculous attraction to a man she'd once found, at the least, unpleasant. "A room at the Gold Spike would be fine," she replied in the primmest, most proper tone she could manage. "And if you can get word to my family, I'd much appreciate it."

Chapter 12

Although the lynch mob had dispersed, an air of excitement still hung over the town. Noisy groups of men, still worked up from the near lynching, packed every saloon. In the crowded lobby of the Gold Spike, the clerk at the counter threw up his hands. "We're full up, Mr. McKenna. No use going someplace else. There's not an empty hotel room in this town."

Darcy turned to Laurie. "Don't worry, you can have my room."

"But where will you sleep?"

"I'll find a bed."

Laurie was about to protest when an attractive woman in her forties, a bit on the plump side, approached and spoke to Darcy. "Are you all right? I heard what happened." She saw the blood on his head and gasped. "Oh, my dear, you're hurt."

"I'm fine, Lucille."

The woman caught sight of Laurie, standing beside him. For the fleetest of moments, her lips parted in surprise, but she quickly recovered and said pleasantly, "We've never met, but I believe you're Laurie Sinclair."

"Yes, she is." Darcy performed introductions, explaining, "Valeria cooked for the Sinclair family, so of course Miss Sinclair's very concerned. She'll be staying here tonight so she can give Valeria all the support she can at the trial tomorrow."

Mrs. Wagner frowned with concern. "Do you have a room, Miss Sinclair? We're full up, and I don't think I can—"

"I'm giving her my room," Darcy said.

"Well then, I guess you'll have to sleep on the floor in the lobby."

"I guess I will."

Whom did they think they were fooling? Laurie immediately caught the subtle significance of their exchange. So that's how it was. She'd never given a thought to the women in Darcy's life, if indeed there were any, but she'd be a fool not to notice the adoration in Lucille Wagner's eyes when she looked at him. She owned the hotel and no doubt lived here. Obviously, he wouldn't be sleeping on the lobby floor tonight. But wherever he slept certainly wasn't her business. She had much graver concerns. "I'm hoping they'll let me in the jail tomorrow. Valeria doesn't deserve this. I've never known a better person, always generous, always kind, and I'll do all I can to help her."

Sympathy filled the hotel owner's eyes. "That poor woman. If there's anything I can do to help, you must let me know." She turned to Darcy. "That cut looks terrible."

"I'll take care of it."

Mrs. Wagner didn't press the point. Whether she shared her bed with Darcy or not, Laurie recognized her as one of those warm-hearted, motherly women she'd always admired but could never hope to emulate.

Declaring how busy she was, Mrs. Wagner soon disappeared. Laurie turned to Darcy. "Just show me where your room is." His head had stopped bleeding but was still a mess. "And we'll tend to that cut before you go."

They climbed three flights of stairs to his room. When he opened the door, and she stepped inside, the stark furnishings surprised her. Bed, bureau, one chair, and a washstand. This was all? She'd be foolish to believe all mine owners lived in a palatial mansion, but considering he owned a successful mine, she'd somehow expected more than a shabby room like this. Not that she'd say so. After he stepped inside and shut the door, a sudden awkwardness overcame her. She'd never been in a man's hotel room before. Not just any man, either, but a man she'd unexpectedly found attractive. "Before you go, let's take care of that cut," she said briskly.

"Don't bother. I can take care of it." He stood with his hand on the doorknob, ready to leave.

"Don't be foolish. You can't see the back of your head, can you? It looks terrible."

"If you say so." He stepped inside and sat on the bed. "There's fresh water in the basin and fresh towels underneath."

Acutely aware of his eyes upon her, she found the towels, dipped one in the water and wrung it out. "I don't suppose you have any iodine?"

"What do you think?"

"I think we don't want your cut to get infected." She walked to the bed and stood over him. "Turn your head so I can see." When he did, she exclaimed, "Good Lord, it's worse than I thought. That rock could have killed you."

"Well, it didn't."

She started dabbing at the cut, trying to be gentle, but now and then he winced. "Sorry I'm hurting you."

"Don't worry about it. Just do what you have to do."

Of course, she'd do what she had to do, but the trouble was, being so intimately close like this had affected her ability to think straight. What was wrong with her? She should be thinking of poor Valeria sitting in the jailhouse expecting to be hung in the morning, but instead, being this close to Darcy had put strange thoughts in her head. She found herself aching for Darcy to touch her, to kiss her again like he had that night in Hangtown. But obviously he had other things on his mind. Since then, his standoffish attitude had clearly informed her his interests lay elsewhere. Now she knew where. After he left the room, she'd wager on her life he'd soon be sharing a bed with the warm and comforting Mrs. Wagner. But then, how could she blame him when she'd made it abundantly clear that her heart belonged to one Brandon Cooper of Philadelphia?

Gently as possible, she cleaned out the cut and wiped the blood away from his thick, dark hair. The trouble was, the longer she stood so close to him, the more aware she became of his long, lean body, the scent of him, the heat of his skin. She could hardly breathe, she was so aware of him, which was just so ridiculous. He'd made it clear he had no interest in her and was no doubt anxious for her to finish so he could get to the welcoming arms of the widow.

He sat still as a statue the whole time. When she finished, she tossed the towel to the washstand. "There, I've cleaned it out. It should be fine now." Right about now, she should back away, tell him goodbye, but a force beyond herself kept her feet from moving. As if it had a mind of its own, her hand reached out and rested lightly on his shoulder. Words she had no control over came to her lips. "Darcy, I…I so admire you for what you did tonight. Most men wouldn't have been so brave. You were truly…truly…"

She heard a quick groan, felt his hands wrap around her waist. Before she could understand what was happening, she found herself lifted high in the air, then flat on her back on the bed, Darcy hovering over her. "You find me truly what?" he asked, his breath coming hard. Before she could answer, he slid his open hand behind her head, pulled her mouth to his, and planted a demanding, searing kiss that lasted until he pulled away and left a trail of kisses from her forehead to her chin.

When he lifted his head, she wrapped her arms around him, whispering, "I find you truly desirable, Darcy McKenna. Kiss me again." Was that really her talking? Right about now she, the properly brought up Miss Sinclair, should be putting a stop to this nonsense. She could think of all kinds of reasons why she shouldn't be in this man's hotel room, on his bed, about to throw her so-called precious virtue to the winds. But more than that, how could they be doing this when poor Valeria sat in the jailhouse waiting to die? But after a night like tonight, the trouble was, she was tired of thinking, tired of always doing the correct thing, not what she really wanted, and right now what she really wanted beyond all reason was Darcy McKenna.

He kissed her again, long and slow, and when his hand began a slow slide down her arm and over to her breast, all she could focus on was the heat of it through the fabric of her dress. He began to fumble with the buttons that ran down the bodice of her gown, and she reached to help him.

* * * *

Darcy had never thought of himself as a passionate man. To the contrary, he'd grown up in a home so cold and loveless, he'd had no idea what true passion was, and figured he'd never find out. True, he'd been with a woman from time to time. Lately he'd been completely satisfied with his comfortable relationship with Lucille, and she, he was sure, with him. But that was nothing more than a convenient arrangement. Never, until tonight, had he known what it was like to make love to a woman in the true sense of the word. To give himself to her completely, forget his own pleasure and think only of her. When they were done and lay spent on the bed, he raised up on one elbow and gazed down at her. Her hair had come loose and spread over the pillow. Her slim body with its inviting curves lay stretched beneath him. "You're beautiful," he said, dropping kisses on her cheek and bare shoulder.

She looked up at him and ran her hands over his damp skin. "I never thought anything could be so...so..." As he watched, her eyes went wide. She was remembering. He'd suspected it wouldn't take long. "Valeria! Sitting in the jailhouse while I—"

"Hush." He silenced her with a soft kiss on her mouth. "Tomorrow we'll think about Valeria, but tonight is ours." He lay beside her and pulled her tight against him.

"It's ours." She snuggled her head on his shoulder and sighed with contentment.

* * * *

At the crack of dawn, Laurie awoke with a start. *Valeria. The trial.* Darcy lay asleep, his arm slung across her. Carefully she slid from underneath, stood by the bed and looked down at his bare body, only half covered by the blankets. She liked everything about him—his muscular arms, bare and covered with silky hairs, his narrow waist and lean hips. They'd made love last night. If this were an ordinary day, she'd be reliving every single minute of it. How it happened, why it happened, how she'd felt when it happened. But no time to think about it now. She must get to Valeria.

The Gold Spike Hotel was so modern it had an indoor bathroom at the end of the hall. She made use of it, washed, dressed, and twisted her hair in a bun atop her head. By the time Darcy woke up, she was just about ready to leave. "Good morning," she said briskly and headed for the door. "I don't have time to talk. I don't care what the sheriff said. I'm going to see Valeria before the trial."

Darcy swung from the bed, wrapping a towel around his middle. "Wait. The streets aren't safe with all those fools running around. You're not going alone." His gaze softened. "About last night…"

"We don't have time." She instantly regretted her edgy reply. "I'm sorry. It's Valeria—"

"You don't have to explain. Just wait."

He washed and dressed in no time. At his insistence, they ate a quick breakfast in the dining room. He made no further mention of what had occurred in his room last night, and for that she was grateful. She needed time to sort it through, and besides that, nothing but Valeria mattered now. She was all they talked about. "Don't get your hopes up," he warned her again.

As they walked to the jailhouse, Laurie looked up at the bright blue sky. What a beautiful, sunny day it was, but poor Valeria wouldn't think so, not when she was sitting in jail, alone, shocked, and she must be terribly frightened. Laurie could only imagine how awful it must feel to be so hated that an enraged mob wanted her dead. She clenched her fists at the thought of it. "They can't kill a woman. Nobody should die on a day like this. I refuse to believe they could do such a terrible thing."

Darcy's somber expression revealed his concern. "By now you've got to know Lucky Creek can be a heartless place. That's the way it is in the West. I've seen brutal floggings for nothing more than petty theft. I've seen men get their ears cut off for cheating at cards, and they were lucky they didn't lose their lives instead of their ears. Listen, Laurie…" He stopped in the street and gripped her arms. "The world's not a fair place, much as you'd like to think so. I said don't get your hopes up, and I meant it. Chances are, they won't let you see her, much less listen to anything you have to say."

"No!" She shook her head and broke away from his grasp. "I don't believe you. There will be a fair trial. I will make them let me testify, and I'll tell them what a fine woman she is, and how I often saw bruises on her face, put there by that lowlife, Emery Finch. I can't believe they won't listen."

Darcy said nothing more. They started walking again and soon arrived at the jail. Already at least a hundred people had gathered in the square in front. In contrast to the ugly mood of last night, this morning's crowd possessed almost a jovial attitude, as if they were looking forward to some kind of entertainment. "Look at them," Laurie whispered to Darcy as they pushed their way through. "You'd think they want her found guilty just so they can have the pleasure of watching someone hang."

Darcy didn't answer. He put a protective arm around her and guided her to the jailhouse entrance. The door was locked. He knocked, and no one answered. He began to pound, and kept pounding until finally, the door opened a crack, and a deputy poked his head out. "You can't come in. Nobody's coming in."

"This young lady is Miss Laurie Sinclair, Valeria's employer," Darcy said with cool authority. "She has every right to see her."

"Wait." The deputy's head disappeared, and the door closed. Minutes went by before he opened it again. "Sorry, the sheriff says no one can come in. Valeria sent a message for Miss Sinclair, though."

Laurie's heart jumped at the sound of her name. "What did she say?"

"She wants you to get her a piece of rope or heavy twine. Six feet or so. She says you can get it to her at the trial."

"But why does she want—"

The door slammed shut. Darcy took her arm. "Let's get out of here."

She pulled away. "This isn't right. Why won't they let me in?" She raised her hand to knock again, but Darcy's quick, firm clasp of her wrist caught her before she could. "You're wasting your time, Laurie. Come away. All you can do now is stand by. At least she knows you're here."

Mixed feelings surged through her. How dare they keep her from seeing Valeria? Part of her wanted to hurl herself against the door, pound with her fists, demand the sheriff let her in. But another, more sensible, part told her Darcy was right. She could pound all she pleased, but they weren't going to open the door again. "All right, we'll wait for the trial."

In defeat, she turned and walked down the steps. So far, she'd done nothing to help Valeria, and the way things were going, doubted she could.

How could she, or anyone, save her cook from the hangman's noose? She'd been so sure she could help, but now her confidence was fading, and she was beginning to wonder.

* * * *

By the time the trial started, a cold knot had formed in Laurie's stomach. As Valeria had requested, she and Darcy had gone to the general store and purchased six feet of heavy twine, although Laurie still couldn't imagine what it was for. Despite the boisterous crowd packing the town square, they managed to push their way to the front row where they watched the sheriff's deputies set up tables and chairs for the judge and jury. They placed a lone chair to one side, no doubt meant for Valeria. After completing the setup, the deputies carried in a long wooden box that looked like a coffin. Laurie gasped when she realized indeed it was a coffin. Inside, the body of Emery Finch lay dressed in a suit and tie, arms crossed, the expression on his face so kindly and serene he looked almost saintly. A great hoot and holler went up at the sight of him. "Old Emery looks better dead than he did alive," someone jibed.

"That's so unfair," Laurie cried. With a sinking heart she watched as they set the coffin directly in front of the judge's table. The jurors had already been selected, Laurie didn't know how. As they took their seats, Darcy uttered an oath. "I recognize most of them. Either they're friends of Emery's, they work at the Palace, or both."

Cheers and whistles erupted when the judge entered and took his seat. "Do you recognize him?" Darcy asked quietly. No, she didn't. "They brought in Judge Bert Sanger from over in Hangtown. He's as corrupt as they come. He's good friends with the owner of the Palace."

Two burly deputies appeared, half hauling Valeria between them. She looked so frail and vulnerable, hands bound in front of her, scarcely able to walk, but holding her head high. As she took her seat, she raised her chin with defiance. Her bowler hat was gone. Despite her bound hands, she managed to flip one braid over her shoulder. She sat rigid and straight backed, staring directly ahead as if she wasn't aware of her surroundings, but when Laurie gave a slight wave, she saw it and inclined her head in the briefest of nods.

The trial got underway. The first few witnesses heaped praise upon that fine fellow, Emery Finch. How generous he was, kind, considerate, a real pillar of the community. Although no one had seen the actual stabbing, several surmised as to how "that Latina woman" had to be the one who stabbed poor Emery. They all agreed hanging was too good for her.

The judge summoned Doc Hansen to the witness chair. In a calm, straightforward manner, he described the stab wound. "Only the one, but straight to the heart, and that's what killed him." The judge told him he could leave, but Doc had more to say. "In my opinion, Valeria Gomez is not in a fit condition to be hanged. As you can see from her face she's been badly beaten…"

He could not continue. A chorus of jeers and boos drowned him out.

The good doctor sat in the witness chair patiently waiting for the taunts and threats to die down. Several times, he tried to speak, but each time the noise of the crowd forced him to silence. Finally, with a sad shake of his head, he cast a regretful look at Valeria, shrugged his shoulders in defeat, and left the witness chair.

Laurie let out a breath that was half frustration, half disbelief. "I can't believe this. They wouldn't listen to Doc, but maybe they'll listen to me. I still want to be a witness."

"No, you can't risk it." Darcy spoke softly, but she heard the alarm in his voice. "You saw what happened to the doctor. Why do you think you could do any better?"

"But I feel so helpless."

"You are helpless. Can't you see this crowd is out for blood? Only a miracle can save her now, and miracles are few and far between around here."

She saw it now. Darcy had known all along, but fool that she was, she'd firmly believed she could save her cook. She'd grown up in a world where right was right, wrong was wrong, and justice always prevailed. Not in Lucky Creek. The undeniable, dreadful fact was, this trial was a mockery. They were going to hang Valeria, and neither she, nor anyone else, could stop it. Now she understood what the rope was for. Darcy was holding it. "We must get the rope to her."

"Don't worry, I'll see to it."

After the doctor left the witness chair, the judge addressed Valeria. "Have you anything to say? If you have, say it now."

A corner of Valeria's mouth lifted in a sneer as she replied, "Why bother?"

Judge Sanger turned to the jury. "That's it, boys. If you want, there's a room in the jailhouse where you can retire and discuss—"

"We don't need to retire." One of the jurors, a bearded man in his forties, stood. "Wait a minute, Judge." He bent to consult the others. They huddled together and whispered among themselves for less than a minute. He raised up and spoke again. "We have a verdict, Your Honor."

"So, tell us."

"We find Valeria Gomez guilty and she ought to hang."

A wild cheer broke from the crowd. The judge pounded his gavel and looked straight at Valeria. "You've had a fair trial. I sentence you to hang." Another roar of approval went up. He spoke again. "How about right now? The gallows is down by the river." Another roar arose from the elated crowd. Laurie closed her eyes a moment, trying to cope with the combination of shock and hopelessness that had overcome her. Nothing could save Valeria now. She gazed at Darcy, too overcome to speak. He put a protective arm around her. "I've got to get you out of here."

She found her voice. "But I want to stay close to Valeria."

"You can't. It's too dangerous."

Stunned and sickened, she hadn't the strength to argue. She remained in the shelter of his arm as he maneuvered his way to the edge of the crowd, then followed as the eager spectators moved toward the river. Last night only men made up the furious mob, but now she was shocked to see more than a few women had joined in. Everyone seemed in a good mood, as if they were going to a picnic, not a hanging. As they drew close to the river, Laurie saw a makeshift gallows had already been erected: wooden scaffold with stairs leading up to it; two sturdy beams extending above, from which a rope with a noose on the end dangled. Sick realization made her cry out, "They must have built this before the trial."

Darcy nodded grimly. They found a place to stand on a small rise at the edge of the crowd, a place where they had a clear view of the gallows but away from most of the crowd. "This seems safe enough. They're in a better mood now anyway." He laughed with irony. "They think it's some sort of picnic. Stay here. I'll be right back."

Before she could ask where he was going, he plunged into the crowd. He'd been holding the rope, but when he came back, it was gone. She didn't ask. All she wanted to do was turn and run from this horror, but she couldn't. Valeria couldn't see her, but that didn't matter. She needed a friend to be there for her. *And that will be me*, Laurie thought, determined she would stay.

"You look pale," Darcy said. "Are you sure you want to see this?"

"I have to see it. I have to be there for Valeria."

As the crowd cheered and heckled, Valeria mounted the steps to the gallows. She held something in her hands. Was it the rope? At the top, she was met by a man dressed in black, head covered by a black hood with slits for his eyes. He untied her hands and bound them again behind her back. He led her to where the rope dangled and dropped the heavy noose around her neck. Taking the piece of rope—now Laurie could clearly see it was the rope Darcy brought her—he bound it tight around her skirts, halfway between her knees and ankles. So even at a time like this, Valeria had kept her pride. She wasn't going to have people looking up her skirts. Laurie wasn't sure how much more she could endure, but endure it she would, for Valeria's sake.

The rest of the horror went quickly. When the hangman asked, "Do you have any last words?" Valeria simply shook her head and stepped into space.

Laurie forced herself to watch the rest, knowing this was a moment that would never leave her. The flighty, frivolous girl she'd been in Philadelphia was gone forever. From this day forward, she'd never be the same.

Chapter 13

It was over. Darcy looked on in disgust as the spectators drifted from the site of the hanging, their cries for blood and vengeance satisfied. The crowd had suddenly turned quiet, almost subdued. Maybe the sight of a woman's body swaying in the breeze had caused those with the least semblance of compassion to realize the awful thing they'd done. His stomach turned every time he thought of it. He'd seen a lot of bad things in his life, but the hanging of Valeria Gomez rivaled his worst mEmery, the scalping of Ned Grimes. He would carry forever the haunting visions of both. Laurie had held together a lot better than he thought she would, but now, as he guided her through the thinning crowd, he noted how pale she'd become. "I'm taking you home."

"Yes, home. I've got to—" Her voice broke.

"Are you all right? We could go back to the hotel."

"I've got to get home, tell the family." She pulled her shoulders back as if bracing herself for the grim task ahead. "They loved Valeria. I can only imagine how devastated they'll be."

They reached the stable behind the hotel where he hitched up his carriage. They hardly spoke as he drove her home. What could be said? After the gruesome scene they'd witnessed, words seemed meaningless. When they reached her house, he asked, "Do you want me to come in?"

"It's best I tell them alone." She quickly climbed from the carriage and looked back up at him, eyes full of pain. "It all seems so unreal. Last night. This morning and Valeria."

He knew what she meant and felt the same. Nothing he could put into words, though. "You'll be wanting some time off from the mine."

"No, I won't. I'll be there tomorrow." She started to turn away, caught herself and turned back. "Goodbye and thank you for everything."

What exactly did she mean by "everything"? He watched after her as she walked to her front door and disappeared inside. He must sort things out, try to figure what was going on in his head because right now he wasn't sure he knew. This wasn't like him. He hadn't become the man he was by acting like some kind of dithering idiot. Things were different when he was younger. His early years had been a nightmare he'd barely survived. He'd gone through so much turmoil he hardly knew who he was or where he was going. But all that was behind him now. Since those priceless years he'd spent with Ned, he'd become the man he wanted to be: honorable, tolerant of others, quick to make decisions, and always sure of himself, and what he wanted. But was that enough? Up to now, all he wanted was sufficient money to make himself comfortable, the satisfaction of a job well done, an unlimited view of the sky, and the comforting arms of Lucille Wagner awaiting him whenever he chose. So, what more could he ask for? Although, to be honest, the thing with Lucille wasn't working out. He'd never wanted to hurt her, but maybe he was, and he'd have to do something about that.

He hadn't asked for a woman like Laurie Sinclair to come into his life. Up to now, he'd done very well without her. But now...? He got a twist in his gut just thinking about last night. He'd been with a few women in his life, gotten his satisfaction, and been on his way. Some he'd liked more than others. Some he'd developed a real affection for, but never had he felt like he did with Laurie Sinclair, and it was hard figuring out why. He'd never made love but what he didn't want to satisfy himself. But last night? All he'd wanted was to please her, not himself, and let her know he cared. Not that he'd said the words. It was all in the caring way he'd made love to her, and what a pleasure it had been, holding her beautiful body in his arms. For once in his life, he'd put himself second, although in the end he'd enjoyed their lovemaking as much as she.

What irony. The man with the so-called heart of stone had met his match. Laurie Sinclair—vain, spoiled, couldn't harness a horse, but now? How could he get through the day without thinking of her—wanting her—again and again, seeing her as she lay naked in his bed.

But why bother? Laurie didn't belong to him and never would. She belonged to Brandon Cooper, a man he heartily disliked even though he'd never met him.

* * * *

When Laurie walked into the house, she wasn't sure what her reception would be. She'd almost forgotten how she'd rushed out of the house to help Valeria—was it only yesterday?—defying her mother, disregarding her brother's advice. It all seemed unimportant now. Perhaps they hadn't heard about the hanging yet, although bad news traveled fast. If they had heard, they'd be devastated. Laurie could only hope they wouldn't be too upset.

She reached the parlor and immediately knew from the somber look on Mother's and Ada's faces they'd heard. "You're safe." Ada leaped from her chair and gave her a hug. "We were worried about you."

Before Laurie could answer, Mother declared, "If you were in that awful lynch mob, I don't want to hear it. Where were you last night? Why didn't you come home?"

If they only knew. Laurie wouldn't lie, but with some careful maneuvering she could avoid the entire truth. "I stayed at the Gold Spike Hotel." Mother gave her a searching look but didn't say anything. Best to get off that subject as soon as possible. "I was there. I saw the hanging. It was horrible, but I want you to know Valeria stayed brave to the end."

Tears glistened in Ada's eyes. "That's so terrible. I can't even imagine what she went through."

Mother remained dry-eyed. "Valeria should never have taken up with that awful man, that Emery what's-his-name. When I saw those bruises on her face, I warned her, but would she listen? Now look what's happened. Here we are without a cook, and I don't know what we're going to do."

For a moment Laurie could only stare. Words failed her until the injustice of it all overcame her, and she burst out, "Don't you care? Valeria was the most generous, kind, thoughtful person I knew. She just died a horrible death, and all you're worried about is you don't have a cook?"

Mother not only remained unmoved, she rolled her eyes as if asking for patience. "There's no need to get upset. Of course, I'm sorry for what happened to Valeria. It's just that we have to be practical. Am I supposed to cook now, along with everything else?"

Laurie opened her mouth to argue, but quickly shut it. What could she say? Mother would never understand, and she'd just be wasting her breath.

Soon after, she went upstairs to talk to her brother and found him sitting up in bed. "You heard about Valeria?"

Hugh shook his head with regret. "She was a great cook. I'll especially miss that *feijoada* she used to make."

"She was a wonderful woman. It's terrible what happened. You've no idea how awful—"

"We all know what happened." Hugh's voice held a note of admonition. "Don't tell me you were part of that mob. How dumb can you get, Sis? You could have been killed."

The family had surprised her many a time, and this was but another example. Only Ada understood. Hugh was simply being Hugh, and she shouldn't expect he'd suddenly developed a big heart. And how could she blame Mother, who'd been brought up in a world where compassion didn't extend to those she considered beneath her. *Maybe I was that way once*, Laurie thought, *but not anymore*. If there was one thing living in Lucky Creek had taught her, it was that people didn't always react like she expected them to. Hard to understand sometimes, but she'd try.

She went downstairs and talked to her mother again. "I know how you feel. Maybe we can hire Mei Ling back. She wasn't a bad cook. I'll look into it."

"Please do." Mother clamped her jaw, a sure sign of anger. "We must get out of here. I've had enough of this awful place. I want to go back to Philadelphia, where the streets aren't muddy, and lynch mobs don't go running around hanging people."

Under ordinary circumstances, Laurie might have found her mother's illogical reply amusing, but today nothing was funny. "They're well underway with digging the new shaft at the Monarch. Mr. McKenna is quite optimistic. It won't be much longer before the money starts rolling in."

"Well, it won't be too soon for me."

Laurie started to add a "me too," then thought better of it. Of course, she wanted to return to Philadelphia, but the prospect didn't seem quite as thrilling as it had before. Why? What was the matter with her? Brandon awaited. Enlightened civilization awaited. Paved streets—the latest fashions—high-class friends who knew which fork to use. And yet... Was this muddy little mining town really so bad? Philadelphia had no snowcapped mountains, no breathtaking waterfalls, no crisp, clean pine-scented air. And after last night? Of course, she still loved Brandon, but how could she leave Darcy McKenna when last night had been so...so...

"I'd appreciate it if you could bring Mei Ling back." Mother's mood had improved, and she was smiling. "She's a tiny little thing, but she's a hard worker. She'll make life easier for the short time we'll still be here. You look tired, dear. Perhaps you'd better go lie down for a while."

Oh, God, maybe she better had. How could she be sure of anything anymore? She'd been prepared for a deluge of shock and grief from her family over the loss of their beloved cook, but that hadn't happened. Now she was the shocked one. She'd been wrong to expect they'd want to hear every little detail concerning Valeria's death. Only Ada cared. Hugh's main concern seemed to be how much he'd miss the *feijoada*. Mother's main concern was that they find another cook. As for Darcy... She wouldn't think about him now. Tomorrow would be soon enough to get her thoughts straight. Right now, she welcomed the excuse to escape. "I believe I need a nap."

She hurried to her room, and had just laid down, when Ada knocked and entered, her desolate expression an indication of how much she cared. She sat on the edge of the bed. "Laurie, were you there? Did you see it when they hung her? It's all so awful I can hardly bear to think about it."

"I saw it all, and I'll never forget it." Laurie sat up, plumped a pillow behind her, and proceeded to describe the unbelievable ugliness of the crowd, Valeria's incredible courage, all of it except for the actual hanging. Some things were best unsaid, let alone, and best forgotten. When she finished, they both wept for the woman who had died so bravely with such dignity. They reminisced about her excellent cooking, her kindnesses, her funny sense of humor.

Not until later did Ada casually mention, "Of course you know it was Kenvern who brought us the message that you weren't coming home."

"Of course." Why was Ada bringing this up?

"I invited him in. He stayed for a while. I fixed him some tea, and we drank it in the kitchen. We talked a lot."

Ada entertaining a male guest? Fixing him tea? How astounding. "It was kind of him to bring the message."

"I find him to be a very nice man."

Aha! So that was it. Ada in love? Laurie had thought she'd never see the day.

"Of course, he's not suitable," her sister went on.

"Really? Who says he's not suitable?"

"Kenvern doesn't speak correctly and doesn't know his manners. Not that I care one single bit, but you know Mother. After he left, she referred to him as 'that ignorant Cornishman.'"

Laurie couldn't argue. A miner from the back country of Cornwall would never in a million years gain Mother's approval. "I'm afraid you're right, Ada. Wait till we get back to Philadelphia. As you know, it's full of handsome young bachelors. Maybe this time you'll find one you like."

Ada sighed and didn't answer. Laurie didn't pursue the subject. After her turbulent relationship with Brandon, she was hardly the one to give advice about love. Now even more so after her night with Darcy McKenna.

* * * *

The next day, Laurie got up early. After fixing her own breakfast, she hitched the horses to the curricle without the least difficulty and drove to the home of Mei Ling. Their former maid would be happy to return. "You want me today?" she asked.

Laurie gave her an enthusiastic yes and headed for the mine. At least one problem solved. Mei Ling's cooking skills couldn't match Valeria's, but Mother should be pleased, nonetheless.

After their night together, Laurie wondered if she'd feel awkward seeing Darcy again, but she needn't have worried. When she entered the office, he gave her a friendly but casual "Good morning," no different than he'd give anybody else. She went to her desk immediately and got to work. Darcy, Tom by his side, was hiring more miners today, and there was plenty to do. He, too, stayed busy all day, and they hardly spoke. Even so, not for a moment was she unaware of his presence. She could hardly keep her eyes off him. Everything about him held her captivated, from his tall, lean body, to the hard angles of his face, to every graceful move he made, so very sure of himself and in control. As if that weren't enough, she couldn't keep her mind off what he'd looked like when they lay in bed and had just finished making love. His hard-muscled chest glistening with sweat—that line of silky dark hair running from his chest, over his stomach, to where it disappeared below. Just the thought of it made her blush. This had to stop. She loved Brandon Cooper. Back in Philadelphia, despite the eagle-eyed chaperones, they'd been intimate more than once, but it hadn't been all that exciting, and she'd never thought of him with lust in her heart, not like she kept thinking of Darcy. And the worst of it was, that night with Darcy had been something so special that she didn't feel the least bit ashamed. It had all seemed so natural, as if this was the way it was supposed to be.

Only once during the day had something other than Darcy captured her complete attention. Again, she noticed the ledgers didn't look right. The records Hugh kept simply didn't match the figures Father had entered in his ledger. Of course, she was at fault for not understanding. She would ask Hugh to explain the discrepancy when she got home.

At the end of the shift, she stood at the entrance to the mine, time ledger in hand, quite sure of herself now, and pleased she knew what she was doing. Like always, the miners filed out in high spirits, happy their shift had ended. Each day, they were digging the shaft deeper, following the newly found vein. After that first astounding find, the vein had provided barely enough rich ore to keep them going, but both Darcy and Tom remained optimistic. It was just a matter of time before they'd hit pay dirt again. After she'd recorded their hours, and the last man had filed by, she noticed Kenvern Trenowden had remained behind. "Can I help you, Kenvern?"

The Cornishman stood twisting his cap in his hands. "Yes, Miss Sinclair. I...uh..."

The poor man. She already had a good idea what he was going to say, and she'd better help him out. "I certainly appreciate your taking my message to my family the other night. It was such a terrible night, as you know, and I really appreciate it."

Kenvern smiled and stopped twisting his cap. "I was happy to do it."

She would help him out even further. "My sister especially appreciated it. I hear she served you tea and enjoyed your conversation."

To her surprise, Kenvern's face fell. "I don't see how she could have when I know I don't talk right."

She quickly sought something kind to say. "There's nothing wrong with the way you talk. Of course, one can easily tell you're from Cornwall, but I find your manner of speaking rather charming."

Kenvern thrust out his jaw. "I don't want to sound charming. I want to learn proper English."

Before she could think of an answer, he spoke again. "I really want to learn, Miss Sinclair. Could you maybe tell me how I can? You see"—he was struggling for words—"I like your sister, but the way your mother be looking at me, she wouldn't want me cleaning out her stable, let alone courting her daughter. Not placing any blame, mind you. I know me place."

So Ada had a suitor? Laurie loved the idea, but Kenvern was right. Mother had already expressed her displeasure over "that ignorant Cornishman." Before Laurie could find an answer that wouldn't hurt his feelings, he blushed, uttered a quick, "Sorry I troubled you," and hurried away.

Tom and Darcy were still in the office when she returned. After she checked the time sheets and was about to leave, Darcy inquired, "How did things go today?"

"Just fine," she replied with the kind of detachment she'd use on a mere acquaintance. He was only being polite, but because Kenvern Trenowden was very much on her mind, she added, "It appears one of your Cornish miners has an interest in my sister."

Darcy smiled. "I'd wager you mean Kenvern Trenowden. He's asked me about her. Think she's interested?"

Not wanting to give any of her sister's confidences away, Laurie formed a careful answer. "Possibly she might be, and that would be fine if we were planning on staying in Lucky Creek. Manners and morals don't count here. The problem is, even if Ada was interested, Mother would never approve. She desperately wants to return to Philadelphia and so does my sister. Unfortunately, Kenvern would never be accepted there. For one thing, he doesn't speak proper English. He'd be out of his depth and considered totally unsuitable for a refined young lady like Ada."

Darcy's dark brows lifted with irritation. "You're right, this isn't Philadelphia, where the streets are paved, and you won't find a crazed mob ready to lynch some innocent victim. But I'll tell you one thing that your fine Philadelphia doesn't have, and that's equality."

"I don't quite grasp your meaning." Actually, she hadn't the faintest notion what he was talking about.

"What I mean is, in Lucky Creek—all the West—a man is judged by the work he does, not by how prominent his family is, or how he talks, or how much money he has. I've seen miners who were lawyers, merchants, college professors, all grades, shades, and classes when they lived back east. Out here what they did before doesn't mean a damn thing." Darcy spoke with an unusual spark of passion in his eyes. "The best thing I ever did was head west."

Harry Peske, Darcy's top employee at the Atlas, happened to be in the office and had overheard. "He's right, Miss Sinclair. You'd never guess by looking, but back in Boston I worked as a lowly clerk in an attorney's office. Twelve hours a day, I sat on a high stool copying documents. Same thing—over and over again—the most boring job in the world. No chance of promotion. I had no future, other than to work till I died. Now look at me. I'm a supervisor at the Atlas, by God. I don't have to stay if I don't want. There's opportunities everywhere, and I'll tell you something. There's not enough money in the world that could bring me back to Boston, or Philadelphia, or any place east of the Mississippi. Maybe Lucky Creek isn't perfect, but a man has a chance here to do what he wants."

Harry Peske's fervent words left her momentarily speechless and searching for answers. Both he and Darcy had caught her off guard. "I never thought of it that way, but I see what you mean. There's no such thing as high society in Lucky Creek, and I find I like it that way."

"You do?" Darcy searched her face, reaching for her thoughts. "You see Philadelphia as the center of your universe. From what I've seen, nothing will change that."

She instantly bristled. How could he think her so inflexible? "As you know, I have certain interests in Philadelphia, but it's definitely not the center of my universe." Or was it? Maybe he spoke the truth, and she just couldn't face it.

Harry burst into easy laughter, as if to smooth the slight friction in the air. "Well, California's the center of Kenvern's universe. He's a hard worker and a fine man."

Darcy nodded in agreement. "He might not speak proper English, but Ada would be lucky to have him. His future is here, and I plan to help him all I can."

Laurie said no more. Darcy had set her to thinking about a lot of things, and so had Harry Peske.

Chapter 14

Did she really see Philadelphia as the center of her universe? The question hung heavy on Laurie's mind as she drove the curricle home. One thing for certain, along with everything else she liked about Darcy, she admired him all the more for his passionate defense of the West. Clearly, his feelings on the subject ran deep. For once, he'd opened up and spoken from his heart. She'd give it more thought later. Right now, she had a plan for Ada and could hardly wait to present it.

Arriving home, Laurie was pleased to find Mei Ling had returned as promised. Not only had she given the house a good cleaning, they all enjoyed the beef stew she fixed for their dinner. Laurie waited until the children had been put to bed and both Mother and Hugh had retired to their rooms before she sat down with Ada in the parlor. She wasted no time presenting her plan. "Kenvern spoke to me today. I'll be blunt. He likes you very much, but he thinks he's not worthy of you."

"But that's not so," Ada answered with a touch of righteous indignation. "Mother's the one who thinks that way, but I certainly don't."

"I know you don't, but since she does, we need a plan, and I have one."

"Tell me." Ada's eyes sparked with interest.

"Kenvern wants to learn how to read and speak 'proper,' as he says. I suspect he'd like to write proper, too, so why don't you teach him?"

"What do you mean? I'm not a teacher."

"He already knows how to read and write. You don't have to be a trained teacher to help him polish his English. All you need is a McGuffey Reader, maybe the one for fourth grade. Kenvern could come over after work once, maybe twice a week. You could sit at the kitchen table and give him a lesson. I'd be there to help, too."

"But what of Mother? She'd never approve."

"Mother doesn't have to approve. We're not children anymore. We're both grown women with minds of our own, and we don't need a mother to tell us what to do. You need to be firm with her, in the kindest way, of course. In other words, you're not going ask her. You're going to inform her, firmly but pleasantly, that Kenvern Trenowden will be dropping over once or twice a week, maybe more, for a reading lesson. He won't get in her way. You'll sit at the kitchen table for an hour or two, maybe twice a week. Surely she can't object to that."

"Dare I?" Ada took a few seconds to ponder, then smiled. "You're right. I'm twenty-three years old, and I don't have to do everything Mother says anymore. I wouldn't hurt her feelings for the world, though."

"You'll find a way. There's no one more tactful than you, Ada. The best part is, you'll be doing a great kindness, helping a man who's yearning to learn. Not only that—"

"We'll get to know each other better. I love your plan, Laurie. How soon do we start?"

"I'll have to ask him first."

Ada's face lit in a smile, the brightest Laurie had ever seen on her face. "He'll say yes, I know he will."

* * * *

Later, Laurie went up to Hugh's room and knocked on his door. He was sitting up in bed writing a letter when she walked in. "You're looking better." She sat on a chair beside his bed.

With a derisive sniff, he tossed his pen down. "I'm sick of being an invalid. I am feeling better, though. The ribs are healing. I can take a breath now without feeling like I've been stabbed in the chest. The doctor says I can get the cast off my arm tomorrow. Looks like I'll be back to work before you know it."

She should have been overjoyed at his news. The sooner he came back to work, the sooner she could leave. But oddly enough, she didn't feel overjoyed like she should. "You don't need to rush."

"Why shouldn't I? Aren't you dying to get back to Philadelphia and your beloved Brandon?"

She couldn't blame him for the mockery in his voice. She'd be in a bad mood, too, if she were confined to the house as long as Hugh had been. "Of course, I want to leave, but we must make sure you're feeling up to it." She wasn't exactly lying, although she had to admit her concern for her brother's health wasn't foremost in her mind. The truth of it was, the thought of leaving Lucky Creek didn't fill her heart with joy, not like it would have a few weeks ago.

Hugh eyed her suspiciously. "Don't tell me you enjoy working in that dirty office, dealing with those grubby miners. Or is it something else? I know. You've forgotten all about Brandon. Instead, you've fallen madly in love with Darcy McKenna."

"Don't be ridiculous." Her brother had hit an area so sensitive she hastened to change the subject. Recalling the problem with the ledgers, she would distract him. "Speaking of work, I've been comparing yours and Father's ledgers, and there's something I'm not clear on." She went on to explain the discrepancies she'd found. When she finished, Hugh regarded her with amusement.

"You shouldn't bother your pretty little head about ledgers. I'll make a note of it and get it all straightened out when I get back. Fair enough?"

"Fair enough."

She said nothing more on the subject and left soon after, relieved Hugh had made no further mention of her being in love with Darcy. He'd only been teasing, a wild stab in the dark, and so untrue, but she found his accusation highly annoying. She'd made allowances because he wasn't well, but even so, she especially resented his condescending attitude when she mentioned the ledgers, implying she didn't know what she was talking about. She would let it go, though. Hugh was simply being Hugh, and besides, surely there had to be a reasonable explanation.

* * * *

Next day at the office, Laurie waited until Darcy had left, and she was alone with Tom. She got out the ledgers she was curious about and carried them to Tom's desk. "Would you take a look at these?" She laid them out in front of him. "There's a few things I don't understand that perhaps you can explain."

Together they went through the ledgers, Laurie pointing out the discrepancies as they went along. Other than a grunt and an interested nod now and then, Tom kept silent until she finished, then shook his head and frowned. "I've only had a quick look, so I really can't say. Tell you what. I'll take these home with me tonight and look them over. Like as not, they contain nothing more than minor mistakes."

Laurie felt relieved already. "Of course, they must be mistakes, but I wasn't sure, and I didn't want to bother Darcy about it."

Tom smiled with understanding. "Of course, you didn't. He's got enough on his mind, what with running two gold mines."

"That's it exactly." No, it wasn't, but of course she couldn't explain what really bothered her. If the figures in the ledgers didn't match, then either Hugh had made false entries, or her father had. Either way, she didn't know which would be more disheartening, to discover her father was a crook, or her brother.

In the afternoon, when the shift ended, she stood in her usual place outside the mine entrance, doing her job with the time sheets. When Kenvern emerged, she asked him to wait because she'd like to talk to him. He stood by patiently until the last miner had gone, and they were alone. "You wanted to speak to me, ma'am?"

What an imposing figure he was, towering over her, gleaming with sweat, his face smudged with dirt, a pick resting on his powerful shoulder. "Yes, Kenvern. You had mentioned you wished you could talk better English and improve your reading and writing skills. I talked to my sister, and we have a plan. We'd be happy to assist you, if you're still so inclined."

A smile wreathed Kenvern's broad face. "I'm still so inclined, ma'am. Just tell me what to do."

"Come to our house after dinner tomorrow night. Say, around seven o'clock. I have in mind a few reading lessons would be helpful, as well as some writing and spelling lessons, too. We'll discuss it further then."

She could see he wanted to throw his arms around her and was about to burst with excitement, but knowing his place, he settled for emitting an elated, "Allycumpooster."

The sight of his enthusiasm warmed her heart. She had done the right thing, even though Mother wouldn't agree. "Yes, indeed, Mr. Trenowden, allycum...cum...what you said. My sister and I shall look forward to tomorrow night."

* * * *

Next day in the office, Tom waited until Darcy had left on an errand before he drew Laurie aside. "I took a close look at the books last night, and you were right. There's a discrepancy, and a big one. Someone altered the books, not in a small way, but in a big, criminal kind of way. Thousands of dollars aren't accounted for."

Just what she was afraid of. She dreaded to ask, but no turning back now. "So, who do you think is responsible?"

"Only two people had access to those ledgers, your brother and your father."

"But which?"

"I don't even have to think about it," Tom answered, his voice strong and sure. "I was friends with your father. Maybe he made some bad decisions, but Sam Sinclair was one of the most honest and trustworthy men I ever knew. He would never have done a thing so sneaky and underhanded as to alter the books. I remember right before he died, he was complaining about the high-graders. Weren't you there that day? He was talking about how he was being robbed blind, how they were stealing the ore every night, and he had no way to stop it, even with a guard. And wasn't Hugh in charge of seeing to it the sluice boxes were guarded? It all makes sense. Hugh was the biggest high-grader of all, stealing that ore behind his father's back. I always suspected. Now I know."

"Then it was my brother." She could hardly get the words out.

"Looks that way, although I suppose you'll want to talk to him, see what he has to say for himself. I'll have to tell Darcy." Tom thoughtfully scratched his forehead. "There's going to be a lot of consequences from this. If Hugh doesn't come back, I don't know as how Darcy will want you to leave anytime soon, being as you've made yourself pretty much indispensable around here. He was telling me just the other day how much he admires the way you've caught on to the job."

At any other time, Laurie would have been pleased at the compliment, but not now. Her brother was a crook. She could hardly think straight. She wasn't sure of anything anymore. "I'll talk to Hugh. Perhaps he has a reasonable explanation."

"You can try, but don't get your hopes up."

The compassion in Tom's voice clearly told her she was grasping at straws and had better face the truth.

Darcy returned. Seeing Laurie talking to Tom, he inquired, "Why the long faces?"

Tom replied, "Looks like we've got some bad news for you."

Laurie returned to her desk and watched as Tom showed Darcy the ledgers. He didn't have to say much. All he had to do was point out the discrepancies. Clearly, Hugh had been stealing from the Monarch Mine. When Tom finished, he discreetly declared he had business to attend to and left the office.

"Will you help me, Laurie?" Darcy sounded dead serious. "I want to go over the ledgers again, make sure I've got this right."

Feeling sick inside, Laurie sat by as Darcy bent over the ledgers, examining each closely. When he closed the cover to the last ledger, he shook his head in disbelief. "My God, the man stole thousands. No wonder Sam was broke. Did your father ever say anything? Wasn't he suspicious?"

"No, never. I knew he used to worry that the mine wasn't paying off like it was before. Apparently, it was Hugh who..." She had to stop a moment. This was so painful, having to reveal the shocking things Hugh had told her in confidence, but if ever there was a time for honesty, it was now. "Hugh told me our father was responsible for the big decrease in profits. He told me how Father gambled every night at the Gold Spike and had lost a fortune."

"At the Gold Spike?" Darcy frowned with puzzlement. "That's crazy. I never saw Sam there, and I live there."

Had her brother been lying? She might as well tell Darcy all of it. "Hugh said Father was carrying on, as he put it, with the owner of the Gold Spike, that Mrs. Wagner, I believe her name is."

"With Lucille?" Darcy looked highly amused. "I assure you Mrs. Wagner was not 'carrying on' with your father."

She almost asked how he could be so sure, then thought better of it. She already knew how. Darcy and Mrs. Wagner were the ones carrying on. This only confirmed what she'd suspected when she saw them in the hotel lobby the night before Valeria's hanging. She could pursue the subject, but at this moment, his relationship with the widow was the least of her worries. "It's hard for me to take this all in. I'm greatly relieved it wasn't my father who did those awful things. I could never quite believe he could be unfaithful to Mother, but Hugh had me almost convinced. Still, it's awful to know my brother is a crook. I'm embarrassed that a member of my family could do such a thing." She had to stop and swallow over the lump in her throat

"This must be hard. I'm sorry you have to hear this about your brother. It must come as quite a shock."

"It's hard, but I'll survive." Nothing more need be said concerning a subject so painful. She'd never admit it, but she wasn't as shocked as he might think. She'd always loved her brother, but she'd grown up resenting the relentless way he teased her. The times he stole her toys out of sheer meanness and broke them or hid them away. His greediness, always making sure he had the biggest piece of cake, candy, or whatever it was. When she complained, Hugh always came back with *I was just teasing. Can't she take a joke?* Their parents always took Hugh's side. They'd glare at Laurie as if she were to blame. Add to that his lack of grief when his wife died, his indifference to his children. No wonder he'd lined his pockets at the family's expense. He'd always put himself first, so why should she be surprised? She rose to leave. "Time to go home. I'll be fine."

He stood and took her hand in his. "You realize Hugh can never come back." His eyes brimmed with sympathy.

"I know." Such a tough man, hard as nails sometimes, but his wholehearted compassion spread like a warm blanket around her and gave her comfort. "Then I'd better stay for a while, since I'm familiar with the time sheets and all."

"I'm surprised." He gripped her hand tighter. "I thought you could hardly wait till Hugh got back so you could return to Philadelphia."

"Of course, I'm anxious to get back, but there's really no rush." Had she really just said that? She could still correct herself. *On second thought, I'm dying to get back to the man I'm madly in love with, so you'll have to find someone else.* But somehow the words wouldn't come out, not when the touch of his hand, the warmth of his compassion sent a surge of yearning within her. His quick intake of breath, the brief flare of desire in his eyes, told her he felt the same. For the briefest of moments, she was sure he'd take her in his arms, but the moment passed, and Darcy pulled back and dropped her hand.

"That's fine, then," he said. "I'll stop by tonight and give Hugh the bad news."

He'd broken the spell and turned strictly business again. So would she. "Thanks, but I'll tell him myself as soon as I get home. It won't be easy, but the sooner he knows, the better. I'll tell him in private. I don't want Mother and Ada to know yet, although I guess they'll find out sooner or later." The passionate moment had ended, if, indeed, it had ever happened in the first place. She went to the coatrack to retrieve her bonnet. Placing it firmly on her head, she remarked, "I hope Hugh takes it well."

"Look, I don't know your brother as well as you do, but I'm guessing there could be trouble. Let me handle it."

"No, I'll be fine." She took up the ribbons of her bonnet and started to tie a bow under her chin.

"Are you sure? Sometimes it's hard to see into the heart of a man. You might find more darkness than you thought was there."

She finished tying the bow and gave it an extra firm tug with both hands. "You mean Hugh? He's greedy and arrogant, but otherwise harmless.

He'd never hurt anyone. I dread telling him, but it has to be done, and I'm the one who'll do it." She gave him a determined nod and left for home.

* * * *

After Laurie left, Darcy settled at his desk and disgustedly shoved the ledgers aside. He'd never liked Hugh, thought him weak and conceited from the first time he met him, and that wasn't all. More than once in his life he'd met a man who set off subtle warning signals in his gut—made him not want to turn his back, check where he'd put his money and his gun. Hugh was such a man. Because he was also a Sinclair, Darcy had kept his mouth shut, but the truth was, he hadn't trusted Hugh from the day he met him. So, fine, he should be grateful he'd seen the last of Hugh Sinclair and no longer need deal with him. But something didn't sit right. Why hadn't he been more persistent? He should have told Laurie he'd take care of informing her brother he was no longer welcome at the Monarch Mine. She might be his sister, but he couldn't get past his suspicion that Hugh Sinclair was a man full of vengeance and hate, and anyone who crossed him did so at their peril, and that included Laurie.

Good God. Darcy leaned back in his chair and gazed in exasperation at the ceiling. He couldn't get his mind off Laurie Sinclair. Holding her hand a while ago, it was all he could do to keep from taking her in his arms again, like that night at the hotel when he'd let his feelings get out of control. Somehow, he suspected she wouldn't have minded if he had, but he must be wrong. She still loved the bug man. If she didn't, she would have said so. Or would she? He'd never understood women and wouldn't pretend to now. And besides, since when had he ever driven himself nearly crazy wondering what a woman was thinking?

But all that didn't matter. Laurie Sinclair belonged to another man. Of course, he would honor that. Any other course of action would be despicable. In future, he must guard what he said to her, how he acted toward her. He'd be friendly, but only to the point politeness required.

Chapter 15

Since Laurie started working at the Monarch, she looked forward to the end of the day when she could relax and play with Mathew and Maryanne, eat dinner, and give her family the latest news and gossip from the mine. Not today. As she drove home, the more she thought, the more she dreaded her upcoming confrontation with her brother. Lately it seemed all he ever talked about was returning to the Monarch. How would he react when informed he couldn't come back? Would he be shocked? Angry? Would he deny everything? What if he confessed what he'd done and begged for a second chance? *But he doesn't deserve one*, she thought bitterly. All her life she'd looked up to her older brother, despite his teasing and meanness. Now she saw him for the man he really was: devious, dishonest, without an honorable bone in his body. He could never be trusted and could never come back. And why would he want to? Father had been easy to fool, but she'd wager either Darcy or Tom, both sharp-witted and shrewd, would soon catch Hugh in the act if he tried to steal again. As of yesterday, she was seeing her brother in a different light. Who knew what he'd try? One thing for sure. He had to be told now, the sooner the better, and no second chance.

Laurie arrived home to find Ada in a high state of repressed excitement. Kenvern would arrive at seven o'clock. She was ready for him, having obtained a copy of McGuffey Reader, the one for fourth grade, as Laurie had recommended. "Do I look all right?" Ada's hair swung prettily away from her shoulders as she twirled around in her best blue muslin dress. Her eyes sparkled. A rosy glow flushed her cheeks.

Ada had always called herself the plain sister. She could never be considered beautiful, but to Laurie's delight, today she was. "You look absolutely gorgeous. Have you told Mother?"

"Yes, and she said she was going to retire to her room directly after dinner." Ada sighed. "She's not happy."

"We'll worry about that later. I must go upstairs and talk to Hugh." He was all Laurie could think of right now, and the more she thought, the angrier she got over what he'd done. Father, the whole family, had trusted him so completely they'd ignored all the signs: his fancy suite of rooms at the Egyptian Hotel; sporty new clothes; the way he'd gone around acting like a rich mine owner when in reality he worked for his father at a mine that was about to go broke. She'd wondered how he was able to afford all the luxuries, and now she knew.

She found Hugh out of bed, dressed and sitting in his room reading. He smiled and got up when she knocked and came in. "Ah, there you are," he said. "Another hard day at the mine? You look tired. Come in and have a seat. I'm thinking of coming down to dinner tonight." He gingerly placed a hand on his left rib cage, the one that had suffered the most damage. "Definitely better. Tomorrow I might even go for a beer at the Gold Spike. I'll be back at the mine before you know it."

Hugh could be charming when he wanted to be, like now, and that made her mission all the more difficult. She had an urge to flee but quickly suppressed it. She'd be a coward if she backed out now. She sank to a chair, returned no answering smile, and solemnly announced, "I've got to talk to you. It's a matter of great importance."

"Really? Oh, my." Hugh got that familiar teasing little smirk on his face, the one that implied nothing she said could be taken seriously.

She had planned on softening the blow by giving him a way out. Maybe she was wrong. Maybe he had an explanation. But not now. For the first time, she found his superior attitude beyond annoying. It had become intolerable. He'd always talked down to her and Ada, treated them like his two sweet but empty-headed younger sisters. She never thought to protest. Weren't women supposed to be empty-headed? She used to think so, but not anymore, and found herself drained of all sympathy. "I've bad news for you, Hugh. You won't be coming back to the Monarch Mine."

He must have been surprised, even though he retained his expression of complete unconcern. "And why is that?"

"Because you were stealing the company blind." She could have gone on, but she'd said what needed to be said, and sat back to wait for his reaction.

Other than a stone-cold stare he had no reaction, at least not one she could see. After a long, chilling pause, he softly inquired, "And what makes you think I'm a thief?"

Ready for his question, she proceeded to give him as complete an answer as she could. The altered accounting ledgers. The conflicting report concerning the daily amount of ore produced. Hugh's high-living style when their father was complaining they were nearly broke. Her anger grew in the telling until she couldn't hold it back. Rising from her chair, she stabbed a finger at him. "You complained about the high-graders stealing our ore. Now it turns out you were the worst high-grader of them all, stealing I-don't-know-how-much from the Monarch, and that's not all. You lied to me when you said Father was gambling all the family's money away when all the time, it was you. How dare you! That man cared for you, loved you, and look how you repaid him."

He sat quietly through her increasingly angry discourse, his expression unchanged. When she finished, he shrugged indifferently and inquired, "Anything else?"

"Yes, something else. Why did you tell me Father was carrying on with that woman who owns the hotel when he did no such thing? I think you did it out of meanness and spite, just to make me feel bad."

A half smile crossed his face. "Ah, so you've been talking to your dear friend, Darcy McKenna. Did he tell you he's also one of Mrs. Wagner's frequent visitors? Her favorite lover, from what I understand. Does that not break your heart?"

She almost gasped but caught herself. Hugh's shrewd eyes never missed a thing. Careful though she'd been, she should have known he'd spot her attraction to Darcy. But she couldn't let him distract her. She'd gone too far to stop now. She took a deep, calming breath and lowered her voice. "To make this easier for all of us, I want you to return to your suite at the Egyptian. You're well enough now, so that shouldn't be a problem."

Hugh's eyes narrowed. "This is my home. You can't kick me out."

She had no intention of backing down. How sad she'd lost all her sympathy for the brother she'd once idolized. "Mother and Ada have got to know the truth. If they don't mind, then come for a visit any time you want. I won't keep you away from your family, especially Mathew and Maryanne, who don't see enough of you anyway. You're lucky, Hugh. If you leave and don't cause any more trouble, we'll do nothing more, and you'll get away with your thievery. Of course, you must agree never to set foot at the Monarch Mine again, or anywhere close."

His eyes blazed with sudden anger, but after a moment he answered pleasantly, "The Monarch is the least of my concerns. As soon as I'm able, and that will be soon, I have other plans."

"Like what?"

He tipped his head and regarded the ceiling, as if pondering whether or not to tell her. "If you must know, for quite some time I've been organizing an expedition. I was, shall we say, out of funds when Father died, but I've recently come across a new source of financing." A smile touched his lips. "Let's just say I have obtained enough money for the expedition and am ready to go."

"Go where?" She couldn't imagine what he had in mind.

"I'm going to find the Lost Lake. Whoever finds it will be rich beyond their wildest dreams, and that, my dear, will be me."

"Are you serious?" She could hardly believe what she was hearing. "There is no Lost Lake. From what I've heard, those rumors have been going around for ages, and there's nothing to them."

He regarded her smugly. "You don't know what I know. Granted, the lake is nearly inaccessible, but others have found it, and so will I."

This was insane, but she didn't care to argue. If he chose to go on a wild goose chase, it was no business of hers. She stood, ready to leave. "I don't care what you do as long as you stay away from the Monarch." She waited for his answer, but he remained silent, giving her a long, contemptuous stare. "Agreed?"

He took his time, deliberately making her stand and wait an uncomfortable length of time for his answer. "I won't be coming down for dinner tonight after all. You may tell Mei Ling she can serve me in my room."

He spoke in a tone cold and clear as ice water. Clearly, he was toying with her, hoping she'd humbly stand there begging for his reply. In the past, she probably would have, but not anymore.

"Tell her yourself." She left without another word, not bothering to close the door behind her.

* * * *

Mother had retired to her room by the time Kenvern Trenowden arrived. Cap in hand, so shy he could hardly speak, he looked as if he might bolt and run at any moment. Both Laurie and Ada went out of their way to put him at ease, and within minutes he began to relax and enjoy himself. As they sat at the kitchen table, Laurie watched with pleasure as her shy, reserved sister blossomed into a talkative, animated young woman who tossed her head flirtatiously and laughed with abandon. And who could blame her? Kenvern might be uneducated and simple-spoken, but with his roguish smile, booming laughter, and masculine good looks, he filled the room with his presence, if not the whole house.

At first, Laurie took an active part in the lesson. She and Ada took turns as they went through the pages of the primer. Soon, however, she noticed that whenever she spoke, Kenvern had difficulty switching his gaze from Ada to her. And Ada could hardly keep her eyes off Kenvern. If nothing else, Laurie could take a hint. When she stood and announced she was tired and going to bed, she knew she hadn't been mistaken. As she left the kitchen, she could have sworn Ada and Kenvern didn't even notice she was gone.

That night, she couldn't sleep for thinking about Hugh. What nonsense about Lost Lake. What did he mean when he talked about "a new source of financing"? He couldn't be serious and was just trying to throw her off. She kept seeing the expression on his face when she told him his theft had been discovered. It wasn't just an angry look, it was a look full of cold fury, of evil intent, a look so threatening the thought of it sent chills up her spine. Darcy was right. She should have let him handle her brother. She'd been foolishly overconfident to think a few words from her would cause the arrogant Hugh Sinclair to meekly give in and agree to stay away from the Monarch. As yet, she hadn't told Mother and Ada. They'd be crushed when they found out, especially Mother, who considered her only son to be the anointed one, the golden hope of the family. Sooner or later they'd have to know the truth, just not tonight. She'd gone through enough for one evening.

So, she was back where she started from. Tomorrow she'd have to tell Darcy she'd failed, and would he please take care of the problem. Which, God help her, she should have done in the first place.

* * * *

The next day, Laurie went to work as usual. She waited until she found Darcy alone in the office before she brought up the subject. "I spoke to Hugh last night."

"And?"

Judging from his clipped answer, he wasn't going to make this easy for her. "And you were right. I don't know if I got through to him or not. He… he…didn't seem to want to cooperate." She hated how she was bumbling. "I did my best. Told him he could never set foot in the Monarch Mine again, but I don't think…" She didn't like the way Darcy was looking at her, so cool, so perceptive, as if he already knew what she was going to say. "All right, I failed. He didn't take it well. You were right, and I was wrong."

"Looks that way."

At least he wasn't gloating. "I guess you're the one who should have talked to him in the first place."

"Looks that way."

"I can't believe he means it, but there's something else he plans to do."

"And what is that?"

"He said he's going to lead an expedition to Lost Lake. You know, the lake that's supposed to have all that gold?"

Darcy started laughing. "Are you serious? That story has been around for years."

"He says he found someone to finance the expedition, so I'm sure he means it."

"Then he's more of a fool than I thought. Where can I find him?"

"He's feeling better. Said he was ready for a beer at the Gold Spike. You might find him there tonight. That would be better than home. As yet, Mother and Ada have no idea what's going on."

"Don't worry, I'll take care of it."

Relief flooded through her. She wished she could tell him how worried she'd been, how very grateful she was, but his distant attitude caused her to respond in kind. "Thank you. I appreciate that."

"So, he might be at the Gold Spike tonight?"

"That's what he told me, but he didn't say what time." She'd said enough but couldn't help adding, "Along with everything else, Hugh told me you were the one carrying on with that woman who owns the Gold Spike."

The strong line of his jaw tightened, ever so slightly. "You mean Mrs. Wagner?"

"Yes, Mrs. Wagner." How dumb could she get? Why had she mentioned the woman? She could kick herself. Darcy might think she was jealous, which she certainly was not. "Not that it matters."

"It doesn't matter at all."

The chill in his voice came through loud and clear. Nothing more to say. "All right then, I'll get back to my time sheets." She turned away, vowing from now on, she'd regard Darcy as her business partner and nothing more. Obviously, that was what he wanted, and she'd be happy to oblige.

* * * *

That night, Darcy ate dinner as usual in the hotel dining room. Afterward, he visited the saloon, a part of the hotel he usually avoided. A tinny version of "Arkansas Traveler" blasted from the piano. Even at this early hour, boisterous crowds of men gathered around the gaming tables. Laurie had said her brother might be here. Sure enough, Hugh sat at the long mahogany bar, taking a swig from a bottle of beer. Darcy slid onto the stool beside him. Hugh looked over, saw who it was and slammed down his bottle. "If it isn't McKenna. Just the man I wanted to see."

One sniff told Darcy this wasn't the man's first beer. His breath reeked of alcohol. "Let's step outside," he said softly. "I want to talk to you."

Hugh snorted. "Why would I want to do that?"

"Because I asked." He rarely resorted to any use of force. Usually a look was enough, especially for someone like this little weasel. "I'll ask one more time. Shall we step outside?" He directed a bullet gaze into Hugh's eyes and held it steady.

Hugh glared back but his gaze quickly faltered, just as Darcy expected. He shifted his eyes away. "Sure. All right. I've got the time," he mumbled.

They went outside and around to the side of the hotel where they could be alone. As they went, Darcy watched Hugh closely. If he was too drunk, no use talking to him. He wasn't staggering, though, and looked sober enough to comprehend good advice. "You already know what I'm going to say. You heard it from your sister."

Hugh's face clouded with anger. "No woman is going to tell me what to do."

"You should have listened. Stay away from the Monarch. Thieves aren't welcome. Out of consideration for your family, no one's going to have you arrested, but don't push your luck, and do not ever again"—Darcy's cold voice grew colder still—"show your face at the mine. Are we clear?"

Hugh's lips quivered with outrage. "By all rights, the Monarch is mine now. I inherited it from my father, and you can't keep me away."

"That's where you're wrong. I own fifty-one percent of the Monarch. That means what I say goes, but I'm not going to argue. Just stay away, and if I hear you've threatened Laurie in any way, you'll hear from me."

Hugh smirked and replied, "Sweet on her, aren't you? But it won't do you any good. She can hardly wait to get back to the love of her life in Philadelphia."

If ever Darcy had an urge to smash his fist in someone's face, it was now. But of course, he wouldn't. This pitiful excuse for a man wasn't worth it. "Are we clear?"

"You high-and-mighty mine owners think you own the world," Hugh answered in a contemptuous tone. "I don't need you to tell me what to do. Mark my words, I'll soon be richer than all of you."

Darcy had to chuckle. "You're going to find Lost Lake? I can only hope you're not serious. It's a myth, Hugh. There's no lost prospector who found a lake covered with a layer of gold dust, no Indians with solid gold fish hooks, no huge gold nuggets lying on the ground."

"Believe what you like, but this time I'll have the last laugh."

Darcy had done his best, but he'd learned long ago some men wouldn't listen to reason, and Hugh was one of them, especially now when he was half drunk and belligerent. "You heard what I said, Hugh. Get back to your beer." He turned and walked away.

Headed for his room, he met Lucille on the staircase. He said hello, and was about to pass by, when she waylaid him with a gentle hand on his arm. "Darcy, what's the matter?" she asked, all motherly concern.

"Nothing. Just tired."

Sometimes she had a shrewd way of looking at him when she didn't believe him, like now. "Come to my room, and we'll have tea," she said.

"Well..."

"Just tea."

Soon he was sitting in the room he'd avoided these past few weeks, a room he always thought of with pleasure for more reasons than one. How could he not find comfort in the faint scent of her lavender sachet, the soft ticktock of her ormolu clock on the mantel, the rich gleam of her fine silver tea service, the teacups so fragile he might break one just by looking at it. He took a sip of the tea she'd just made. "I've always liked this room. I feel at peace here."

"Thank you." She cocked her head. "Now tell me what's wrong."

Knowing he could trust her completely, he told her about Hugh, how he'd stolen God only knew how much from the Monarch Mine, and now might cause trouble.

She listened carefully, as she always did. When he finished, she remarked, "That's terrible. What an awful man, but I'm sure you can handle him."

"Not only that." Darcy added, "He's planning on finding the Lost Lake. Says he'll soon be richer than all of us."

"That old story? How ridiculous." She gave him her familiar piercing gaze. "Now what else is wrong?"

"Nothing."

"Oh, yes, there is. It's that Sinclair girl, isn't it?"

"She's already taken. I told you that."

"Oh, really?" Lucille looked faintly amused. "Then what were you two doing in your room that night? Playing tic-tac-toe?"

"How did you know?"

"Good heavens, I own the hotel, Darcy. Nothing escapes me. And don't think you've hurt my feelings. Nothing would give me more pleasure than to see you married and settled down. As for your Miss Sinclair—"

"She's not *my* Miss Sinclair. I'm an honorable man, Lucille. I'm not taking another man's woman, and that's final."

She sighed patiently. "Sometimes honor can be overdone. She's not married to him, is she?" He shook his head. "Then she's fair game, far as I'm concerned. You're not yourself, Darcy. No one would notice but me, but ever since you met her, you've had an unsettled look about you, like something struck you, and you're not sure what. Obviously, you care for her, and I'd wager the young lady cares for you, although she might not want to admit it, maybe not even to herself."

He took another sip of tea before he answered. "I'll think about it."

"You do that, and here's my final word on the subject. The next time you get the chance, and I'm sure you will, forget about honor and seize the opportunity. You may be surprised."

Chapter 16

Hugh moved out some time during the night, so quietly no one heard him leave. "Why didn't he tell us?" Elizabeth lamented the next morning. "He didn't even leave a note."

Ada had no idea. "I don't think he even said goodbye to his children."

"You don't need to worry," Laurie said. "I'm fairly certain he decided to move back to the Egyptian."

"Seems odd he left in the middle of the night," Ada commented.

"But why wouldn't he at least say goodbye?" Elizabeth asked in a plaintive voice.

Laurie braced herself. The moment she dreaded had arrived, and no escaping it. She could conceal the truth no longer. "You'd better sit down. I have something to tell you."

By the time she finished revealing the grim facts about her brother, Ada had run to her room, and her mother was staring in shocked disbelief. "You're saying Hugh's a liar and a thief?"

"That's what I'm saying." At least the truth was out. Ada would be all right after she recovered from the initial shock, but this was a terrible blow for Mother. "There's no way I can make this go away. From what I gather, Hugh was stealing from the Monarch over a long period of time. He wasn't simply pilfering now and then. He stole thousands. Maybe we should have questioned his extravagance, but I trusted him so completely I never thought to ask."

Plainly, Elizabeth had yet to believe her and glared at her defiantly. "I've always had Hugh on a pedestal. He could do no wrong."

"We all had him on a pedestal. We were blind to his faults because we loved him."

"He's my firstborn child, my one and only son. I'll always love him no matter what you say, and frankly, I don't know if I believe you or not."

"I understand. Nothing's going to change that." Laurie gave a silent prayer of thanks that she'd been wise enough not to mention Hugh's despicable lies about Father's supposed gambling habit, let alone his carrying on with Mrs. Wagner. Mother was suffering enough already without knowing the whole story. For herself, Laurie wished her brother well but had lost every last shred of love and respect she'd ever had for him, and that would never change.

Elizabeth dabbed at her eyes with her handkerchief. "Why are we even here? What reason do we have for staying in this awful place?"

Laurie patiently explained what Mother already knew, that the new vein they'd discovered had yet to pay off, but it could happen any day now. When it did, they could go home, not defeated and broke, but as the richer-than-ever Sinclairs. Heads held high, they would resume the same life of luxury they'd left behind, maybe better than before. "It could happen any day now. We mustn't give up."

Laurie's words of encouragement didn't seem to have any effect. Elizabeth sat listening with her shoulders slumped, looking as if her world had ended, and from her point of view, perhaps it had. "Nothing good will happen," she said morosely. "We're doomed, and I know it."

Laurie hated seeing her mother like this. There was a time when she'd resented Elizabeth's overbearing attitude, and the way she tried to run her daughters' lives. How ironic that now she'd give anything to see her mother back to her normal self again, issuing orders, bossy, and demanding. Anything would be better than seeing her as she was now, sad and grieving, her spirit crushed and defeated.

* * * *

During the next two weeks, except for Darcy's still-distant attitude, Laurie enjoyed working at the mine. The more she learned, the more she didn't want to leave. Early on, she realized doing the time sheets wasn't enough. Now she wanted to know all there was to know about mining. Aware of her desire to learn, Tom went out of his way to teach her.

"If you're gonna run a mine, you got to know how to grade gold. It's the number of grams per ton of ore," he told her. "The value of a gold mine is determined by the grade of the ore and how difficult it is to extract and distribute." She listened carefully and took in every word. As she became better acquainted with the miners, she lost her fixed ideas about how uncouth some of them were and gradually came to realize how much these hardworking men sacrificed, toiling ten hours a day in the dark, and all to put food on the table for their families. She admired them all and enjoyed their down-to-earth humor when she checked their time sheets at the end of the day.

Hugh hadn't shown his face, thank God, either at home or the Monarch. She could only hope Darcy had scared him away for good.

Brandon must have received her letter by now. His letter in reply should arrive any day. At first, she'd eagerly awaited the arrival of the daily mail, but not so much anymore. She'd been so busy she'd given little thought concerning whether he'd wait for her or not. Of course, he would, and she wouldn't waste her time worrying about it.

One day she noticed a worried frown on Tom's face. When she asked what was wrong, he first told her nothing was wrong. When she persisted and asked again, he replied, "Did you notice our daily output of ore has dropped? I don't want to worry you, but that new vein of gold we got so excited about is petering out. You never know, though," he hastened to reassure her. "It might pick up again or we could strike a new vein tomorrow that'll be twice as rich."

Although Tom told her not to worry, of course she did. By now, she was avoiding talking to Darcy alone, but that evening before she left, she got him aside. "Tom says the new gold vein is petering out. Is that true?"

He gave her a reluctant nod. "We're down to about fifty tons of ore a day, and that's not good."

"And you didn't think to tell me?"

"I didn't want to worry you."

"Don't treat me like some empty-headed female. You may own fifty-one percent of this mine, but the Sinclairs own forty-nine percent, which, if you ask me, is a significant enough figure that I should be informed of all that's going on."

He solemnly nodded in agreement. "You're right. I let a lot of old prejudices mess with my thinking, and I apologize. As a member of the Sinclair family, you're entitled to be told everything." He proceeded to tell her pretty much what Tom already said. Unless they discovered another rich vein soon, the Monarch Mine was in deep trouble. He ended with, "Again, I apologize. In future, I'll forget you're a woman and keep you informed, be it good news or bad."

His thorough explanation and sincere apology swiftly dissolved her hostility. "Thank you. I appreciate your honesty." With a trace of laughter in her voice, she added, "Of course, you needn't entirely forget I'm a woman. I shouldn't like that."

She expected he'd make some flippant remark in reply, but the look that came over his face was anything but humorous. His eyes drilled into hers so intently she caught her breath. "More than you'll ever know, I could never forget you're a woman, Laurie. Can't you understand?"

Before she could even think to form a reply, he walked out of the office, leaving her watching after him, her heart racing. So, he did care about her. And here she'd been thinking he'd been acting cool because he didn't want to be around her anymore. It all came clear. She'd been blind not to reach beyond her own hurt feelings enough to see that he, being the honorable man he was, would not interfere with her plans to marry the man she loved, the man she'd been dying to get back to. She needed to remind herself that soon she'd be leaving Lucky Creek. Before she knew it, she'd be back in Philadelphia planning her wonderful wedding to Brandon. The best of Philadelphia society would attend. She'd wear the most beautiful wedding dress ever…

What's the matter with me? Why am I not excited?

What happened to the elation she'd felt every time she thought about marrying Brandon? She tried to picture him, but her mind stayed blank. Surely all the wonderful memories would soon come flooding back. Surely, she'd soon be yearning to be in his arms. She just had to think about it for a while, and put her lustful, totally inappropriate thoughts of Darcy out of her head forever.

* * * *

That night after she'd arrived home and done her chores in the stable, she found her mother alone in the parlor, knitting at a furious pace, a sure sign she was upset.

"What's wrong, Mother?"

Elizabeth tossed her head with indignation. "Ada is entertaining that Cornishman in the kitchen nearly every night now. I didn't mind when you claimed you were trying to help a poor, illiterate miner, but this is ridiculous. I'm beginning to think she likes him, despite his background. Will you please do something, Laurie? Ada's bent on having him here and won't listen to me."

She might have known Mother wouldn't stay silent and depressed for long. Now she was demanding answers, and who could blame her? She'd been assured Kenvern would be coming over twice a week, at most, for reading lessons, which Laurie and Ada, in the spirit of generosity and concern for those in need, would be happy to provide. Their contribution to charity, so to speak. But things hadn't quite worked out that way. Kenvern Trenowden could be found in their kitchen nearly every night now. So could Ada, but not Laurie, as she was well aware she wasn't missed at all. Ada had proven to be an apt teacher, and Kenvern an amazing pupil. Already he'd easily read his way through all the McGuffey Reader and had started reading a collection of short stories by Edgar Allan Poe. Kenvern's reading skills had increased tremendously. His Cornish dialect was fast disappearing, replaced by the proper English he'd longed to speak. Not that the kitchen had become a solemn area of learning. Every night, the sound of Kenvern's booming laughter filled the house, punctuated by Ada's giggles. Obviously, they were having a delightful time together, which Mother couldn't fail to notice. "It appears they fancy each other," Laurie replied, aware she was stating the obvious. "He's a fast learner and quite bright."

"That's not the point." Elizabeth threw her knitting down. "He's nothing but an uneducated Cornishman, far below our class."

Laurie concealed her exasperation. She would try to explain, although her words would doubtless fall on deaf ears. Darcy had discussed this very subject once. She remembered what he'd said, and it was worth repeating. "This isn't Philadelphia, Mother. This is the West, where no one's concerned about what class someone's in. Kenvern is a fine man, a little rough around the edges, maybe, but who cares? No one's judging him by his fine manners, or lack thereof, and you shouldn't either." She'd surprised herself. Never had she spoken to her mother more firmly.

Elizabeth sat back in surprise. "Have you no concern for your sister? Don't tell me you want her married to some Lucky Creek oaf who's just now learning to read and write. She needs to return to Philadelphia where she can find a man of quality, a man with connections who comes from a fine family."

Her mother didn't understand, and probably never would, but she'd give it one more try. "Haven't you noticed how Ada goes around the house singing these days? She's happier than I've ever seen her. I don't know what's going to happen, but would you at least agree to leave her alone for now?"

"What choice do I have?" Elizabeth asked in a martyred tone. "All I can say is, this family is ruined if we don't get back to Philadelphia soon. And might I ask why you aren't more anxious to return? Aren't you dying to get back to Brandon?"

"Of course, I am," Laurie quickly replied. She'd given the answer she was supposed to give, but did she mean it? These days she so enjoyed working at the Monarch. She loved what she did, and she loved working with Darcy, even though he kept her at arm's length. She'd adjusted, and she was fine with that, or so she kept telling herself. And meanwhile, she hardly thought of Brandon anymore. Whenever she tried to picture him, his exact image got blurry, like he was disappearing into a heavy fog.

Later that night, Laurie knocked on her sister's door. "Ada? I've come to talk."

"Please do come in." Perched cross-legged on her bed, dressed in her voluminous white nightgown, Ada looked as perky as Laurie had ever seen her. Laurie joined her on the bed. "Sounds like you and Kenvern had a lot of fun tonight."

"Isn't he wonderful?" Ada blissfully responded. "I love his laugh. I love everything about him."

"I do believe you're in love with him."

Ada's face lit with happiness. "And he loves me. He's told me so."

Laurie wanted to laugh and cry at the same time. How wonderful Ada had finally found a man who loved her. How sad he had to be a man their mother could never accept. "I'm happy for you, Ada, truly I am. Kenvern has many fine qualities, but—"

"Have you ever seen a man so handsome?" Ada burst out. "He's so kind and caring and gets those adorable dimples in his cheeks whenever he smiles."

Plainly Ada was so smitten she'd never listen to anything resembling common sense. Yet Laurie couldn't ignore the one problem that loomed large on her sister's otherwise bright horizon. "Mother's not happy about Kenvern."

Ada's smile faded. "I know. You would think he was some sort of criminal, the way she looks at him. So far, she hasn't said anything, but it's obvious how she feels, and I don't expect she'll stay silent much longer."

"She thinks you should wait until we get back to Philadelphia where you can find someone more suitable."

"But I don't want to go back to Philadelphia. I want to stay right here and marry Kenvern Trenowden. Good grief, I'm twenty-three years old, and know what I'm doing. He's going to ask me soon, and when he does, I'll say yes, no matter what Mother thinks."

Startled, Laurie sat back and asked, "Where has my meek, shy little sister gone? I've never known you to act this way."

Ada burst into laughter. "I've never been this way. Part of it is, I'm so in love with Kenvern I'd do anything to be with him. Another part,

I think, is that living in Lucky Creek is different from living back east. There's more freedom here. People do what they want and aren't tied to rigid rules. Remember in Philadelphia how we had to have tea at exactly four o'clock every afternoon?"

"And we wouldn't dream of going visiting without our calling cards."

They both laughed, thinking how silly that would look in Lucky Creek.

Laurie continued, "I think I've talked Mother into giving the whole situation more time."

"Thanks for that, although it's not likely I'll change my mind. And by the way"—Ada got a playful grin on her face—"lately you haven't seemed all that anxious to leave yourself. What's going on? Have you fallen out of love with Brandon? Or could there possibly be someone else?"

From the shrewd way Ada was looking at her, Laurie knew she'd guessed the truth. "I'm in a bit of a dilemma."

"It's Darcy McKenna, isn't it? The man you *don't* like?"

Laurie took a playful swipe at her sister. "You've guessed, haven't you? The more I'm with him, the less I find myself thinking about Brandon."

"It was getting pretty obvious. You talk about Darcy a lot lately, all of it good. What changed your mind?"

"I like that he makes decisions fast and doesn't dawdle around. He's firm but fair with his employees and keeps his temper, no matter what."

"That's all?"

She'd always been completely honest with her sister and would be now. "Of course, that's not all. I never used to find him attractive, but now the more I look at him the handsomer he seems."

"Have you kissed?"

"Yes."

"More?"

"Yes."

Soon, to Ada's titillated delight, she was recounting the night she spent with Darcy at the Gold Spike Hotel. She had to explain at length about how they could have possibly done such a thing on the very night before Valeria was hanged. "I hardly understand it myself. Maybe part of it had to do with how wrought up we both were because of the near lynching. I just know we couldn't keep our hands off each other, and that's how it started."

"You were so swept away on the wings of love you couldn't help yourselves," Ada volunteered.

"Perhaps." Laurie laughed to herself, picturing Darcy's reaction if told he'd been swept away on the wings of love. Still, Ada could be right.

"So what are you going to do?" Ada asked in her practical voice.

"I honestly don't know. I've committed myself to Brandon. I haven't heard from him yet, but I'm sure he expects me to return soon as I can. Since that night, Darcy has been friendly enough but standoffish, like he wants nothing more to do with me, other than as someone who works at the mine. After all, I'm not the only woman in his life. He's cozy with Mrs. Wagner, the woman who owns the Gold Strike. Perhaps there are others, I just don't know."

"There's no one like you, Laurie. You're bright and you're beautiful. Have you forgotten all those suitors in Philadelphia who wanted to marry you? Darcy's just being honorable. He thinks you're dying to go back to Brandon. Unless you let him know otherwise, he'll stay away."

"I'll think about it."

"I think you better had before you head back east to marry a man you no longer love."

No longer loved? Could it be true? "I have a confession to make. Whenever I try to picture Brandon, all I can see are his bug collections. I can't see his face anymore."

"Shame on you," Ada exclaimed, and the two collapsed, laughing, onto the bed.

Chapter 17

What had happened to the gold-bearing ore? As the next week went by, an atmosphere of gloom hung over the office of the Monarch Gold Mine. Iron cars heaped full of ore still rolled from the entrance, but as Tom pointed out, the quality of the ore "just ain't worth a damn." As yet, no one acknowledged they'd soon be shutting down, but the obvious threat hung over everyone, from the owners down to the lowliest shoveler.

In an unexpected fashion, the Trenowden brothers were first to make a change. One night, in the midst of a reading lesson, Kenvern blurted, "I'm quitting the mine, Ada. My brothers and I will be going into business for ourselves." He explained that he, Petrok, and Steren never had any intention of spending the rest of their lives toiling in the darkness for somebody else. They'd been saving their money for years and now had enough to escape a life in the mines. Kenvern would be leaving first, being as he was now the educated member of the family. He would soon be opening a much-needed dry goods store in the town of Lucky Creek.

"Think of it." Kenvern's eyes sparked with enthusiasm. "I can see the sign, Trenowden Brothers Dry Goods Store. Petrok and Steren can soon be sending for their wives, and as for me"—he gazed at Ada with adoring eyes—"I'm only waiting until I have plenty to offer, but you know how I feel."

Since then, Ada had been walking around in a blissful cloud of happiness, although she still hadn't got up courage enough to tell her mother.

Since her frank conversation with Ada, Laurie had been in a quandary. She wanted very much to have an honest talk with Darcy, but he remained standoffish and never gave her an opportunity to speak her mind. But that would be difficult because what on earth was in her mind? Was she ready to forget Brandon? She wished she could sort out her feelings for Darcy, but how could she when she could never get past the rigid boundary of politeness he'd set up for himself? She still wasn't sure. Pride alone would keep her from asking, and possibly making a fool of herself, and so she kept silent.

One day, when the day's production of valuable ore had fallen to nearly zero, Darcy spoke to Laurie, a grim look on his face. "It's not looking good. I'll give it a few more days at best, but if nothing happens, we'll have to shut her down."

She'd been expecting this, but still, his news hit her hard. "The whole mine?"

"All of it. I hate to disappoint you. This is my fault. If I hadn't expected that vein to keep going, I'd have told you a long time ago to get out, go back to Philadelphia."

"No one's to blame. You warned me of the risk." She could hardly speak in a normal voice, just thinking what the consequences would be if they lost the Monarch. Mother's worst nightmare come true. They could scrape up enough money to get home, but then the family would be poor, and Mother would be at the mercy of Aunt Florence. At least Ada would be spared. Laurie couldn't imagine her lovestruck sister returning to Philadelphia now that she'd found Kenvern. As for Hugh, aside from a few quick visits with Ada and Mother, he wasn't in their lives anymore. But no doubt Mother would be devastated. "There's no chance at all?" she asked.

"Not much. We'll go down a few hundred feet more, but I'm not expecting anything. I'm sorry, Laurie. I wish this had had a better ending. But at least you can feel free to go home now."

And marry Brandon, she knew he was thinking. The unsaid words stood like a stone wall between them. She so wished she could unburden her heart, tell him she hardly thought of Brandon anymore, but how could she when his every word, look, and gesture were so guarded she never had a chance to speak her mind. "Thank you for being honest with me, Darcy. I know you tried." She hated giving such an impersonal answer, but at least she could walk away from him with her pride intact.

That night, she got Ada alone and gave her the bad news. As expected, Ada stubbornly clamped her jaw and declared, "Rich or poor, you couldn't drag me back to Philadelphia now. I dread telling Mother, but one of these days I've got to."

Laurie hated giving Mother even more bad news, but she had a right to know about the impending closure of the mine, the sooner the better. When told, Elizabeth took the news more calmly than Laurie expected. "Are you sure?" she asked.

"Darcy said they'd dig a couple of hundred feet more, but he's not expecting anything."

"Then I shall pray for a miracle."

"Let's hope you find one," Laurie replied, although she highly doubted any such miracle would occur.

* * * *

Late the following afternoon, Darcy, Tom, and Laurie were in the office when Petrok Trenowden burst in. "Mr. McKenna, Mr. Crain, you've got to come look." The two rushed out of the office and headed for the mine, Laurie following. At the entrance, she stood anxiously waiting while the three men disappeared inside. She could hardly dare hope for good news, but why else had Petrok been smiling? After an agony of waiting, she heard a faint cheer go up from deep inside. She waited, hardly able to breathe until Tom and Darcy appeared again, both with broad smiles.

"By golly, we hit it!" Tom exclaimed.

In a quieter but still exuberant voice, Darcy told her, "We've found another vein, Laurie. It's even bigger than the first one."

She clasped her hands in front of her heart. "Then the Monarch won't be closing?"

Both men broke into laughter. Tom grabbed her and swung her around. "You're rich, little lady. You should see the size of that vein, a stream of golden ore at least thirty inches wide. I'd wager it'll take years before it gives out."

Men started pouring from the entrance, everyone in a jubilant mood. They'd been given the rest of the day off and were on their way to town to celebrate. "You should come along," a beaming Tom told Laurie.

Happy though she was, she couldn't picture drinking beer with a bunch of boisterous miners in a saloon. "Thanks for the kind offer, but I'll just close the office and go home." As the miners scattered, headed for town, she started back to the office and soon noticed Darcy following. "You're not going to celebrate?" she asked.

"There's time enough for that later." He held the office door open for her, and they stepped inside. "I'll close the office if you'd like to get home. You must be anxious to tell your mother and sister. Just think, you can go back to Philadelphia in style now. From what I saw of that vein, you'll never have to worry about money again."

He might be making a show of sounding calm and detached, but she hadn't missed the suppressed excitement in his voice. Hearing it, a reckless mood possessed her. For once, she wouldn't hide her true feelings like she usually did and would say exactly what was on her mind. "You're not fooling me for a minute, Darcy McKenna. You're just as excited as I am, and you might as well show it."

He stared for a moment, then tipped his head back and burst into laughter. "Of course, I'm excited. But this means you'll be leaving soon, and I won't like that." His gaze traveled over her face and searched her eyes. "I won't like that at all."

The next move was up to her. Common sense prompted her to step back, thank Darcy again for his efforts in saving the mine, then leave for home. That's what she ought to do, but she wasn't going to. She reached out to touch his arm and looked directly into those deep, amazingly blue eyes. "Finding that vein means a lot to me for a lot of reasons, and you're one of them."

For a moment, he didn't move. Had she made a mistake? The prolonged anticipation became almost unbearable until he gripped both her arms and asked in a voice harsh with emotion, "What reasons, Laurie?"

"For one thing, I don't want to go home."

"And why is that?"

It was time to throw caution to the winds. She slid her hands up his chest and rested them on his shoulders. "Because I don't want to leave you. And because—"

She never finished her sentence and soon forgot what she was going to say as he pulled her into his arms. With a pent-up emotion explosively released, he devoured her mouth with a kiss that ignited a heat that spread through her blood and made her forget everything except how much she wanted him.

"God, how I've been wanting to do that," he said in a whisper when he came up for air.

"I haven't forgotten." Her heart slammed in anticipation as she pressed against the hard, flat planes of his body. Within the next few minutes, a blur that later she barely remembered, they had made sure the door was locked and the old couch in the corner cleared, its contents tossed unceremoniously to the floor. This was the second time they'd made love. After the first, she'd thought it couldn't get any better, but it did. Afterward, as they lay exhausted on the rickety old couch, totally content, he asked, "So you want to stay here in Lucky Creek?"

She snuggled closer, running her hand over the hard muscles of his chest. "I don't want to leave you."

"What about Brandon?" Before she could answer, he touched a finger to her lips. "Wait. Don't answer. You've got enough on your mind right now. You'd better get home before your family hears the good news from someone else."

She agreed she better had. Together they straightened the office, carefully replacing the items so hastily tossed from the sofa. "Tom will never know," Laurie remarked when they were done, and the office was neat again.

Darcy chuckled. "Tom doesn't miss a thing, but don't worry, he'll be happy for us." They left the office. He helped her hitch the horses and said he'd follow her down the mountain on Champ. "It's almost dark, so be careful."

By the time she got home, night had almost fallen. She brought the buggy to a halt in front of the house. He pulled Champ to a halt beside her. "Any regrets?" he asked.

She smiled and replied, "None, whatsoever."

"Tonight belongs to your family. You'll be wanting to give them the good news." His eyes brimmed with tenderness and passion, sending the message she wanted to hear. "We'll talk tomorrow."

"Of course." On a whim, she added, "I'd wager Mrs. Wagner has already heard the news. I'm sure she'll be very happy for you."

"I'm sure she will," he answered straight-faced but with a faint grin that told her he knew she was teasing.

"Tomorrow." He gave her a quick salute and rode away.

As she watched his horse disappear in the growing shadows, she repeated, "Tomorrow," in an ecstatic whisper. A simple word, commonly used, but spoken in a tone that held a promise of wonderful things to come. In a matter of hours, her life had done a complete turnaround, so swiftly she could hardly absorb it. The new vein of gold meant they wouldn't be poor after all. Darcy had revealed he cared, putting an end to those miserable weeks she'd spent thinking he didn't. Tomorrow they would talk. She already knew what he'd say and what she'd say in reply. How could her life get any better?

Anxious to get inside with the good news, she drove around back to the stable, hurriedly unhitched the horses, gave them a quick brushing and fed them their oats. Stepping inside the house, she heard voices coming from the front parlor. Good. She'd hoped to find Mother and Ada together, and the children, too. But wait, was that a man's voice? How strange. What man would come visiting at this hour? At the parlor door, she paused. All the family was there, and a man sat in their best giltwood chair. When he saw her, he stood and smiled. "Hello, Laurie, are you surprised?"

Surely her eyes had deceived her. But he was still standing there, real and in the flesh. She heard herself say, "Why, yes, this is quite a surprise."

"Well, it's me, sweetheart. I've come to fetch you home."

She hoped she didn't look as thunderstruck as she felt as Brandon Cooper strode across the parlor and swept her into his arms.

Chapter 18

Brandon had become a myth in her mind, so remote, so far away, he could have been living in the cloud palace over Mount Olympus. Now here he sat in her parlor, handsome as ever with his golden hair and wide smile, his teeth strikingly white against his tanned face. Both Mother and Ada were going out of their way to be cordial. How delighted they were to meet him after all the wonderful things Laurie had said about him. How deeply impressed they were that he'd traveled clear from Philadelphia just to see her. "Aren't you thrilled, Laurie?" Elizabeth asked.

"Uh, yes, thrilled." While her family was giving Brandon the warmest of welcomes, Laurie made a valiant effort to conceal her shock. As if someone else were speaking, she heard the correct phrases coming from her mouth with just the right amount of delighted disbelief.

"My goodness, what a surprise. I can't believe you're here."

"You're looking well, Brandon. How was your journey?"

Brandon appeared to be in a buoyant mood. "My journey was amazingly easy. I took a steamboat from New York to Chagres, Panama. Crossed the Isthmus in a day on that new railroad they built. Caught a ship to San Francisco, and here I am." Sitting next to Laurie on the settee, he took her hand and gave it an affectionate squeeze. "So wonderful to see you again."

Elizabeth beamed with sheer joy, her most ambitious dreams for her daughter come true. "We're just so delighted that you're here, Mr. Cooper. Laurie has told us all about you, and of course I'm familiar with the prestigious Cooper family. I can't imagine why you and Laurie didn't meet sooner, being as we also lived on Society Hill."

"I, too, regret we didn't meet sooner, Mrs. Sinclair," Brandon replied deferentially. "Until recently, I've been deeply devoted to my entomological pursuits. Dedicated myself to science, so to speak, but now I've rearranged my priorities. By the way, my sincere condolences. When I heard the sad news about Mr. Sinclair, and how Laurie was actually working in a gold mine, I couldn't stay away any longer, and I—"

Laurie let out a little gasp. "I forgot about the mine." The shock of seeing Brandon had knocked the exciting discovery at the Monarch right out of her head. "Excuse me for interrupting, Brandon, but I must give my family the good news. How could I have forgotten?" She described the newly found vein of gold at the Monarch. "Mr. McKenna says it's the richest he's ever seen, and it may produce for many years to come." She wanted to add, "So we won't be poor after all," but a guest was present, so she refrained.

"That's wonderful!" Ada exclaimed. The children were too young to completely understand, but they caught the excitement, laughed, and clapped their hands.

Mother looked as dazed as Laurie felt. "I can't believe it. This means we can all go home now, does it not?" As realization hit, her face lit with happiness. "Just think, Laurie, you can get married in Philadelphia. Oh, how exciting. You'll have a wonderful wedding with all the best families invited. We'll start planning the minute we get back."

Laurie didn't know how to answer. Still shocked and dumbfounded, she couldn't get her thoughts in order. Did she want to go home? Plan her wedding to Brandon? *No.* She desperately needed time to clear her head. If she spoke up now, revealed her doubts, she'd shock them all and ruin the evening for everyone. She must have a discussion with Brandon, but she'd wait until tomorrow. Yes, by far the better plan. She would get him alone and tell him...what? That she'd fallen in love with someone else? That she loved her job at the mine? But what about her commitment to Brandon? How could she hurt him when he'd come all this way? But she must. There was no other way. "We'll see about the wedding later," she remarked noncommittally. "There's too much else going on."

"It's never too soon to start planning," her mother replied, not the least daunted.

The family spent the rest of the evening in a jovial mood. Mei Ling fixed a fine dinner. Mother decided they should open a bottle of the champagne Sam had stored in the cellar. "So, we can properly celebrate the finding of the new gold vein," she announced. "As well as our happiness that Laurie and Brandon will soon be married." She invited Brandon to stay in the guest room, but he declined.

"Thanks, but I've already booked a room at the Egyptian Hotel, where Hugh's staying."

For a fleeting moment, Laurie wondered how Brandon knew where her brother was staying, considering no one had mentioned it. But by the time he left, she'd forgotten such a trivial concern. He'd said he would return in the morning, take her to breakfast, and she could show him the town. He hadn't asked if she was busy, had just assumed she had nothing more important to do than be with him. Why hadn't she spoken up? Told him she was needed at the Monarch Mine? The more she thought, the less she admired her spineless behavior. By the time they all went to bed, she was disgusted with herself, and for more reasons than one.

She was in her nightgown when Ada came in and perched on her bed. "Are you excited?" she asked.

"More like astonished and concerned."

"I didn't think you were all that thrilled to see him."

"How could you tell?"

"Because I caught that horror-struck look on your face when you walked in. Mother missed it of course. You covered it up fast, but I knew what you were thinking."

"Not so long ago, I would have swooned with delight if I'd found Brandon sitting in my parlor."

"What a shame. The man's gorgeous—all that blond hair and those gleaming white teeth." Ada's brow creased with worry. "Are you sure? Maybe you haven't had time to think it through. When you do, maybe you'll find you're still in love with him."

If there was one person Laurie could talk to, it was her sister. She wouldn't hold back. What a relief to let it all pour out. "For years I waited for him. You wouldn't believe the number of times I cried myself to sleep because I loved him so desperately, and he kept postponing our wedding date. Now he's come clear across the continent to see me. Fancy that. I should be thrilled, my most heartfelt wish come true, but instead my heart sunk when I saw him."

"Is it Darcy McKenna?" Ada asked, regarding her with sharp, assessing eyes. "It is, isn't it?"

At the mention of Darcy's name, Laurie couldn't help but smile. "I told you how standoffish he's been, but not today. We celebrated finding the gold vein together. It was…quite a warm moment, I would say. We're good friends again, and more."

"Oh, my goodness." Ada took a moment to digest this latest. "When will you tell Brandon? What about Mother? She's already planning the wedding, and I can only imagine how crushed she'll be when she finds out how you really feel. What a mess this is, Laurie. Why didn't you speak up when he first got here?"

"I have no excuses," Laurie replied honestly. "Other than I was so shocked at first I didn't know what to say. Then I got all wishy-washy and didn't want to make a big scene."

"You were only being thoughtful and considerate."

Laurie vigorously shook her head. "No, I wasn't. I was being a coward. Men have the right idea. Darcy wouldn't have dodged and evaded the truth like I did tonight. He wouldn't have worried about spoiling the evening for everyone. He would have said straight out, "Sorry, Brandon, but you need to know there's somebody else now.""

"That's because men are more direct about such things," Ada answered in her soothing voice. "They don't care about hurt feelings. We women have more compassionate hearts."

"Don't make excuses for me, Ada. I should have spoken up. Forget about compassionate hearts. Brandon gets told first thing tomorrow."

Ada heartily agreed Brandon must be told, and quickly. "If you don't, what's Darcy going to think? From what I've seen, he's a man you wouldn't want to mess with."

A sudden fear gripped Laurie's heart. Ada was right. Darcy was indeed a man not to be messed with, a man who'd never understand her cowardly hesitation.

After Ada left, Laurie lay in bed for hours, trying to absorb the amazing events of the day. How elated she'd been over the finding of the new gold vein. How shocked at the sight of Brandon sitting in her parlor. His unexpected arrival had turned her world upside down. So terrible that he'd come all this way for nothing. She hated to disappoint her mother, but what choice did she have? When she thought of Darcy, his passion and tenderness, the way he'd made her feel this afternoon, she knew she must tell Brandon her true feelings in the morning, painful and embarrassing though it would be.

But first she must tell her mother, a task which, upon reflection, was what she dreaded most of all.

* * * *

Next morning, Laurie knocked on her mother's bedroom door and found her already dressed and ready to come downstairs. "Good morning, Mother, I need to talk to you."

"Of course," Elizabeth answered in a jubilant voice. "Isn't it a lovely day?"

Laurie hadn't seen her mother in such a cheerful mood since they left Philadelphia. This would be harder than she'd expected, and she'd already prepared for the worst. She'd made up her mind, though, and nothing could make her change it now. "Sit down. I have something to tell you." When both were seated, she began, "I know this will come as a surprise, but I'm not sure about my feelings for Brandon." Hearing how weak that sounded, she tried again. "What I mean is, I'm not sure I love him." What was the matter with her? That wasn't strong enough, either. "Actually, what I mean to say is, I positively don't love Brandon, and that's because I've fallen in love with someone else."

To her astonishment, Mother started to laugh. "You're not the first bride with the jitters, and you won't be the last."

"It's not jitters. I meant what I said."

Elizabeth rolled her eyes in disbelief. "And just whom are you supposed to be in love with?"

"Darcy McKenna."

"What? Are you out of your mind?" A combination of scorn and disbelief filled Elizabeth's voice. But only for a moment. She started laughing again. "Really, Laurie, you must be joking. What college did Darcy McKenna attend? What degrees does he have? What are his family connections? Have you gone insane? Do you honestly expect me to believe you prefer him over a man of exemplary character and achievement like Brandon?"

"Actually, yes."

Laurie's resolute answer must have finally got through because Elizabeth shot up from her chair and started pacing the floor. "I cannot believe what I'm hearing. All we ever heard was Brandon, Brandon, Brandon, and now you don't love him anymore?" She clenched her fists and stamped her foot. "How could you do this to me?"

Laurie hated to see her mother so distraught. *And it's all my fault.* "I didn't mean... I never thought..."

"You never thought," Elizabeth raged. "Well, it's time you did think." She paced for a while, seeming to calm herself down, and finally sank back into her chair. "You think you don't love Brandon anymore?" she asked in a quieter voice.

"I know I don't love Brandon anymore."

"Will you at least do this for me?"

"Anything." Laurie would have added *within reason*, but seeing her mother in such a state, she didn't have the heart to deny whatever she wanted.

"Then don't tell Brandon yet. Have breakfast with him. Take him to see the town. Give yourself time to get over the shock of seeing him again. Wedding jitters is all it is, you know." Mother had regained her composure, her voice steady and assured. "You'll soon remember why you fell in love with him."

"For how long am I not supposed to tell him?"

"It won't take long for you to come to your senses. Give it a day. You know I always have your best interests at heart. Just twenty-four hours, and you'll see I'm right."

No, I will not, Laurie thought. Never in her life had she seen things more clearly. No more dithering. She didn't have the wedding jitters. Whether she put off telling Brandon for twenty-four hours or twenty-four years, she was done with him. Her mother was wrong, and neither she, nor anyone else was going to tell her what to do. "I'm not going to marry Brandon, and I'm going to tell him so this morning. I'm sorry, but that's the way it is, and I'm not changing my mind."

Elizabeth sank back in her chair looking as if she'd been struck. For a few moments she could only sputter. "You're making a terrible mistake," she finally managed.

"Perhaps, but it will be my mistake and nobody else's."

She must have sounded as if she meant what she said because Mother threw up her hands and declared, "Fine then. You're a grown woman. Do as you please."

"I'll do just that."

Laurie left her mother's bedroom with a burden lifted from her shoulders. She'd almost faltered, followed Mother's demands yet again, but thank goodness, not this time. Now all she had to do was give the bad news to Brandon. What a heady moment. At last she'd be free to do what she pleased. She dreaded telling him. Of course, he'd be devastated. Especially after he'd come all this way, but she'd made up her mind. No turning back now, despite how wretched she felt about hurting him.

* * * *

Elegantly dressed in a cutaway coat and derby hat, Brandon arrived early. The horse and buggy he'd rented awaited Laurie in front. He smiled broadly as he assisted her into the buggy with a flourish. "I hear there's a good restaurant at the Gold Spike Hotel. Shall we eat there?"

What if Darcy was there? She almost said no, then remembered he was an early riser and surely would be at the mine by now. "The Gold Spike would be lovely." She would tell Brandon at breakfast. They would say goodbye, and then she'd head for the Monarch, the only place she really wanted to be. A stab of guilt struck her. How callous she was being! How coldhearted and insensitive. She was about to break a man's heart, but all she could think about was getting to the mine and Darcy.

They arrived at the Gold Spike. Even though she was sure Darcy had already left for the mine, when they entered the Bonanza Restaurant, Laurie looked cautiously around. Of course, he wasn't there. She couldn't relax, though, not until she had that talk with Brandon. She would wait until they'd placed their orders, then tell him.

The waiter had come and gone, but finding the right moment was harder than she thought. Brandon was a talker. Why hadn't she noticed all he did was talk about himself? Halfway through breakfast, she'd as yet to get a word in edgewise. He'd hogged the conversation with lengthy descriptions of his successful expeditions, his latest highly acclaimed discoveries in the entomology world, his journey from Philadelphia to California, which he described in excruciating, boring detail. So different from Darcy, who never rambled or talked about himself, and always got straight to the point. She had just finished the last of her pancakes when she reached the end of her patience. Brandon had just started a discourse on the superiority of Philadelphia restaurants when she laid her fork down and interrupted. "I have something to tell you."

"Oh?" He looked baffled. "Do go ahead, my dear."

"I can't marry you."

He didn't look the least alarmed, just regarded her curiously. "And why is that?"

"Because…" She must be tactful. Mustn't hurt his feelings more than she had to. "I've never known a finer man than you, Brandon, but the thing is, since I've been in California, I've changed. I'm not the same person you knew in Philadelphia. I've gone on to other things, other interests. You wouldn't want me now. I'm…just…different, and it wouldn't be fair to you if I didn't tell you." She'd started out strong and ended up pretty weak, but at least she'd got her message across.

He remained silent as he picked up a piece of toast and buttered it slowly and deliberately. Finally, he looked up at her, a mocking smile on his face. "Are you sure, Laurie?"

"Very sure."

"Is there someone else?"

This would wound him, but she must be honest. "Yes, there is."

"Very well then." With great deliberation, he took a bite of his toast and washed it down with a sip of coffee. If he had a broken heart, he was hiding it well. "I'm disappointed, of course, but if you must know, you weren't my entire reason for coming to California."

She'd been prepared for just about anything but not this. "I'm not?" she asked, knowing how inane that sounded, but his response had left her so astounded she couldn't think what to say.

"No, you're not," he replied, a note of satisfaction in his voice. "Far from it, actually. I did plan to marry you, and I daresay we would have been happy enough, but since you'd rather not"—he raised his chin and peered down his nose at her—"this may sound immodest, but in Philadelphia I'm considered quite the catch. I can have my pick of lovely brides dying to marry me, so rest assured, I'm not in a state of despair because you've rejected me." His lips twisted into a cynical smile. "Now I can concentrate on the real reason I'm here."

"And what is that?" She couldn't imagine what it was.

He settled back in his chair, unruffled and sure of himself. "You don't know this, but for the past few months I've been engaging in correspondence with your brother, whom, by the way, I greatly admire. He had sought my advice on how to form an expedition. I became so interested in his plan that I finally agreed to help him with more than just advice. I became financially involved. That's why I've come here, to watch after my interests, and also, I must admit I'm greatly intrigued by your brother's plans."

She could hardly believe what she was hearing. Hugh had never mentioned any of this. "You mentioned an expedition?"

Brandon's grey eyes suddenly gleamed with excitement. "Hugh has a map, and with it we're going to find Lost Lake. Think of it, Laurie, a lake covered with a sheet of gold. I know it's out there. Besides the map, Hugh has some solid leads as to exactly where it is."

She was about to give Brandon her honest opinion concerning the insanity of such an expedition when, out of the corner of her eye, she saw a man and woman enter the restaurant. She paid no attention until they came closer, and then...

Darcy and Mrs. Wagner were about to pass by.

Chapter 19

Never in his life had Darcy awakened in a better mood than that morning. As he opened his eyes, the events of yesterday came flooding back. The discovery of the new gold vein alone would have filled him with elation, but it paled in comparison to what had happened between Laurie and him. Like he did every day, he climbed out of bed, walked to the window, and looked up at the sky. This morning it had never been bluer. The sun had never been brighter. Soon he'd be seeing her at the mine. They would talk, start making plans.

He had dressed and was on his way downstairs when he encountered Lucille. She took one look and declared, "You look as if your ship just came in. What happened?"

"Wait till I tell you."

She invited him to her room where he related the news of the gold find, and then, the most important news of all, his new understanding with Laurie. "Turns out she doesn't love that jackass in Philadelphia after all."

Lucille caught his jubilant mood. Laughing, she asked, "So are you going to marry her?"

"If she'll have me."

"Then we must celebrate. Have breakfast with me, Darcy. The Monarch can wait. It won't hurt if you're late. After all, you own it, don't you?"

He readily agreed, and they proceeded to the Bonanza Restaurant. As he walked in, his heart took a jolt. There sat Laurie at one of the tables, and not alone. What was she doing here with a man he'd never seen before? "Wait a minute, Lucille." He walked to the table.

When she saw him coming, her eyes widened with surprise. "Darcy? I didn't think you'd be here."

"Good morning, Laurie." Why was she staring at him like she couldn't believe he was standing there? He flicked a glance at her companion. "I don't believe I know your friend." She continued to stare at him. What was wrong with her? Had she lost her tongue? The stranger tossed down his napkin and rose from his chair. Handsome. Well dressed. Big wide smile.

The man held out his hand. "The name's Brandon Cooper. Are you a friend of Miss Sinclair?"

Brandon Cooper? If there was one thing Darcy had learned in the years he'd lived in the West, it was how to keep a poker face. He did so now, even though he felt like he'd just been kicked in the teeth. He shook Cooper's hand. "Pleased to meet you. I'm Darcy McKenna. I work with Miss Sinclair at the Monarch Mine."

Laurie finally got that stunned expression off her face and remembered her manners. "Uh, Mr. Cooper has just arrived from Philadelphia. I…uh, I'd ask you to sit down, but we were just—"

"Not a problem." He got a kind of perverse satisfaction in seeing how flustered she was, and she damn well should be. All the more reason he must remain calm, collected, and looking as if he couldn't care less. Casually he gestured toward Lucille who stood waiting. "I was about to have breakfast with Mrs. Wagner. Nice to meet you, Mr. Cooper. Good day, Miss Sinclair." He gave them a pleasant nod and turned away. He and Lucille continued to their table. As he sat down, out of the corner of his eye, he saw Laurie and her companion get up and leave. He picked up a menu. "What are you ordering, Lucille?"

During breakfast, he shut his mind to the shock he'd just received and acted his normal, unruffled self. Or tried to, but Lucille saw right through him. He might have known she'd sense his shock at seeing Laurie with the man she'd planned to marry. Lucille had sense enough to realize he didn't care to discuss it, but toward the end of the meal, he could see she was itching to ask. "I suppose you think I'm upset," he finally said.

"The thought crossed my mind." She chose her words carefully, like he might fall apart any second. "Did you know he was coming?"

"What do you think?" He intended to sound amused but couldn't keep the tinge of disbelief from his voice, which of course, she would notice.

She arched an eyebrow. "What do I think? You just received a blow you didn't expect. You must be devastated."

"I got over being devastated about anything a long time ago, Lucille. Nothing touches me now."

"But…" She started to protest but changed her mind. "What will you do?"

What would he do? Laurie Sinclair was the woman he figured he'd never find, if, indeed he'd even been looking. He loved everything about her—her laugh, those beautiful eyes, and rounded curves. But far more than the physical things, as he'd grown to know her, he'd seen what determination and true grit she had. Like when she carried Maryanne in her arms all the way to Hangtown. Like when she stuck with poor Valeria to the very end. Like how she chose to stay with her family because she was needed and didn't hightail it back to Philadelphia when she had the chance. Last night, she'd led him to believe she loved him. But did she? Brandon Cooper had everything. Handsome, good family, college educated. Whereas he? Never let it be said Darcy McKenna would ever feel sorry for himself. He'd spent a lifetime staying tough and wouldn't give in now, despite the sick, despairing feeling in his gut. Maybe he should confront her, ask what the hell was going on, but why ask? Why else would Brandon Cooper be here other than to claim his bride? "I won't do anything. If she wants him, she can have him."

Lucille frowned. "You're making a mistake if you're assuming Laurie's still in love with him. How do you know? Shouldn't you at least talk to her?"

"Why? I won't stand in the way of Laurie's happiness."

"Don't be ridiculous. For heaven's sake, Darcy, you can't just walk away. At the least, you must find out how she feels. Who knows? You might be surprised."

"If you think I'm going to beg and plead—"

"Of course not." She rolled her eyes in exasperation. "Why must you men be so stubborn? Do what you please then, which of course, you will. You're a smart man. I can only hope your pride doesn't get in the way of your common sense."

* * * *

"Just take me home," Laurie told Brandon when they left the restaurant. She had nothing more to say to him and could hardly wait to get rid of him. Thank goodness, she'd fought off her impulse to leap from her chair and run after Darcy as he walked away from their table. She had desperately wanted to explain, but a lifetime of deference to good manners kept her in her place. Besides, he wasn't alone, and she wasn't about to make a spectacle of herself in front of Mrs. Wagner. What must he be thinking? She must get to him as soon as possible. Surely, after breakfast, he'd go to the mine, and she'd have a chance to talk to him then.

When Brandon brought the buggy to a stop in front of the house, Laurie scampered down, not waiting for help. She didn't want him to touch her. "Thanks for the breakfast," she called over her shoulder as she hurried inside. She'd loved him once. Now she couldn't remember one reason why she had. She had no interest in his utterly foolish plans to search for a lake that didn't exist, or anything else about him, for that matter.

She found her mother and Ada in the parlor. They both sat wide eyed as she marched in and ranted, "I'm done with Brandon Cooper. Sorry, Mother, but if I never see him again, it will be too soon." Calming herself, she told them what happened. "Brandon lied. He didn't come all this way for me. It's the gold he's after."

"But you must be wrong," Elizabeth replied, reacting just as Laurie expected.

"No, I'm not." Laurie described Hugh's upcoming expedition to Lost Lake, which, she gathered, Brandon was financing. "They've been corresponding for quite some time. That's why he couldn't wait to get to California."

Elizabeth listened with growing dismay before saying, "I can't imagine my son doing anything so foolish, and dangerous, too."

Laurie wasn't surprised that the first mention Hugh might be in danger brought a shift in her mother's concerns. All else paled in comparison to her worry over her beloved son. But much as Laurie wanted to talk about the insanity of Hugh's plan, she didn't have time now. She must talk to Darcy. That's all she cared about. She must get to the Monarch, find him, and explain. "We'll talk later," she said, fled the parlor, and hurried to the stable.

With frantic haste, she hitched the curricle and drove up the road to the Monarch faster than she'd ever done before. Champ was tied to the hitching post in front of the office. So, Darcy was there, thank God. Inside, she found him talking to Tom. She waited until Tom left, but just as he did, a wagon loaded with new mining equipment arrived and she had to check it in. She could never seem to find Darcy alone. Her impatience grew as the day went by until finally, toward the end of the shift, the office emptied out except for the two of them. She walked to his desk where he seemed engrossed in some kind of paperwork. "I've been wanting to talk to you."

He looked up with mildly inquisitive eyes, as if he expected something trivial. "About this morning?"

Why the indifference in his voice? How galling. "What else? Last night when I came home and found Brandon sitting in our parlor I was shocked. I had no idea—"

"There's no need to explain." His gaze softened. "I want you to be happy, Laurie. Maybe you were shocked, but this is Brandon Cooper we're talking about, the man you've been in love with for years, the man you were longing to marry. Maybe, because of what's happened between us, you think you owe me something, but you don't. I'm fine. I'm happy for you. You don't need to say another word."

Say another word? As she stood looking down at him, she doubted she could say her name, let alone put a sentence together. Maybe he thought he was being kind and magnanimous, but he might as well have thrown a bucket of ice-cold water in her face. Why hadn't he asked for an explanation? She'd been eager to tell him she was finished with Brandon and had told him so in no uncertain terms. But now? If that's the way Darcy felt, she wasn't going to stand here and beg him to listen. "Then I have nothing more to say."

She walked away, hoping he might call out to her, but he didn't. She gathered the time sheets, left the office, and walked to the mine entrance where the daily exodus of miners kept her busy for the next hour. Darcy had left by the time she returned to the office. For a while, she sat at her desk and blindly stared into space. How ironic that only a day ago, she'd truly been giddy with happiness. Now, in the space of twenty-four hours, she'd lost not one man but two: Brandon, whom she thought she loved but didn't. Darcy, whom she loved with all her heart, but about whom she now hadn't the faintest notion what to do.

* * * *

That night, she arrived home to find Hugh sitting in the parlor, Mathew on his lap, Maryanne cuddling beside him. At least he was paying some rare attention to his children for a change. Surprisingly, Mother and Ada were listening with enthralled attention to what he was saying. Laurie had informed them of all the terrible things he'd done, but where was their outrage? She should have known. With her extra-kind heart, Ada would forgive anybody anything. Mother, with her blind love for her son, didn't believe her in the first place, and even if she had, she would have instantly forgiven him.

When Elizabeth saw Laurie in the doorway, she motioned her to join them. "You must hear this," she said. "Your brother's telling us about his plans with Brandon."

At the moment, the furthest thing from Laurie's mind was Hugh and his stupid expedition, but she dutifully entered the parlor and sat down. In no mood for niceties, she looked at her brother and inquired, "So what makes you think you'll find a lake covered in gold?"

Looking smug and sure of himself, Hugh was eager to tell. "Ever since I've been in Lucky Creek, I've wanted to find it. I know it's there—the golden lake, high in the mountains, hidden and unimaginably rich, those sheets of gold dotting the lake's surface like leaves in autumn—"

"Don't forget those Indians fishing with golden fish hooks." She made no attempt to hide her scorn.

Hugh threw her a look of contempt. "Not long ago I met an old prospector by the name of Stubbs who convinced me beyond all doubt he'd been there. What he told me was unbelievable. In the course of only hours, with no labor other than bending down, he'd walked along the shore and gathered nuggets ranging in size from marbles to walnuts. The only problem was whether his mules would collapse under the load of gold heaved onto their backs. I asked if he was going back, and he told me no, he didn't need to. That man is set for life. I practically begged him to tell me where the lake was. He drew me a map, for a price of course, which I gladly paid. I call it my treasure map. With it, I'll know exactly where to go."

Elizabeth didn't look convinced. "But, Son, such an expedition must be extremely dangerous, especially with winter coming on."

"Of course, there's drawbacks and dangers. For one thing, the lake is nearly inaccessible. Stubbs said his party had to crest the last high mountain before they could see the lake hidden below. The descent to the lake was so steep the mules had to be lowered and raised by rope. And then there's the Indians. Fierce and hostile, he says. Several attacked his party. Some were wounded, and the rest had to flee. I don't worry, though. Our expedition will be well armed."

Both Elizabeth and Ada stared in alarm. Elizabeth pressed a hand over her heart. "You can't do this, Hugh. It's far too risky."

"You're taking a terrible chance," Ada declared. "I still don't believe it exists."

"I know what I'm doing," Hugh replied. "Have faith, ladies. When I return with a mule train loaded with gold, we'll all be rich for life."

Laurie couldn't keep her mouth shut. "Really, Hugh? What if something happens to you? What about Mathew and Maryanne? Not that you're supporting them now, but it would be nice if you could start contributing again."

Elizabeth appeared shocked, just as Laurie expected she would. "Laurie, how can you say such a thing when poor Hugh is still recovering from the accident?"

"Because it's true, Mother. You just don't know…" She had to bite her tongue. Mother needed to be reminded of the truth about Hugh, but what good would it do? "This expedition is a terrible idea. Sheer insanity, as far as I'm concerned."

Hugh laughed, not the least daunted by her candid opinion. "You'll soon be proven wrong, my dear little sister."

She hadn't missed the contempt in his voice but why argue? Nothing would stop Hugh from doing what he wanted to do, and that was worrisome. Even now, knowing what she knew, she wouldn't want anything bad to happen to him. More than Hugh, she worried about Mother. After all she'd gone through, if anything happened to her cherished son, Laurie didn't think she could bear it.

* * * *

The next morning, before Laurie went to work, she heard a knock and found her neighbor, Agatha Harrison, standing at the back door. Laurie invited her in, always happy to see her. The loss of little Ruthie had been a terrible blow, but strong woman that she was, Agatha had bravely held together and carried on. Over a cup of coffee, she said, "I hoped to catch you before you went to the mine this morning. Wait till you hear…"

Laurie listened as Agatha described the meeting she'd attended the night before. A group of determined ladies had gathered at the church. As solid citizens of Lucky Creek, they were disturbed at all that was wrong with the town. The lawlessness and high rate of crime, the muddy streets, the lack of cultural events, along with the disgrace of Mein Street with its drunkenness, lewd behavior, and only God knew what other debaucheries that went on every night. "At last we're taking some action. We formed the Association for the Improvement, Beautification, and Enlightenment of Lucky Creek, and tonight we're holding the first official meeting. We very much want you to join us, Laurie. Ada and your mother, too."

Laurie had never given any thought to the subject but agreed that it was a fine idea. "I don't know what I can do, but I'd be happy to come to the meeting."

Agatha beamed. "That's wonderful. We need more women like you. You're a born leader. You may have your hands full with the mine, but if you can spare the time, you can do a world of good for our community."

Agatha left soon after. As Laurie drove up to the mine, she couldn't get over her surprise. She, a born leader? She'd never thought of herself in any such way. All her life she'd been a follower, never thinking for herself, always content with others telling her what to do. But now? Definitely she'd be there.

Entering the office, she wondered what she would say to Darcy. What would he say to her? Why did it matter? They'd go on as before, friendly enough but restrained, two people who worked together and that was all. And yet, wouldn't it be wonderful if he told her he'd thought about it and changed his mind? *I love you, Laurie. Brandon be damned, you're mine now, and I want you to marry me.*

But she found the office empty except for Tom. He smiled when he saw her. "Looks like Darcy won't be around for the next few days. He got real busy at the Atlas."

So, Darcy wouldn't be here? Fine. She had work to do and would not allow the likes of Darcy McKenna to ruin her day. The time went by swiftly as she immersed herself in time sheets, checking deliveries, solving small grievances among the miners. At the end of the shift when she headed for home, she drove the curricle at a slow pace, grateful she at last had time to think about something other than work. Such a pretty ride. Usually she had so much on her mind she hardly noticed the squirrels, porcupines, and all sorts of little creatures that occasionally scampered across the road. Bigger creatures crossed her path, too, like deer, and an occasional lumbering moose or elk. Each morning, a chorus of awakening birds serenaded her as she drove up the mountain. In the evening, another chorus entertained her as the birds settled in for the night. And when she lifted her eyes to beyond the tall conifers, the majestic, snow-covered peaks of the Sierra Nevadas loomed above in all their splendor.

She wouldn't find anything like this in Philadelphia. She hadn't thought she would, but when she moved back, she'd miss this spectacular scenery. But was Philadelphia still her home? Why would she want to go back there? Certainly not for Brandon. She didn't hate Lucky Creek anymore. In fact, Agatha's invitation to join the new association had set her to thinking. Lucky Creek should have an opera house, and what about a library? The town should also have a decent courthouse, along with an honest judge who wouldn't take bribes. She could do a lot to help. She wanted to help. What would her life be like if she returned to Philadelphia? She could wear fancy clothes, give elegant teas, attend boring parties where white-gloved beaux would treat her as if she didn't have a brain in her head. Not so in Lucky Creek, where each day brought new challenges, new excitement. She knew her job at the mine, did it well, and they all respected her. And she loved working there, being a part of it all.

I am not going back to Philadelphia. I like it here, and I'm going to stay.

And then there was Darcy. She laughed aloud. *We'll see about that.* Touching the reins to the horses' backs, she gave a decisive nod to herself as she continued guiding the curricle down the mountain.

Chapter 20

Early one morning, Darcy was riding Champ along the upper part of Mein Street when he came upon a line of pack mules, loaded and ready to move out. A dozen men milled about, including several Miwok Indian guides he recognized. "What's going on, Elki?" he called to a guide who worked for him from time to time.

A small man, heavily muscled, the Indian usually wore an impassive expression on his face and had little to say. Not this morning. He walked to where Darcy had pulled Champ to a halt. "We go to find Lost Lake," he said in a voice loaded with scorn. He spat with contempt on the ground. "Fools."

Hard to believe, but this must be Hugh's expedition. The man was crazier than he thought. Not his business, though. He was about to move on when he spotted Hugh Sinclair walking toward him, Brandon Cooper directly behind. Something in Hugh's walk reminded him of a strutting peacock, all cocky and arrogant. When he got close, he looked up at Darcy with a sneer on his face and remarked, "If it isn't McKenna. Come to see us off?" Without waiting for a reply, he turned to Brandon. "You've met my friend, Darcy McKenna, have you not? Mr. McKenna's a self-made man. Born in West Virginia, weren't you, Darcy? Spent your boyhood in a coal mine?"

Darcy refused to recognize Hugh's laughable attempt to demean him. He swung off his horse and looked the idiot in the eye. "What the hell are you doing, Hugh? Don't tell me you actually expect to find a lake covered in gold."

Hugh's laugh brimmed with confidence. "You're a good man, Darcy, but you see only what's under your nose. Like most men, your foresight is limited, whereas I… Well, I don't wish to brag, but I'm a man of vision. I see things you don't. I know things you don't."

"Hugh's right." Brandon clapped his newfound friend and partner on the back. "Nothing can stop us. I have every confidence in our success."

Darcy didn't tolerate fools easily, but he would try one more time. "Winter's coming. We could get our first snow any day now. You might want to reconsider. Rumors about Lost Lake have been floating around for years, none of them verified, none of them—"

"My good man," Brandon interrupted, "I've no wish to insult you, but your somewhat narrow and, if I may say so, ignorant opinion, will get us nowhere." He addressed Hugh. "Let's not waste time. Shall we be off? Good day, Mr. McKenna."

In silence, Darcy watched the two walk away. He knew a losing battle when he saw one. The poor fools. At least he'd tried.

* * * *

Although Laurie tried to persuade her to come, Elizabeth had no interest in the first meeting of the Association for the Improvement, Beautification, and Enlightenment of Lucky Creek. Why waste her time when she'd soon be returning to Philadelphia? "And why should you girls want to join?" she asked Laurie and Ada. "We'll be gone soon, so why waste your time?"

As yet, neither daughter had informed Elizabeth of her decision to remain in Lucky Creek. Despite declaring her everlasting love and devotion to Kenvern, Ada hadn't worked up enough courage to deal Mother what would surely prove a devastating blow. Laurie wanted to tell her and get it over with, but she hesitated to add to Mother's constant, growing worry over Hugh. Before leaving on his expedition, he'd come to say goodbye, brimming with confidence he'd return with riches beyond their wildest dreams. Elizabeth had her doubts. Her beloved son had left on a trek through an unknown wilderness with little protection against the weather, wild animals, savage Indians, horrible accidents, and God knew what. She wouldn't rest until he was back safely.

Despite Elizabeth's objections, both Laurie and Ada decided to attend the meeting. Independent though she'd become, Laurie knew better than to drive the streets of Lucky Creek after dark. Much too dangerous with the lawlessness that still existed in this town. Kenvern Trenowden gladly volunteered to drive her and Ada to the church where the ladies were meeting. He picked them up in his new wagon marked TRENOWDEN BROTHERS DRY GOODS STORE. Laurie climbed in by herself, then watched with concealed amusement while Kenvern assisted Ada up to the wagon seat, cautiously handling her as if she were a delicate porcelain doll. Eyelids all fluttery, Ada didn't mind a bit. Laurie's heart lifted just watching them. In the few weeks Kenvern had taken lessons, he'd gone from hesitant and unsure of himself to confident and poised, an on-the-rise entrepreneur whose business was already prospering.

The meeting went beyond Laurie's most optimistic expectations. It seemed every respectable, upstanding, God-fearing woman in town had chosen to attend, and that included the esteemed hotel owner, Mrs. Lucille Wagner, whom the association voted president by popular acclaim. Immediate needs were discussed. Fix the terrible streets. Hold honest elections. Build a courthouse. Beyond that, ambitious, far-reaching concepts flew thick and fast. Lucky Creek should be officially incorporated into a town, the sooner the better. Why not change the town's name to something more dignified than an accidental gold discovery? The town must expand beyond serving the drunken miners who crowded the streets each night. It could serve as a mining hub as well as an important mining supply center. Why couldn't they have downtown festivals and special events? And most important of all, hadn't they had enough of vigilante justice and crooked officials who accepted bribes? Laurie joined the fervent chorus of women who leaped to their feet, shouting, "Yes we have. Enough is enough." Before the evening ended, she'd volunteered for two committees: Rename the Town and Elect A New sheriff.

Inspired by the ladies' positive attitude and buoyant enthusiasm, the sisters agreed the time had come to be honest with Mother. After Kenvern dropped them off, they found Elizabeth sitting in the parlor waiting up for them. Ada went first. In a steady, sure voice, she gently explained, "I've been wanting to tell you for the longest time and didn't have the nerve, but I can't put it off any longer. Mother, Kenvern and I have fallen in love. He wants to marry me, and I've said yes. From now on my home is here, in Lucky Creek. I can only hope you understand and forgive me because I'm not ever, ever going back to Philadelphia."

Before Elizabeth could answer, Laurie joined in. "I'm not going back either. I never thought I'd say this, but I love living in Lucky Creek. Tonight, I joined the association that will work to make it better, and so did Ada."

Elizabeth didn't look all that surprised. After heaving a resigned sigh, she asked, "What about Brandon Cooper? You don't think—"

"No, I don't think," Laurie replied with a trace of laughter in her voice. "I wish him well, but we are totally, completely done."

"What about Darcy McKenna?"

What about him? Laurie was asking the same question herself. "I love him, Mother. That's all I can tell you." What else could she say? All she knew was, the very sound of his name caused her heart to turn over in response. She must talk to him, and soon.

Ada spoke up in that new, self-assured voice she had. "Why must you go back, Mother? Why not stay here and be with your family?"

"I wouldn't dream of it," Elizabeth said with a firm shake of her head. "Once Hugh comes back, he'll be wanting to get out of this place and go back where we belong. That's what he told me, and that's what we'll do."

Laurie knew better than to argue. *We'll see about that,* she thought to herself, but kindly didn't say.

* * * *

Nearly three weeks had passed since Hugh and Brandon's expedition had headed out. Darcy had pretty much put it out of his mind. With two mines to run, and the discovery of the new gold vein at the Monarch, he had more than enough to keep him busy. As much as he could, he'd put Laurie Sinclair out of his head. He was good at that. Maybe those long, mind-numbing hours he'd spent in the coal mine had trained him well. Only at night, when he lay in bed listening to the sounds of revelry from below, did he ache with longing for the only woman he'd ever loved or could love. The woman he valued and cherished. The woman he'd lay down his life for if the need arose.

Darcy was hard at work at his Atlas Mine when he received a message from Doc Hansen. Elki, the Miwok guide, and two other guides had staggered into town half dead and starving. They'd been taken to the hospital where Elki had asked to see Mr. McKenna. Darcy rushed to see him. What a shock to find his Indian friend lying flat in bed, thin and gaunt, so weak he could hardly talk. Darcy had to bend low to hear him. "We were lost the whole time," Elki whispered. "No more food. Gang of Paiute stole mules and horses."

"What about Sinclair and Cooper?" Darcy asked.

"In bad shape. They need help. Mr. Sinclair said send rescue party."

Darcy clamped Elki's shoulder. "Get well, my friend. We'll find them."

He left the hospital with a sole purpose in mind: organize a party to rescue the remains of Hugh Sinclair's ill-fated expedition. He wasted no time contemplating whether Hugh and Brandon deserved to be rescued. They were two men lost in the wilderness who needed help, and in Lucky

Creek, when help was asked for, help would be given. Brock Dominick, the Hudson brothers, they'd all want to pitch in. By early tomorrow at the latest, the rescue mission would be ready to go.

* * * *

Upon hearing the bad news about Hugh, Elizabeth sank into a state of despair. Laurie kept trying to console her. "I'm sure he's still alive," she kept saying. "The rescue party will surely find them in time." For herself, she wasn't so sure. According to the Indian who'd brought the message, Hugh and Brandon were trapped in their tent in deep snow with little to eat and a scant supply of firewood. How could they possibly survive? More than once, she sent up a heartfelt prayer that both would be found in time and return safely. Now she knew for certain she was done with Brandon Cooper forever. If he died, her heart would not be broken. She'd mourn for him as she would for any friend, but nothing more. When she thought about Hugh, a deep anxiety overcame her. Even now, despite the terrible things he'd done, she remembered the good things about him and ignored the bad.

She might have known Darcy McKenna would be the one who organized the rescue party and led the way as it began its treacherous journey into the mountains. Busy though he was, he was the kind of man who put others first, another reason why her love for Darcy had grown to the point where stupid pride would no longer prevent her from telling him so.

As soon as he returns.

* * * *

Mercifully, the snow stopped shortly after the expedition's survivors staggered back to town, enabling the rescue party to follow their tracks to where Hugh and Brandon were stranded. After a three-day trek, the rescuers came upon the pitiful remains of Hugh's expedition, one small tent with the blackened remains of a campfire in front. Accompanied by Brock, Darcy approached the tent and yelled a greeting. They were met by an ominous silence. No one came out to greet the rescue party. Fearing the worst, Darcy lifted the flap and stepped inside, Brock behind him. In the dimness, he made out two bodies, each lying beneath a pile of blankets. "Looks like they're both gone," he said as he squatted beside the one on the right. He placed his hand on what he expected to be an ice-cold forehead and jerked it back when the man's eyes suddenly opened. Despite the heavy growth of beard and the red-veined eyes that stared at him with mad desperation, he saw who it was. "This one's alive. It's Brandon Cooper."

Brock squatted by the body on the other side and looked closely. "This one's Hugh, all right, but he didn't make it. He's gone."

Brandon stirred and tried to lift a hand. "Save me," he feebly whispered, his hand dropping limply to his side.

Darcy patted his shoulder. "Don't worry, we'll get you out of here." Hugh dead. The once-arrogant Brandon Cooper begging for rescue. How the mighty had fallen, but Darcy had no desire to gloat. Right now, all he could focus on was getting Brandon to Doc Hansen's hospital as soon as possible and carrying the remains of Hugh Sinclair back to his family.

Chapter 21

For the second time within months, Laurie stood beside a grave in the small cemetery overlooking the town. As the minister read a eulogy, she looked out at the good-sized crowd. Not as many as had gathered for Father's funeral, but a respectable number, nonetheless. Mother should be pleased. Despite her grief, she'd held together better than Laurie expected and would notice how many had come to mourn her son.

Laurie hadn't noticed Darcy at first, but there he stood on the other side of the grave on the fringe of the crowd. Their gazes locked. She should be listening to the minister, but she couldn't pull her eyes away from the man who overwhelmingly occupied her thoughts. She hadn't had a chance to speak to him since he'd returned from the rescue mission. She must speak to him now. Judging from the urgent way he was looking at her, he wanted to speak to her.

"Ashes to ashes, dust to dust…"

The minister finished his eulogy. The last handful of dirt was tossed in the grave. Standing with her daughters, Mother graciously accepted condolences from mourners passing by.

At first, Laurie couldn't break away, what with people offering their hands, murmuring how sorry they were about her brother. Finally, when the last of the mourners began to leave, she saw Darcy still waiting for her. She walked toward him, aware she didn't look her best in the borrowed black dress, but it didn't matter. He started walking toward her, eyes intent upon her. "I'm sorry I couldn't save him," he said when they met.

"You did your best. More than enough. I deeply appreciate that you tried."

"At least Brandon's alive." He peered closely into her face, as if searching for her reaction.

"I hear he suffered some frostbite, but he'll be good as new."

"You haven't been to see him?"

At last, the opening she'd been waiting for. "I haven't been to see Brandon, nor do I intend to. Do you remember when you saw us in the restaurant?"

A corner of his mouth pulled into a slight smile. "I recall."

"What you don't know is, I had just told him I could never marry him, and believe me, I meant what I said." How could he not understand? How much more plainspoken could she get?

"So…" Slowly a smile spread over his face. "So, you and I…?"

"You and I, Mr. Darcy McKenna."

They weren't alone. A few stragglers had yet to leave the cemetery. The site of her brother's funeral was hardly the proper place, but certainly Hugh wouldn't mind, and she couldn't care less what people might think. She raised her hands to his shoulders and pulled him toward her. His breath caught as he took her into his arms. Sighing with pleasure, she sank into his warm, welcoming embrace.

"Forever," he murmured.

"Forever," she whispered back. Not much of a conversation, but from a man who didn't talk much, what more did she need?

* * * *

If she'd had her way, Elizabeth Sinclair would have organized the most elaborate wedding Lucky Creek had ever seen. It would have been a welcome distraction from Hugh's death, but Laurie said no. What with the ever-increasing output at the Monarch, she was much too busy, and so was Darcy.

Despite her mother's protests, Laurie married Darcy McKenna in a small ceremony attended by family and close friends only.

Elizabeth's disappointment didn't last long. To her delight, the wedding of Ada Sinclair and Kenvern Trenowden turned into the most extravagant, highly attended event the town of Lucky Creek had ever seen. It hadn't started out that way. In her modest fashion, Ada had declared, "Just a simple wedding is fine, just like Laurie's. A few friends, some sort of refreshment afterward, that's all I want."

But the Trenowden brothers had other ideas. Wouldn't she like to have a big Cornish wedding? "Outdoors by a clear brook," Kenvern reminisced about weddings he'd attended during his early days in Cornwall. "Under tall ash and oak trees. The smell of salt water in the air, coming from the ocean. A band of Cornish musicians playing sea shanties and polkas."

Ada quickly warmed to the idea. And so, too, did their mother. As the weeks went by, Elizabeth kept putting off her return to Philadelphia. How could she leave when Ada needed her help planning the wedding? The winter months passed, and on a sunny spring day, the wedding of Ada Sinclair and Kenvern Trenowden turned into the grandest Lucky Creek had ever seen. Mother and Ada couldn't arrange for salt air from the ocean, but finding a brook was no problem, nor was substituting pine and fir trees for oak and ash. There'd been a small difficulty with the menu. Kenvern had requested his favorite, stargazy pie, but when Ada discovered it featured fish heads sticking through the piecrust, she firmly put her foot down. They settled for oggies, which the brothers explained were savory meat pies.

Practically the whole town was invited, and from what Laurie could see, everyone was having a fine time. They all loved the oggies, and declared the wedding cake, made from clotted milk, a Cornwall specialty, to be the best they'd ever tasted. And of course, the bride and groom glowed with happiness, a delight to look upon. Little Mathew and Maryanne were part of the wedding, too. Already Kenvern treated them as if they were his own. In turn, they adored him and were already calling him daddy.

Increased responsibilities at the Monarch had kept Laurie so busy that not until Ada's wedding day did she take the time to think about where she'd been and where she was going. As she stood for a moment alone, watching the guests dancing in a clear spot beneath the trees, she could hardly remember how much she'd hated Lucky Creek when she first arrived. Amazing, how it had changed since then, thanks in large part to the Association for the Improvement, Beautification, and Enlightenment of Lucky Creek. To her daughters' astonishment, Elizabeth not only joined the Association, she and Mrs. Wagner had become a powerful force for good in the town. A new, honest sheriff had been elected. Trash no longer lay uncollected on the streets. Construction of a new courthouse was well underway. In both looks and temperament, Elizabeth Sinclair and Lucille Wagner couldn't have been more different from one another, yet they'd become fast friends and greatly enjoyed each other's company. Mother hardly mentioned Philadelphia anymore. Both Laurie and Ada agreed, she'd never go back now.

As Laurie stood watching the dancers, two arms went around her waist. Darcy had slipped up behind her. "Care to dance?" he asked.

"Not now." She pressed back against him, warm and secure, aware of the life growing within her. "I think I felt it move a while ago."

"I love you," he whispered in her ear, and she could hear the slight tinge of wonder in his voice. She had never realized how much a baby would mean to him until she saw the tears in his eyes when she told him.

"I decided you're right about the window," he said.

"I know I'm right." Once, in a moment of candor, he'd told her of his need for a big window facing east so he could see the morning sunrise. "Our bedroom will face east," she'd told him when they were drawing plans for a house of their own. "You'll have that window."

"It's not necessary. I don't need it anymore," he'd told her.

"Yes, you do. If I'd spent my childhood in a coal mine, I'd always want to see the sunrise."

Nestled beneath tall trees, overlooking the river, their new home was almost complete, and that included a big bedroom window facing east.

Now, on Ada's wedding day, standing under a bright blue sky, he gently gripped her shoulders, turned her toward him, and gazed at her with adoring eyes. "I'm glad it's there but still don't think I need it. With you, I can always see the sun."

Never had he uttered anything so flowery, so sentimental. "That's the nicest thing you ever said to me, Darcy McKenna."

"This is just the beginning," he said and pulled her into his arms.

Meet the Author

Shirley Kennedy was born and raised in Fresno, California. She lived in Canada for many years and graduated from the University of Calgary, Alberta, Canada, with a BS in computer science. She has published novels with Ballantine, Signet, and several smaller presses. She writes in several different genres including Regency romance, western romance, and contemporary fiction. She lives in Las Vegas, Nevada, and is an active member of the Romance Writers of America, Las Vegas chapter. Please visit Shirley at www.shirleykennedy.com, or follow her Twitter account @ ladyk360, or on Facebook at https://www.facebook.com/shirley.kennedy.52.

Bay City Belle

If you enjoyed *Lucky Creek Lady*, be sure not to miss all of Shirley Kennedy's
In Old California series, including

Before the war, Belle Ainsworth led a life of pleasure and privilege in the
deep South. Five years after losing her fiancé at the Battle of Gettysburg,
she is still alone, with no prospects for marriage among the remaining men
of her acquaintance. But out west, there are possibilities. And when Belle
answers an ad for a mail-order bride and boards a train to San Francisco
to meet wealthy restaurateur Robert Romano, it's with the hope of at last
making her dreams of family come true.

When the train is robbed, Yancy McLeish, a disillusioned Union Army hero,
rescues Belle from her attackers—and lays claim to her heart. But Belle
has pledged her troth to Romano and intends to honor that commitment.
It's a decision she soon regrets, for her groom-to-be is nothing like his
letters. As she plots a course to escape Romano, Belle prays that road can
lead her back to the safety of Yancy's arms, where she believes she was
always destined to be…

Keep reading for a special look!
A Lyrical e-book on sale now.

Chapter 1

Savannah, Georgia, 1870

Miss Annabelle Ainsworth, known as Belle, never missed the semi-weekly meeting of the Georgia Ladies of the Confederacy. At today's meeting, held in the parlor of the Elihu Barnes residence, visits to veterans' hospitals were arranged and the annual report from the Committee Dedicated to the Beautification of the Graves of the Glorious Dead was heard and approved. Soon both old and new business had been efficiently dispatched. As they always did, the members conducted themselves with profound dedication. The war had ended over five years ago, yet the consequences of that terrible conflict lived in the hearts and minds of everyone present. As far as the ladies were concerned, General Lee's surrender at the Appomattox Court House happened yesterday.

Refreshments and social chitchat followed. Ordinarily Belle enjoyed this part best, but at the moment, her mind kept wandering. If there was anything more boring than listening to the endless prattle of Miss full-of-herself Allegra Barnes, she didn't know what it was. Not that she'd let it show. She sat, teacup in hand, face carefully arranged in an expression of attentiveness, as if she couldn't hear enough of Allegra's account of her struggles with her latest achievement in the art of embroidery.

"So I decided to go with the dollhouse cross-stitch," Allegra rambled on. She paused and got a curious grin on her face. "But enough of all that. Ladies, I have something exciting to tell you."

"What?" came a chorus of curious female voices, including Belle's and that of her sister, Victoria, who sat beside her.

"I'm going to get married."

Everyone gasped. Belle set her cup down with a clatter and exchanged stunned glances with Victoria. In the old days before the war, such an announcement wouldn't have come as such a shock, but now? Who on earth was Allegra going to marry? More to the point, who was left to marry? The war had cut a deadly swath through the male population of Georgia. The battles at Gettysburg, Bull Run, Wilson's Creek, and more had taken countless Confederate lives. If a bullet hadn't felled their brave soldiers, then dysentery, typhoid, and God-knew-what diseases did. And even if they'd lived… Belle felt a twinge of sorrow, as she always did when she thought of Bridger, her brother. He'd survived the war but would never be the same. Come to think of it, neither would she. At the age of twenty-five, she should have been comfortably married by now, with at least a child or two, but she'd lost Jeremy, her fiancé, at Gettysburg. In fact, most of the beaux who'd courted her were gone now, so here she was, single, childless, living with Victoria and her husband. Not that she led a useless life—far from it. Her busy sister depended upon her to help care for her three children who all adored their aunt Belle. In turn, she loved them so dearly she hardly missed having children of her own, or so she told herself.

Victoria was the first to respond to Allegra's stunning marriage announcement. "That's wonderful news. Is it someone we know?"

"Not exactly."

"But of course he's a Southerner."

"Not exactly." Allegra got that smug, superior look on her face that annoyed Belle to no end. "Don't worry, dear, he's not a Yankee."

"Then who?" came the chorus. "Tell us! We're dying to know."

"His name is Edward Smith, and he's a respectable merchant in the city of San Francisco." Amidst a sudden, shocked silence, Allegra continued, "We've corresponded. He's asked me to marry him, and I sent a letter this morning telling him I accept."

Like everyone else in the room, Belle could hardly believe what she was hearing. "You mean you're marrying a man you haven't even met?"

"Why not?" With a defiant gleam in her eye, Allegra reached for a newspaper that lay on the table next to her. "Have you not heard of the *Matrimonial News*? It's printed every week in Kansas City, a most respectable publication. Here's the ad I answered." She opened the paper and began to read. "'A respectable gentleman of thirty years old, six feet tall, 170 pounds, doing a good business in the city of San Francisco, desires the acquaintance of a young, intelligent, and refined lady, of a loving disposition from eighteen to twenty-eight, one who could make his home a paradise.'" Allegra laid the paper in her lap and flopped out her hands. "How could I resist? I wrote back. He responded and wants me to come. He's sending me a train ticket, and that's all I'm waiting for. When it arrives, I'm off to San Francisco."

Mrs. Beauregard Bedford Stuart cleared her throat. All eyes turned to the group's highly respected president, a formidable figure with her silver-grey hair worn in a stern knot, and her starkly plain, black bombazine dress. She gazed at Allegra with a mixture of alarm and incredulity. "Are you actually going to become one of those mail-order brides?"

Allegra tossed her head. "Indeed I am, Mrs. Stuart. You can say what you want about staying loyal to the South, and I would if I could, but I can't. My beloved Frederick was killed at Bull Run, so where does that leave me?" Her gaze swept the room. "I'm as loyal to our glorious dead as you are, but that won't warm my bed at night, now will it?" She sat back in her chair, pleased her indelicate remark had caused a few nervous twitters. "Look at me. Twenty-five years old, young and pretty if I do say so. But who's to care if I'm pretty or not? Our men are gone. What am I supposed to do? Drink tea and decorate graves until I'm fat and wrinkled and wither away?"

"But, my dear…" Seldom at a loss for words, Mrs. Stuart seemed unable to speak, as if she'd choked on something.

Victoria spoke up. "But Allegra, think of the chance you're taking. What if you travel clear across the country only to find this Edward Smith isn't who he says he is?"

"Then I'd come home." Allegra turned her attention to Belle. "Your sister is married and has her children, so how could she possibly understand? But you know what I'm talking about, being as we're the same age and both of us still unattached. You're such a pretty girl. Like me, if it weren't for the war, we'd both be married by now, with children of our own." She picked up the *Matrimonial News* and opened it again. "Listen to this, Belle. 'Established restaurant owner of good character, thirty-three years old, six feet tall, 170 pounds, brown eyes, seeks to correspond with respectable young lady of pleasing appearance, preferably of full form. If interested, write to Robert Romano,' and it gives the address." She raised her eyes. "You fit his requirements perfectly. Just think, we could be neighbors in San Francisco. Wouldn't that be lovely?"

Belle could think of nothing more unappealing than living next door to shallow, arrogant Allegra Barnes. But she would conceal her aversion to such a prospect and be polite, like she always was. "I'm flattered you'd ask, Allegra, but I'm happy as I am, thank you. Marriage isn't everything.

I like my life as it is, and who knows? Perhaps someday the right man will come along."

Allegra met Belle's remarks with an annoying burst of laughter. "Highly unlikely, and you know it."

Yes, she did know. Only too well did she know, especially when she lay awake in the middle of the night, her heart aching because she must face the unbearable truth that she would never be married, never have children of her own. Not for the world would she reveal her true feelings, though. She shrugged with feigned indifference. "Whether the so-called right man shows up or not, I'm perfectly content with my life."

Allegra folded the *Matrimonial News* and dropped it back on the table. "I suppose you think I'm crazy, but I'm not. Give it some thought. You might change your mind."

"Thank you, Allegra. I'm always open to new ideas." Nothing like a polite lie to avoid any further discussion.

* * * *

As Weldon, their stableman, drove them home, Victoria couldn't stop talking about Allegra Barnes. "That poor man in San Francisco doesn't know what he's let himself in for."

Belle nodded in agreement. "If he expects she'll make his home a paradise, he's in for a rude awakening."

"How nervy of her to imply you'd be interested in that ridiculous ad. If she thinks you'd actually leave your beautiful home for a man you've never met, she's lost her mind."

Belle took a moment to answer. "Actually I don't think Allegra has lost her mind. It's that awful war that's turned our lives upside down and twisted our thinking."

Victoria returned a disdainful sniff. "The war has nothing to do with it. Allegra's always been a meddler."

Belle didn't bother to argue. Victoria would never understand. She was one of the lucky ones. Before the war started, she married Harlan Beeman, a well-to-do young trader. When the time came, like every other able-bodied man from the South, he joined the Confederate Army. Through what the family considered a small miracle, he'd returned home unscathed. Now, although his business had greatly suffered, he provided a good home not only for his wife and three children, but for Belle and their brother, Bridger, as well.

Belle threw her sister a rueful smile. "You wouldn't understand. Despite what you might think, Allegra's only doing what she's driven to do. It's human nature for a woman to want to be married and have children."

"So what am I not understanding? What about you? Do you mean you're not happy living with us? I thought—"

"Of course I'm happy. What would I have done without you?" Belle meant what she said. Before the war, the Ainsworth family lived a comfortable life among the genteel citizenry of Savannah. Her father had made his fortune on the Savannah Cotton Exchange. Her mother reigned as one of Savannah's leading social figures. Their four children grew up in a city considered one of the most serene and picturesque in the country, known for its grand oaks festooned with Spanish moss, elegant architecture, fountains, and green squares. But their paradise didn't last. By the time the war ended, the Ainsworth family had been decimated. Belle's father, who'd been made a colonel, died at Antietam. Her oldest brother, Gregory, died a hero's death at Chickamauga. Bridger, next to the oldest, survived but at a terrible cost. Their beloved mother died of typhoid before the war was over.

When Weldon pulled the buggy to a stop in front of the Ainsworth mansion on the outskirts of the city, the Beemans' three children tumbled out the door to greet them. "Aunt Belle! Aunt Belle!" Tommy, who was ten, Ellen, five, and Amy, three, rushed to their aunt and threw their arms around her.

Ellen asked, "Did you bring us presents?"

Belle bent to untangle all the little arms. "Not today, sweetheart, but maybe next time."

As they went inside, the children crowding around her, she noticed a peculiar expression on her sister's face but didn't think to ask why.

* * * *

"Bridger? Are you awake?" Belle knocked on her brother's bedroom door. He hadn't come down to dinner tonight, and she wanted to know why. "Bridger? Answer me!"

"Come in if you must."

Her brother's sullen voice came as no surprise. More than ever these days, he kept to his room, isolating himself from his family and the few friends he had left. Almost total darkness met her when she opened the door. "Good heavens, Bridge, let's get some light in here."

He lay on his bed and watched while she took a match and lit the paraffin lamp on his dresser. "If you've come to scold me for not coming down to dinner, you can go away."

"I didn't come to scold you about anything." Belle sank into a chair beside her brother's bed. The sight of him filled her with sadness, even though she should be used to the way he looked now with his pale, thin face, emaciated body, his left sleeve folded and pinned because his arm wasn't there anymore. "We missed you at dinner."

"Of course you did. I'm such charming company these days." With his one arm, he pushed himself into a sitting position, his face twisting with pain.

"Is it worse today?' She wasn't asking about the arm. He could have easily survived that and gone on with his life, but at Bentonville, during the last days of the war, he'd been wounded in the stomach. Miraculously he'd survived, but at what cost? The mini-ball that tore through his intestines had caused irreparable damage. Her heart wrenched whenever she remembered Bridger before the war: handsome, strong, confident with a touch of arrogance, a devilish gleam in his eye as he flirted with the young belles who adored him. But now? Everyone knew, Bridger most of all, he wouldn't be around much longer.

"The pain's the same. Let's not talk about it. Tell me about the latest meeting of your Georgia Ladies of the Confederacy." A shadow of the old Bridger appeared in the playful grin he gave her. "I can hardly wait to hear."

She welcomed the opportunity to make him laugh. "Well! You would never in a million years guess what that awful Allegra Barnes is up to now..."

She related the events of the afternoon, including, with a trace of laughter in her voice, Allegra Barnes's shocking announcement that she was going to get married, and her hilarious reading of the ad from the *Matrimonial News*. When she finished, she sat back and grinned. "Did you ever hear of anything so ridiculous? And what's funniest of all, she read another ad aimed at me. She thinks I should be a mail-order bride same as she."

Bridger didn't laugh as she expected. For a time, he remained silent, as if mulling over what to say. "I think you should answer that ad."

"What! You can't be serious."

"I am serious." He paused as if mulling some more. "You've got so many days on this earth. No one's more aware of that than I, especially now when I don't have much time left." She opened her mouth to protest, but he raised his hand. "Don't bother. I face the facts and I'm fine with it. I worry about you, though."

"But why? I'm doing fine. I lead a full life and am perfectly happy."

"Are you?" A corner of his mouth pulled into a slight smile. "All during the war, when I was slogging through the mud in Tennessee, and God knows where else, thoughts of home were all that kept me going. In my head I carried a special mEmery of you. We were at a ball, the last one I ever attended if I remember right. You had ribbons and roses in your hair, and you were wearing that purple dress, the one with the puffy sleeves and big skirt." He grinned. "You looked like you were floating in the thing, like a big, upside-down tulip."

She smiled, remembering. "The purple velvet. I wore it only the once at the Debutante Cotillion, right before Fort Sumter happened and the war started."

"You looked beautiful that night, and that's the image I carried. At every ball, do you remember how the boys were after you? Charlie Sawyer, Tom Peterson, both Ackerman brothers. You had your pick."

Her smile faded. "There're gone now, all of them."

"That's my point, Belle. That damnable war wrecked your life as well as mine. Now here you sit, trying to convince yourself you're blissfully happy when you're not, and don't tell me otherwise."

She opened her mouth to protest but changed her mind. His words had struck deep in that secret part of herself where she hid her unceasing despair. In silence, she looked toward the ceiling, then finally back at her brother. "You know me too well, Bridge. I try not to think of the old days. What a silly, shallow little fool I was, nothing more on my mind than the next ball and who would fill my dance card. I simply assumed I'd marry and live happily ever after."

"I think we all did. But why look back? All we really have is not yesterday, not tomorrow, but now."

"I've adjusted. I thank God for my family. Harlan, Victoria, the children"—she placed an affectionate hand on his one arm—"even you, you grumpy old rascal. But that's not... That doesn't... What's hardest for me now are those awful moments when I realize I will go through my life without someone special to love, without someone special who loves me. I'll never have children of my own. I'll never..." The words stuck in her throat. If she didn't watch out, she'd start to cry, and she wouldn't have that. Her problems were nothing compared to those of her doomed brother. She forced a laugh. "Look at me, feeling sorry for myself. Don't worry, I'm happy. I feel needed. What would the children do without their auntie Belle?"

"They'd survive." Bridger gazed into her eyes with a blazing intensity that surprised her. "To stay in the South is to rot away. There's a man for you somewhere, but not here. You need the guts to go find him."

Poor Bridger. He sincerely meant what he said but had no idea how totally impractical, how absolutely absurd he was sounding. "I'll think about what you said. Meantime, will you promise you'll come down for breakfast in the morning?"

"You can change the subject all you want, little sister, but if you want a life of your own, I suggest you answer that ad."

* * * *

The next morning, Belle joined Harlan, Victoria, and the children for breakfast in the dining room. Bridger hadn't appeared, which, she reflected, was just as well. Ordinarily Harlan, with his balding head and slight paunch, presented the perfect picture of a levelheaded businessman, but today he was on one of his rants. "Damn Yankees!" he raged between bites of his omelet.

"What have they done now?" Belle asked calmly. They'd been through this before.

"Kept us under their thumb is what they've done. Thanks to the carpetbaggers, our taxes get higher and the price of cotton sinks ever lower. After five years, we're still under military rule. My God, haven't we suffered enough?"

"Don't remind us," Victoria said. "Those terrible days are best forgotten."

Belle heartily agreed. Living through the war was bad enough, but at the end, when General Sherman's troops took Savannah, the nightmare began. At least the Union soldiers didn't burn the city, like they'd done in Atlanta, but they wreaked their devastation just the same. They destroyed the railroads, digging up the rails, heating them over fires, wrapping them around tree trunks and telephone poles. "Sherman's Neckties" they were laughingly called. The soldiers broke into homes and businesses and stole what they pleased. Worst of all, they blockaded the port and seized all the livestock and food from the local farms, leaving the population to starve. To this day, Belle could hardly look at a Union soldier without remembering those terrible days when they had nothing to eat. When Victoria's children were crying, weak from hunger. When she feared they'd all starve to death, and they about did. "It's hard to forget those days, Victoria. Whenever I see a blue uniform, the old fury rises inside me and I can hardly be polite."

"I will hate the Yankees until the day I die," Victoria exclaimed. "And General Sherman the most." She picked up a bread basket. "More biscuits, Harlan? At least we're not starving anymore."

Her husband's agreeable grunt told them his rant was over. Actually Belle could hardly blame him. He'd been rich before the war. Now, like nearly all Savannah's merchants, he'd lost his fortune and was just squeezing by, constantly beset by rules, regulations, and new taxes decreed by the Northern-influenced state legislature.

Tommy spoke up. "Aunt Belle, are you taking us out today?"

"Indeed I am." Belle looked at her sister. "I hope it's all right. I promised I'd take the children to the riverfront. You know how Tommy likes to see the ships. Maybe there'll be one coming in."

Victoria smiled. "Of course. They do love to be with you, Belle. What would I do without you?"

How good to be wanted, and needed. Bridger meant well, but he failed to understand how thoroughly she'd adjusted to her new role in life. "It's my pleasure, Victoria. You know how much I love the children, and you, too."

The children finished their breakfast and were eager to leave. Belle shepherded them from the dining room, had them wash up, and was leading them to the stable when Amy, the little one, declared, "I forgot my doll. I left it in the dining room."

Amy was hardly ever without her favorite doll. Belle turned back toward the house. "I'll get it, sweetheart. You children go ahead. Tell Weldon to hitch up the buggy."

Back in the house, Belle headed toward the dining room. She was almost there when she heard voices. Harlan and Victoria must be still there, no doubt lingering over another cup of coffee. She was about to enter when she was struck by the peculiar tone of Victoria's voice, a stressed, near-desperate sound she'd never heard before. Belle never snooped, but something made her stop outside the door and listen.

"...it's hopeless, Harlan. She's stolen my children away from me. They'll probably start calling her 'Mother' soon, and I'll be left completely in the cold, just someone who happens to live in the same house."

"That's nonsense." Harlan was using his most soothing voice. "*You* are their mother, Victoria. No one can ever take your place."

"Ha! The other day when Amy cut her finger, who did she go running to? It wasn't me, it was her wonderful aunt Belle, and that's because my children love her the best now."

"Then why don't you talk to her? Seems to me that would be the most sensible solution. Just tell her to back off, don't give the children so much attention."

"I could never do that. Belle's been wonderful to the children, and to us, too. I would never dream of hurting her feelings."

"Then I don't know what to tell you."

"What can you say? There's no solution. Belle will be with us for the rest of her life, and I'll just have to live with the pain of knowing my children love her more than they love me. Oh, look, Amy forgot her doll. I'll try to catch them before they leave."

The scrape of chair legs told Belle she'd soon be discovered. She darted away, barely making it to the stable before Victoria arrived, doll in hand. "I found Amy's doll." She smiled at Belle. "So sweet of you to do this. What would I do without you?"

Belle accepted the doll. She forced a smile, not easy considering her insides had turned numb and a dry sob burned in her throat. "Always my pleasure, Victoria. I feel the same. What would I do without *you*?"

River Queen Rose

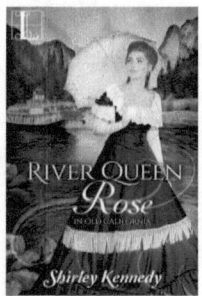

The ramshackle River Queen Hotel is home to vagabonds, gamblers, and heathens—and now, to new widow Rose Peterson. The rundown Gold Rush establishment is the only thing her late husband, Emmet, left her. Despite its raucous saloon and ladies of the evening, Rose can see the hotel's potential. Her late husband's family claims that sheltered Rose isn't capable of running the Sacramento inn herself. But she is determined to make a new life for herself and her young daughter, even if it means flying in the face of custom and propriety. She feels as if she hasn't a friend in the world.

Except, perhaps, one. Decatur "Deke" Fleming, a tall, lanky Australian who once served as Emmet's farmhand. Pride prevents Deke from revealing his moneyed past; conscience keeps him from confessing his feelings for the still-grieving widow. But when Rose is tempted by wealthy civic leader and hotel owner Mason Talbot, Deke may be the only person who can save her—and the one man capable of reviving her bruised and battered heart . . .

Gold Rush Bride

Letitia Tinsley's well-ordered spinster life is thrown into chaos when she learns her beloved brother has mysteriously disappeared from his gold mining claim in California. Determined to discover the truth, Letty sets out on the treacherous journey west. But there's only one thing more perilous than a single lady traveling alone into the rugged frontier—and that is sharing the passage with Garth Morgan. The wealthy bachelor is astoundingly arrogant—and dangerously handsome. Worse, Letty is forced to lean on his strong shoulders, again and again . . .

Humbled by the harrowing expedition, Garth resolves to keep Letty safe—though the courageous beauty is unwilling to give an inch when it comes to trusting him. Still, despite her defiant resistance, he's ready to stand with her as she faces the truth about her missing sibling. And by the time they reach California, Garth is determined to stake his own claim on the lovely Miss Letty—if only she will let him . . .

Wagon Train Sisters

After the death of her abusive husband, Sarah Gregg is free to join her family along with thousands of others in the nation's westward march for gold. But in the middle of the hard journey, Sarah's younger sister, Florrie, disappears. Devastated by the family's failed attempts to find her missing sister, Sarah now wants only to settle into a quiet, uneventful life when she reaches California . . .

But Jack McCoy, a drifter and one-time gambler riding along their wagon train, sees so much more for Sarah. In the roaring mining town of Gold Creek his attentive persistence points Sarah toward new vistas. Then unexpected news of Florrie arrives—and it's worse than anyone expected. But driven by a new hopefulness, Sarah seeks help from Jack, despite his troubled past. The two have traveled a rough road together, and only their hearts can tell them where they are headed . . .

Wagon Train Cinderella

1851, Overland Trail to California. As a baby, Callie was left on the doorstep of an isolated farmhouse in Tennessee. The Whitaker family took her in, but have always considered her more a servant than a daughter. Scorned by her two stepsisters, Callie is forced to work long hours and denied an education. But a new world opens to her when the Whitakers join a wagon train to California—guided by rugged trapper, Luke McGraw . . .

A loner, haunted by a painful past, Luke plans to return to the wilderness once his work is done. But he can't help noticing how poorly Callie is treated—or how unaware she is of her beauty and intelligence. As the two become closer over the long trek west, Callie's confidence grows. And when disaster strikes, Callie emerges as the strong one—and the woman Luke may find the courage to love at last . . .